DEATHSPEAKER—

"You should be careful with those around you," the alien said to So Pak. "You have the look of death about your aura."

So Pak politely tried to pull himself away, but the alien was insistent. "Listen to me," it hissed. "I know you have no curiosity about your future, but I must tell you."

And suddenly So Pak understood that the alien was near its end and had begun Deathspeaking, drawing upon telepathic and clairvoyant powers mysteriously unlocked by its own approaching death.

"I see you for a strong and compassionate man," the alien whispered. "Off-planet you will find what you are searching for, to no one's great advantage. Your crew will perhaps succumb to madness and strife, and I do not know if you will disperse the clouds of darkness surrounding you. . . ."

So Pak couldn't bear to hear any more. Breaking away from the Deathspeaker, he fled the club. But as fast as he ran he could not escape his own fear that the alien's prediction of doom for those aboard the *Bushido* might prove only too true. . . .

THE BUSHIDO INCIDENT

BETTY ANNE CRAWFORD

DAW BOOKS, INC.
DONALD A. WOLLHEIM, FOUNDER
375 Hudson Street, New York, NY 10014
ELIZABETH R. WOLLHEIM
SHEILA E. GILBERT
PUBLISHERS

Cover art by Vincent DiFate.

DAW Book Collectors No. 884

First Printing, July 1992

1 2 3 4 5 6 7 8 9

DAW TRADEMARK REGISTERED
U.S. PAT. OFF. AND FOREIGN COUNTRIES
—MARCA REGISTRADA.
HECHO EN U.S.A.

PRINTED IN THE U.S.A.

This book is for Lawrence Kahn
with special thanks to
Sheila Gilbert
and Elsie and Betsy Wollheim

CHAPTER ONE

September 2095, the Year of the Dragon, was said to be ill-aspected. Astrobio Masters claimed it was a transitional period when the souls of those whose destiny ran counter to that of ruling entities, cadres, or, in a more beneficially aligned chart, personal enemies were in danger of violent death due to foul play. On the surface, it was one explanation of Kim Pak's sudden death. But then, the life of So Pak's brother Kim had never been particularly fortunate.

To be born in the Year of the Dragon was thought by some to be of great benefit. To die during that year was to bring a curse upon one's ancestors and friends. The Dragon-born were lucky, dramatic, courageous, and, if they were more independent than the average individual, it was generally for the good of the whole. Kim had, however, been born in the Year of the Ox. He had been a strong, dutiful son and a thoughtful younger brother. So dutiful that, when So Pak, the eldest son, announced he would have nothing to do with his family tradition, had no intention whatsoever of becoming a Historian like their father, it was Kim who put aside his dreams of a reclusive life in the mountains, and reluctantly began to study History. There were those who had, in the last three days, muttered darkly over Kim's prone body, that his had been no accidental death. The voices disrespectfully insisted he had been at odds with the Iwaski Dictatorship, the most powerful Japanese conglomerate in the world, regarded with distaste by several ecologically focused conglomerates as well as by the Japanese ruling family. It was odd that a second son, carefully quiet in all his ways, could excite such a reaction.

So Pak had lived long enough among Historians to conclude that there are no real secrets in life, that sooner or later everything is known, and all that stands between mystery and disclosure is time. He had no theories. He stood silently beside his brother's grave, so thickly washed by morning mist it seemed the mourners were standing ankle-deep in a ghostly milky liquid that washed over their feet and poured down the mountain in long trails of tears. The silence of the countryside was shattered by wailing women. Bedraggled red ribbons inscribed with Buddhist prayers flapped limply against the wooden grave markers.

The graves were strewn with flowers and dotted with small, finger-pocked piles of rice no larger than the palm of a tiny hand. The grave site clung to the side of a steep mountain pass; the mourners and grave offerings were a smeary blur of red and white against the vast gray-green wash of the earth. The mourners, in white, looked like the ghosts of the buried dead. Kim's wife, her bare pale face whipped by her waist-length black and ropy hair, wailed more loudly than the others. But Reoke's voice cracked and broke, as if torn by the granite mountains, and that, too, was an evil omen. So Pak was not a superstitious person, but even he could not ignore the malevolent signs surrounding his brother's departure. It seemed to confirm his suspicions that perhaps his brother hadn't died accidentally. However, to give energy to this thought was to allow too much importance to political schemes. Despite his natural tendency to notice and catalog detail, So Pak stilled his mind.

When Historian Pak, standing at the foot of his son's grave, turned to look at So Pak, So Pak returned only the briefest glance before lowering his eyes in what he told himself was a sign of respect. Despite the calm resignation shown by his father, So Pak knew the old man considered it a perversion of the natural order for the oldest son to request off-planet exploration clearance from the Japanese. The fewer dealings with the Japanese, the better. That was not only his father's feeling but the opinion of most of Korea. His father's look was a reprimand.

They were a people made sad by war, So Pak thought. For fifteen hundred years his country had been plundered by the Chinese and the Japanese, both fighting over Korea's strategic location.

Many Koreans had left the country in the last hundred years, but So Pak's family stayed, as devoted to the land as a race of poets, which is what they had been before literature was banned throughout the world and the Historians rose to take the place of the deposed literati. So Pak couldn't bring himself to become a Historian, to have his words twisted into stories of self-serving propaganda. He decided that, since he had to lie, he'd do it honestly and become a subliminals and censorship expert in ironic protest. But irony being what it was, he had begun a long unwinding kata of mindless revolt. His stand hardly mattered to anyone except perhaps his father and brother. The World Council of Historians continued to direct the Histories, bending their observations to the dogma of the Iwaski Dictatorship. Once the Histories were written, they were approved, censored, politically corrected, subliminally doctored, and made into Entertainment Holos, then processed once again through the Entertainment Guild. By then there was little left of the original stories at all. Except what the subliminal masters added. In fact, it had become habit for the Historians to talk among themselves in long elaborate folk tales, the only way left to actually say anything meaningful.

Although Kim Pak lacked imagination, he had tried to change the direction of his Histories. Perhaps it was a good thing his brother had died rather than use up his life in bitterness and frustration as, in So Pak's opinion, their father had.

Over the last ten years, So Pak had watched as talent dried up inside the man, as the fire that went out of his father's eyes was replaced by stoic simplicity. For his father insisted on believing he had chosen this time, this system, and this family in which to reincarnate.

In the beginning, he kept his dreams safe in secret books in which he wrote diaries, stories, and songs; real things that had nothing to do with the Histories. But they were found and burned, scattered from the mountaintop before his eyes and the eyes of his family. At sixteen, So Pak stood with the rest on Nakhwaam Rock, thinking the Japanese should have chosen a better site. As the white ashes of his father's torched imagination cascaded over the mountain, it seemed like a synchronistic echo of the legend of the 3,000 Paekche court virgins, who leapt to their death to avoid becoming concubines of the Japanese. Nakhwaam Rock became the Rock of Falling Flowers.

The memory of his brother and of his father's public humiliation knotted in sorrow in So Pak's chest. He was smothered by loss and more determined than ever not to allow himself to be forced to join the ranks of

Historians fostered and financed by the Japanese. Nor did he choose to become one of the Ronin Historians, whose lives were short, who died secretly, nothing left to remind others of their passing but quick whispered conversations in dark alleyways or behind the walls of safe houses.

So Pak was a man of action. He had, by his nature, to channel his sorrow into physical activity, not into the unproductive labyrinth of the mind. He was too direct. Not for him the thankless escape of constructing Histories that never happened. It had taken him only three years to obtain inside knowledge of KR4, and the Japanese then had finally no choice but to give him a directorship, monitored almost beyond So Pak's endurance. Now, with his brother's death, he would have to explain once again to his father and, once again, he would see his father's gaze turn inward and would be forced to endure his father's disapproving silences.

Historian Pak agreed with the Chinese on one thing, that a single outburst of anger shortened one's life by a year. He'd learned to hold his anger inside and wait for revenge. How that revenge would come about was no concern of his. It might take generations, but that was not his problem. So Pak knew his father well.

The ceremony completed, he stood a moment longer than the rest, watching over his brother's grave before turning with the family to walk back down the trail that twisted across the face of the mountainside to the ancestral farm. As they wound, single file, along the mountain paths, the mist lifted and the sun burnt through the clouds. They passed rice paddies, azaleas, persimmon trees, and villagers on bicycles who gave them wide berth and averted their eyes. The lush, teal-colored countryside was ripe with vegetation, watched over by the eternal mountains. Nothing changed here. It had been this way forever.

Once his father had spent many years in Seoul but, as the first son, he had come back to look after his father and rejoin his wife and children. After that he left only on short uneventful trips to be honored by the World Council of Historians, traveling to Europe, Japan, and once to Germany, which he called the Western Japan. But he didn't take the family, not even his sons when they came of age.

Historian Pak was not a cold man, but he was a traditionalist. His way was in keeping with that of his country which, oddly, became more entrenched in tradition as the years progressed and the Japanese and the ten-country European economic authority which was dominated by Germany took control of world monetary concerns, holding smaller world powers in economic thrall. The United States was now a kind of International Port Authority, a country blasted apart to make way for landing strips, interstellar vehicles, clearinghouse offices for world customs and import/export traders, all of their business computer-monitored by the Japanese. Europe had become a giant experiment in sealed environments, studded by nuclear wasteland, a legacy of neutron bomb testing. The world of six billion people was crowded and famine ridden and tottering on the edge of ecological extinction, as it had been for one hundred and fifty years. Unlike his father, So Pak did not believe his soul had chosen to incarnate in this time and space for any particular reason.

Imperiled existence seemed a curious accident. It was the attitude of one living in a defeated time on a defeated planet. The only real alternative was to go off-world, but off-world colonies were either penal, luxury, or populated by ranting idealists politely requested to make a planetary exit—or else. Mining communities, driven to find core minerals on other worlds, limped along but most of them had been abandoned as not cost efficient by Iwaski, a corporate dictatorship with zero environmental concern in a time of dwindling resources and global warming.

A cool breeze touched So Pak's face and fluttered his loose white mourning trousers against his thighs. He watched the women walking before him, leaning their bodies into the comfort of the breath of wind as they moved down the mountain path. Reoke stumbled and his mother reached out to touch her elbow. The slight small hesitation in his sister-in-law's body seemed a marked refusal to take what little comfort was offered her. It was not her place to mourn alone, but it seemed her dignity demanded it. Kim and Reoke had no children; life had been difficult for them. Childless couples in Korea were looked upon with scorn, even though the government allowed only one child per couple because of the danger of mutation. Reoke's grief was tangible, surrounding her like the dust of a drought-stricken road. She had many years left to live, perhaps she would find another husband with whom to share her life.

Drugged by his own grief, So Pak surprised himself by worrying about the future of his sister-in-law. It seemed as though in self-defense he couldn't stop thinking. He had never thought of her as more than a ghost living in the shadowland of his brother's life. She had no strong personality traits to distinguish her from her husband. There was some talk of her liking children and animals, but she was childless and the family did not keep animals. Occasionally, So Pak met her quite by accident in the early morning, walking by the ornamental lake beside the house, but she rarely looked at him and never said a word. She was a country girl who had married above herself and she took his brother's brooding silences as a blessing, thankful that at least she was not beaten.

Unreasonable anger boiled up in So Pak as he considered the waste of two human lives. The hidebound traditions of his country angered him in times like this: there was no economical use of life and breath. He could not understand how such a gentle, loving people could be so ignorant; their insistence on clinging to the old ways angered him beyond belief. After less than two weeks with his family, he was choking to death on tradition. The placidity of them all overwhelmed him. They were like great dense-eyed cows, continuing with forms that had no meaning in the world beyond the valley.

When the family arrived home, they were formally greeted by the servants. The women retired. There was nothing more to cling to; it was over. All that was left to do was burn his brother's clothes and give his jewelry to the village poor. Now there was one more to honor on Ancestor Day. His brother's writings, meager as they were, would be incorporated into his father's body of work. That was the way.

Standing in the foyer of the country house, his back to the rice paper wall panels, So Pak waited courteously on the wishes of his father and looked across the mountain at the small spiraling column of smoke rising four miles away at his brother's cremation site. The old man slid open the bamboo doors of his study and motioned his son into the room. Despite his distaste for his father's work, So Pak felt his body relax immediately as he walked into the study. His father's study was the only modern room in a house which held room upon room of celadon sculpture, tatami mats, rice paper walls, and worn cedar ceilings.

So Pak sat in the large leather chair which faced his father's writing table. The room looked out over an ornamental garden. The library of exquisitely and delicately carved microchips lined the left wall of the room like an ancient mosaic of tiny, meticulously laid tiles. The library was immense, a sign of his father's stature in the Guild. Environmental holos played over the surface, shimmering color and images designed to soothe the mind and aid its journey to a state of alert mental conditioning.

In the left corner of the room was the most valuable relic in the house; an ancient stone stupa full of images—clouds and lotus designs, lions in a variety of poses, mystic birds of paradise known as Kalavinkas, the guardians of Buddhism named Lokapalas and the Apasarases, heavenly fingers playing celestial music.

His father's writing table was a mess of technological toys. There were two tiny computer terminals, a voice-activated computer, which in an odd way returned his father's Histories to the oral story-telling tradition, and a giant wall screen for vids or text reading. The salt tang of the seashore was piped into the room to raise the level of endorphins in the bloodstream and make the Historian more relaxed and comfortable in his work. String quartets gently played in the background, complementing the movement of the images that changed with the shifting holos. So Pak liked this room because it reminded him of the world he'd left. But he hated the technology because he knew it was designed to do one thing; to lull the Historian into an alpha state, which negated all conflict and guaranteed that the Histories written in such an environment would be without passion, intellectual puzzles of a sedate mind, at one with its condition.

A boy brought them tea in white porcelain cups so thin So Pak could almost see the garden through the cup he held up to the window before him. His father sat down at the table and ignored his tea.

So Pak sipped his tea and set the cup gently down on the armrest of the chair. He watched the steam cloud the surface of the green tea, gathering strength and disappearing into the air around him, its fragrance filling his head.

His father reached under the table and flicked a switch. Long ago, Historian Pak had found the location of the hidden cameras and worked out an ingenious way to train them on the stupa, although had the censors been observing at this moment, they would only have seen a man seated in his study talking to his son. His computers were input into the master system to enable the monitoring of his Histories during the course of their creation, but because of his age and loyalty his study was no longer bugged and he could converse without being overheard.

Historian Pak bore himself with dignity. When he was thirty-five, he had looked much as So Pak did now. In thirty years, So Pak, if he were lucky, could expect to have the quiet, handsome dignity of his father. The older man's pale, dim eyes often reflected lightning flashes of wit, though the jokes he appreciated were as studded with black humor as currants in a cake. So Pak attributed this to negativity and a melancholy temperament, but he couldn't deny that his father's gallows humor had taught So Pak that amusement at the injustices of the world was necessary for survival.

"It has been two years, then, since you first approached the Iwaski Dictatorship to request permission to outfit the *Bushido*?''

''Yes, Father.''

''They have agreed?''

So Pak nodded.

Historian Pak reached for the tea and drank thoughtfully, his eyes calm and steady. ''Despite the fact that you resigned from KR4? Iwaski doesn't tolerate employees storming out of its corporations.''

''KR4 is technically a government censoring arm.''

Historian Pak looked at his son in disbelief.

''They allowed it because they consider me difficult and unplaceable in technocratic society.''

''Which is unfortunate. Both for you and the family. And, as you know, they allowed your youthful folly for one reason only. They knew you were planting subversive subliminals in the Histories it was your job to censor.'' His words hung in the air. Both So Pak and his father knew the source of disappointment, now made worse by Kim's death. He had disqualified himself from ever becoming a Historian. For the first time in family history there was no longer anyone to carry on the tradition. And So Pak's determination to pursue his own seemingly fruitless exploration could be construed as an act of utter irresponsibility in the face of his family tragedy. If one were suspicious, it could be interpreted as a red flag, thrown up before the faces of the members of the Dictatorship, a convoluted plan for revolutionary social reform through utilization of the mysteries upon which Iwaski industrial power was based. So Pak had thought his family beneath suspicion. Theirs was an artistic family, not one of industrialists. They had never been notable, individually or collectively, for their revolutionary activity or nationalistic fervor. If anything, they were violently disassociated from politics, preferring to observe events around them rather than wreak havoc on the system. So Pak had his father and his ancestors to thank for that; all of them had chosen the Buddhist way.

"The *Bushido* is an unfortunate name," his father mused. "The Japanese way of the warrior."

So Pak smiled. "That is what the council said."

"You must take care youthful exuberance does not lead you down paths not meant to be taken."

So Pak tipped his head, bowing in respect for the admonition. He saw his father's restless fingers moving over the writing table as though it were a keyboard, probing, curious, unsatisfied.

"I find it odd that anyone would permit a Korean to investigate a questionable Korean-Japanese mining incident on Zeta Reticuli," Historian Pak said flatly. His fingers trembled, but whether the man was overwrought because of the events leading up to the violent death of his son, or whether he was anticipating uncovering some deep mystery, So Pak could not tell. His father was difficult to understand at the best of times, as transparent and opaque as rice paper, and often, when it seemed he was being the most open, he was in actuality the most guarded. Now he leaned his elbows against the ancient teak desktop, thrusting himself toward his son, his face suddenly still in the unnatural envirolighting. "Did you even wonder why it is they have approved a subliminals expert to lead an off-planet expedition, and a failed one at that?"

"I have captained a probe before."

Historian Pak crossed his arms over his chest. "A lot of dream-chasing."

"It was a successful probe, Father. There were no incidents."

Historian Pak wove a hand through the air. "Yes,

yes. You found some obscure reference to a new plant strain in some haranguing history, just a bare hint of possibility and you went chasing off-planet on a botany field trip like a fool, used by Iwaski, of course. . . .'' Historian Pak paused. He stared at the stupa for a moment, his complete attention on his thoughts. ''But,'' Historian Pak added in a softer voice, ''you brought the plant strain back. An admirable feat. And you returned with your crew intact.''

He pulled at the waist of his funeral jacket. ''And what is it this time? Doomed explorers, two competitive probes thrown together off-world, the development of an invaluable ultrasonic mining patent, lost ships and so forth,'' he said sardonically. ''Historian Conglaugh's account was not enough?''

''There are confusing layers of subliminals in that History.''

''Your historical bias. Locate the author's bias; it is often more essential to understanding the work than the work itself. This was not always so. But at the end of the twentieth century, when it was obvious the only common vocabulary the world had was a series of electronic images, moviemakers began teaching the grossest histories in the guise of storytelling, seeded with neurolinguistic programming to give the movies more commercial appeal.''

So Pak waved the history lesson aside. ''They say they want the History retold.''

''And who exactly is it who wants the History retold?'' Historian Pak asked, his eyebrows raised in irony.

''Bauer and Honura.''

''The information, storage, and retrieval conglomerate?''

''Yes.''

Historian Pak's eyes cleared and he thought a moment. "They began a holo business in the 40s. Bought rights to a good deal of the exploration stories. It would make sense. It's legitimate enough for quick clearance."

"The historical account is conflicted."

"You loved it as a boy."

"There is a great deal of layering. I don't know what they were attempting to cover up."

"You haven't wondered why they would allow a subliminals programmer probe clearance?"

"An attempt to put tragedy in its place."

"You speak as though you still believe the Histories are an art." Historian Pak chuckled. "I know I have to. It's all I have left."

"Father . . ."

"You are not as old as I and you are operating from a strong bias and nonattachment." Historian Pak's voice echoed with resignation and patience. He turned in his chair to regard the ornamental garden outside the window. When he looked at his son again, his face was expressionless. "The last thing the Japanese need right now is a great heroic Korean legend and I am inclined to think there is something heroic there."

"Perhaps it is only Iwaski's way of testing allegiance."

At first Historian Pak said nothing. "It is not a day to discuss such things."

"You mean to warn me."

"You have no need of warning. It is the reign of the Buddha Padma Sambadhra, whose characteristics are charisma, magnetism, wealth, and indestructible hardness."

"Yes, Father."

"You have the first three qualities in abundance. But

indestructible hardness? We shall see.'' Sadness gathered in the old man's eyes. So Pak waited. His father's was a sensibility strongly rooted in the shifting seasonal changes of nature. Material rhythms reflected the universe and his links with the natural order seemed to strengthen with each year of life. Some said it was his attention to the nuances of change and transformation that gave his histories such believability. The human agents in his work played out against a much larger canvas of mutability.

''And what of your marriage?''

''Wei is Chinese.'' It was an old discussion. He would not marry a Chinese woman. Korean women did not enjoy marrying an older son. It meant they became responsible for caring for their husband's parents in old age, and necessitated living in the same household all their married life.

''That is a point we have all taken into consideration.''

''I cannot marry now to leave another widow to my family.''

''Perhaps you would be leaving a first son.''

''There is no time. It is most unlikely.''

''It seems to me that the *Bushido* is an unintelligent risk, whereas Wei. . . .'' His father's voice rose and fell. Historian Pak looked at the polished teak surface of his desk and, with one crabbed finger, traced a rough design upon its surface. So Pak watched and waited.

''There is an ancient Chinese tale,'' his father began, ''about a young woman and her child. Walking in the woods one day, the girl saw the footprint of a giant in the forest floor. As she was curious and loved adventure, she stood in the footprint.

''Thunder echoed over the hills and the girl's body

was jolted with energy. She thought nothing of it. However, she became pregnant. When the time came, she birthed a large ball of flesh which frightened her so much that she threw it into the woods. It was avoided by all living things, and every morning the girl rose to see it back outside her house. A passing messenger did her the favor of taking the flesh ball and throwing it into a frozen lake, but it was rescued by a large bird. The bird dropped the ball, and the messenger heard a baby wail. The ball cracked and a baby crawled out.

"The messenger took the baby to the young woman and she decided to be its mother. The baby grew and became the god of agriculture." Historian Pak looked at his son. "The old tales have much to tell us of correct response in the passage of time. Not only have you decided not to become a Historian, you have decided not to have children who might become Historians. Do you hate the way so much?"

His father, understanding, had gone straight to the point.

"Perhaps you think you are different. Perhaps you are wrong. As events unfold, one's destiny is met. It matters not, this affair of the *Bushido.* You are like a small swallow trying to fill the ocean with pieces of stick and pieces of stone. It makes no difference to the ocean."

"But will you give me your blessing, Father?"

"It is not you I bless, but the workings of eternity. The ways of a bird upon the wind. Perhaps for now, you will choose the way of the swallow, but the end is not near. It is Wei about whom I am concerned."

"Why? Wei is a compromised arranged marriage."

"Precisely. It requires less loss of energy to follow

the ways of heaven. All things must bow to the gates of heaven in humbleness and surrender.''

''That is not a Buddhist feeling, Father.''

Historian Pak laughed. His laughter was as pure and swift as the ringing of temple bells. ''Only a Historian would question my theology.''

The coils of his father's will seemed to tighten about So Pak's throat. It would be so easy to bend to the demands of his father. His days would be full of light and peace. But he folded his hands stubbornly on his lap. ''I am sorry I cannot do what you would have me do, Father. I will not marry Wei. I must go off-world.''

''There is more to this mission than an exploration probe.''

''There is not. But human eyes must see what is there and I am determined those eyes will be mine.''

His father looked at him, amused. ''Human memory is fallible at best. And it can be forcibly changed to suit the circumstances. Witnessing truth meant later to be twisted is agony and torment.''

So Pak looked down at his empty teacup. It was no use arguing with his father. ''Are you advising me not to be a witness?''

Historian Pak was not an insensitive man. He turned his chair to face the garden. The interview was over. So Pak looked at the back of his father's head, gray, weary, yet still heroic against the still beauty of the formal garden. There was no blame here. Perhaps, in the wisdom of his years, or his secret access to the workings of the Iwaski Dictatorship, he knew more than he could tell his son. Certainly, he knew more than he was letting on. He had not bothered to dispute, even halfheartedly, mention of Wei's impending widowhood, should he recant and make her his wife. That alone filled So Pak with cold, dreaded certainty. He could not stay in this room one moment longer.

"I must say good-bye, Father," he said, standing up.

"Very well." His father would not see him off. He made it a policy never to see members of his family off and he would not be likely to change now when he had made it clear he did not approve in the least of the excursion, when he believed it was So Pak's duty to stay home and raise heirs.

"I await the day of your return." But it was form and nothing more that led his father to say these words. So Pak could wait forever and he would get no closer to his father's approval. He could not expect his blessing. Although they were very different, father and son, they shared the same unrelenting stubbornness.

"I do not act from disrespect."

"It hardly matters." His father's voice was thin. He waved his son away with a twisted, arthritic hand.

So Pak stared at the room in an attempt to commit even the smallest detail of it to memory: the curling electrical wires upon the stark tatami flooring, the smell of the ocean in a room hundreds of miles away from the sea, the clear north light, the wispy hairs of his father's head, the arrangement of burnt orange chrysanthemums in the beaten bronze bowl, and the stupa on which the cameras were trained. His eyes burned. The air of the house itself seemed changed since his brother's death. Something had departed, leaving the air still and sterile. So Pak shivered at the image of his home dessicated by grief.

A funereal breeze drifted through the window, rustling the dry leaves of the chrysanthemums. Two blood-bright petals fell from the corollas, spun momentarily in the air, catching the light of the deep afternoon sun, and floated to the carpet where they lay on the tatami like abstract gouts of flesh.

"I will lay a bright path of flowers before you, please walk the path of my love," So Pak recited in a rush of anguish. The chrysanthemum petals were an accusation. They lay waiting for his brother's footsteps, his brother who would never walk into this study again.

Windchimes whispered in the garden. It was time to leave. There was nothing here for him now but the twisting, unrelenting ghosts of a badly remembered past. It was madness to allow them to grab tightly to his imagination.

So Pak turned on his heel and went to his room to pack.

CHAPTER TWO

One week later, he sat in a borrowed office in Newark, Federation of Eastern States. Newark had not changed. It was still the grubby, gray-spirited center of transportation it had always been. Through his unwashed polywindow, So Pak could see the airfields with their bristling control towers, reflecto strips, and carousel loading decks.

The north section of the interstellar field was littered with torched and patched carriers in various stages of dismemberment. Sometimes a captain could get good value on a used ship if he spent time and paid attention to the inventory lists of north field carriers before they were transferred to auction at Teterboro. Teterboro was where So Pak discovered the *Bushido*. It was nothing special to look at on the outside and beat up beyond belief, but her builder and mechanic had the eye of a genius and the balance of interior machinery was worthy of a Chagall. The ship still amazed him.

Beyond the scrapped hulls and busted flight decks of the north field were the official ships of the Iwaski Fleet, arranged on the field like sushi on a lacquer tray. The ships were tinted black and salmon, some round, some cigar-shaped, some designed like boomerangs to make maximum use of air currents. Geodesic walkways led to the ships and, at night, floodlights bathed the area, turning the freighters, ex-carriers, and lumbering flagships into grand pieces of ground sculpture. When he thought about it, So Pak couldn't remember the last time he had used an official vehicle for flight. He had forgotten the observation decks, the silk kimonos provided for first-class passengers, the laser environments created to make the physical effects of warp speed less strenuous through meditation. There had been a time when he had traveled for the Iwaski Dictatorship himself, when he had lived on the interstellar ships flying from potential investment to potential investment, meeting client after client until, finally, he had given it up. And for what? A crammed gray quonset office hastily thrown up on the landing field of the north terminal, nailed aluminum sheeting and polywindows that baked with heat in the summer and deafened inhabitants during rainstorms. It wasn't that the office bothered him, it was that the office wasn't adequate for his needs. But he was learning adaptability, and once his work here was done, what did it matter? It made no real difference that he was a slave to his computer's power surges, that his phone was tapped, or that getting any kind of office supplies was practically impossible.

The office was stacked four feet high with piles of printouts through which roaches crawled. Velcroed to the wall and spotted with water stains from the last rainstorm was a star map of the Pleiades. Facing the star map was a floor plan of the *Bushido,* alterations marked in streaky glo-pen, the only writing utensil, it seemed, available for his use. Incoming vidphone calls were interrupted by the unrelenting whine of the com system because neither he nor his assistant Chosyam could figure out how to adjust the com system when the vidphone was in use. The Japanese might have given him permission for probe clearance, but they were certainly not in the business of making it easy.

So Pak sat at the desk with the terminal in front of him, a stack of printouts describing accepted crew members at his left elbow and a growing, ever-changing travel itinerary at his right. The one chair in the room facing the desk was used by interviewees, assuming they could make it past the giant plastic bag by the door which overflowed with garbage.

So Pak sifted through the crew files. Many members of the crew had been assigned him, some he had recommended, some he had still to handpick. He pulled at the collar of his starched black flight uniform. Three appointments were scheduled for this afternoon. Once they had been performed he had to speak with the contractor about the alterations on the *Bushido* and perhaps take time to look over the ship itself. And then something to eat—at a local Fish Bar, if he got desperate before he returned to the barracks room to get some sleep.

So Pak didn't like to eat at the Newark Fish Bars, the last time he had been served a five-headed fish. Maybe it was true that people shouldn't consume great quantities of beefsteak, but it was equally true that people shouldn't consume vast quantities of five-headed fish. It was true that they had closed the Hudson to fishing, but the river hadn't closed until August and the five-headed fish had turned up in early June, random events that lent credence to the saying that the only reason anyone survived Newark was because no one stuck around long enough to die.

Still, Newark was an interstellar port, briefly exciting. People could discover valuable bits of information if they could find the right places, blend in with the crowd, and keep their mouths shut. There was a restless impermanence about the place So Pak liked; people and goods passed through tidelike, leaving no trace. Even the Transit Authority employees left quickly. The longest any stayed was about a year, and then they were off to a new Transport Field, an entry-level corporation job, or else they signed on as crew members on one of the off-world probes. Like Chosyam.

Chosyam Kim, the American operations officer, had been assigned to So Pak's last probe for God knew what reason, other than that he was genetically Korean, of questionable stability, and best kept off-planet. He had already been assisting in arrangements for the *Bushido* for a month. Well, perhaps assisting was in its way a feeble word. Chosyam helped well enough when he managed to show up. So Pak knew one thing and that was that he didn't want to know what occupied Chosyam's spare time. It wasn't, for instance, a woman. Some days So Pak got the feeling Chosyam was a walking arsenal of tiny martial arts weapons no larger than the hand of a child.

Chosyam was twenty-eight and dark-skinned. He had a stringent and original code of ethics derived from being part American street kid, part traditional Korean. His great-grandfather first came to America at the turn of the last century to open a market on Thirty-fourth Street.

With a little savvy, a backbreaking schedule, and a certain amount of violence, the man managed to do well enough. He had become a produce czar and established a family dynasty. Chosyam was a renegade who had married a Korean wife from the ancestral village. He lived for change and believed all things must first be acted upon before they could be completely understood. To So Pak, this seemed like a new kind of backward American logic bordering on, at worst, illogic, but he had been assigned Chosyam and that was that. On his optimistic days So Pak suspected Chosyam was involved in the Korean nationalist movement. When pessimism threatened to overwhelm him, So Pak was convinced Chosyam was a petty arms dealer. On almost all days, he suspected that if Chosyam didn't calm down, he might not live long enough to leave with the crew of the *Bushido.* From what So Pak knew about Iwaski, it wasn't impossible that they had Chosyam pegged as a candidate for removal. But So Pak didn't enjoy pursuing that line of thought—it led irrevocably to conjecture about the fate of the expedition. He tried hard to avoid thinking the Japanese considered it a kamikaze mission and were stacking the crew with those who, in their opinion, couldn't possibly meet a better end.

In any case, Chosyam's mechanical brilliance aside, So Pak knew he could rely on his assistant's street smarts and fine-tuned reflexes as long as Chosyam didn't decide to start thinking for himself. Beyond that, his operations officer was so inconsistent as to be almost useless.

A good operations officer required a methodical and organized mind completely devoid of passion. However, reflecting on Chosyam's shortcomings was getting So Pak nowhere. The more he thought about Chosyam, the more driven he became to visit the tiny tin trailer two quonset huts away from his office in order to petition St. Jude. Chosyam had a tendency to cause people to reach out superstitiously for intervention from unseen presences.

"Captain, you there? Or what?"

So Pak pressed the acupuncture points on his temple to relieve the headache he could feel coming on.

"I think you might want to do something about the sprinkler system on the ship."

Chosyam strolled into the room and slammed the door closed behind him. He was wearing his requisite flight suit but his official haircut was fast growing out and his hair stood, spiked up on his head like tiny knives. The left arm of his flight suit had been torn out at the shoulder, his Iwaski insignia hung off of his elbow, and his boots looked as though he had been scrambling over moon rocks for the past ten years.

"Chosyam, take those knives out of your boot and put them in this drawer."

"Knives?"

"Knives are five years and you are under my jurisdiction."

Chosyam handed over the knives. When he tried to palm the last one, So Pak struck him on the wrist and Chosyam dropped it.

"What you do on your own time is your business, but I do not wish anything to endanger the success of the probe." It seemed important to go through the forms with Chosyam, but they both knew he would do whatever he wanted to do. Sooner or later, going through the motions would become a singular waste of time. "You walk in with an arsenal like that again and you're off the crew," So Pak bluffed. There wasn't much he could do with someone who'd been assigned him.

"Right." Chosyam knew it, too. "As I was saying about the sprinkler system."

"What about it?"

"There isn't a useful one. The *Bushido* was a war carrier. There's foam, workable enough for the electrical fires, but we need something for your regular chemical fire. The kind that can break out in a lab."

"Yes, you're right."

"I can rig something up." Chosyam stood, waiting for permission, his hands behind his back, rocking on his heels. "It's no problem to just jimmy stuff here and there."

So Pak nodded. Chosyam had a positive genius for fixing machinery. If it hadn't been for Chosyam, he wouldn't have considered trying to transform a carrier into a science ship, despite his slim budget. "All right, go ahead."

"And the appointments?"

"What about them?"

"Do you want me to hang around?"

"Just leave the door open and do what you can about the sprinkler system."

Chosyam didn't answer. There was dead silence so palpable that So Pak looked up to see a young woman standing in the doorway.

"I don't know if I should go," Chosyam said, his gaze riveted on the woman, "This one might be perfect."

The woman took in So Pak, seated behind his desk, the office, and the floor plan of the *Bushido.* Then she looked at Chosyam and asked him frankly, "Do you always go around wearing your heart on your sleeve?" She pushed by him on her way over to the room's only unoccupied chair.

"That's not exactly the part of my body I had hoped you'd be interested in," Chosyam said.

In response, the woman sat down in the chair with her back to Chosyam.

"You are dismissed," So Pak informed his operations officer.

"Certainly, sir," Chosyam answered, pulling at his

torn sleeve as he left the office and walked into the reception area.

''Operations Officer Chosyam Kim,'' So Pak told the woman seated before him.

The woman shrugged. ''They're all like that. I'm Jaffee Potter. I'm hoping to board your ship as communications officer.'' She gave him a big smile and handed him two pages of computer printout. When she settled back in her chair, she didn't look around, she kept her attention focused on the matter at hand.

He scanned her resumé. ''This is not your first off-world probe,'' he said.

''No. I was eighteen on my first probe. I'm twenty-three. I like it off-world. I grew up across the river in Manhattan. I didn't have a lot of options.''

''You can operate the old, hand-held sets as well as the standard laser systems?''

''Sure can. Daddy was good for something.''

''Pardon me?''

''Daddy.'' She caught the expression on his face. ''Never mind. Growing up across the river, there's not much you can do if you're working class. It's a jungle. Nobody with values. Just them Japs and Chinks. Excuse me, you're Korean, aren't you?''

''Well, yes.''

She smiled. ''I thought so. Koreans are like the Italians of the Orient; they have class and taste without having it interfere with having a good time. The Japanese have been hitting on them for centuries. See, the Koreans have morals. They're not like the Japs. Manhattan is full of Japs,'' she said bitterly. ''Took the food out of our mouths.'' She paused. ''This is, of course, only my opinion.''

''What is your interest in the probe of Zeta Reticuli?''

So Pak asked as he carefully placed her resumé on his desk.

"I don't know. It's as good a place as any. I'm getting restless, truth to tell." Jaffee's voice faded. She began to pick at her fingernails, which had been recently manicured and painted in a frosted burnt-orange color. She shifted around in her chair and her defenses fell. "You want the truth?"

So Pak sighed and checked his digital watch. "Yes, it would be just as well to hear the truth," he said patiently. He reminded himself to remain in the moment, not to let his attention wander off to the thousand and one things that still had to be done.

"The truth is, my boyfriend broke up with me. We've been together ever since I was seventeen and he turns around and tells me I'm too old for him, he's found this fifteen-year-old. So that leaves me unmarried, childless, and I just don't care. Meanwhile, my parents are trying to set me up with all the eligible guys in the neighborhood. I mean, no thank you. There's not much left to do but go off-world. He'll live to regret it, of course. I'm not all that worried. Not for a minute. Well, maybe I am a little, but not about him. It's good I found out now, in my opinion. The girl will make his life a living hell. It's time for me to concentrate on my work. You know what I mean?" Jaffee was looking at So Pak sincerely, her gold eyes large and limpid. "I mean, that's not too much to ask, is it? I know you understand what I'm saying because you're Korean and the Koreans still have a strong family unit, am I right?"

"You're quite right, Ms. Potter."

"I knew I was right. So what do you think?"

So Pak thought he could do worse. Her credentials were excellent and, if she talked incessantly, well, communications officers tended to run off at the mouth. It was a vocational characteristic.

She stood up and reached over the desk to shake his hand. "I can depart this bucket of blood any time you're ready."

So Pak allowed himself a small smile. "Thank you, Ms. Potter. I must get clearance from the Japanese, of course."

"Of course."

He watched her leave, a tiny figure in a pressed flight suit. She was energetic. None of her movements, unlike her words, were wasted. It was a characteristic of probe travelers, used to living in confined spaces. He could do much worse. She certainly could be trusted not to have any secret political affiliations, which was always something to be desired in a communications officer.

When his second appointment showed up, So Pak was so deeply engrossed in ration quotas that he did not at first recognize the fact that she was unscheduled.

"Excuse me," This woman stood hesitantly in the doorway with a briefcase clutched to her chest. She was medium height. Her wavy red hair was pulled back from her face in a tight knot. She wore a navy suit and a white blouse.

"Mr. Pak," she said, holding out her hand and walking across the floor to the chair. Her heels made stacatto taps on the floor. "I am Alice Drukker."

"The Archivist."

"Quite right." Despite her smile, she looked far more tense than the extreme informality of the office warranted, but, So Pak reasoned, Archivists were probably always tense when they were outside of the actual archives and dealing with human beings rather than data chips and ideas.

"It's quite all right, Ms. Drukker," So Pak said, meaning to soothe her.

"Well, of course, it is. Why wouldn't it be?" she asked, looking at So Pak directly from the bluest eyes he had ever seen. "I wanted to stop by to introduce myself informally, as it were. A courtesy call to inform you how happy I am to be aboard your ship."

So Pak appreciated the gesture, but surely the woman must know that she was an interruption in an already busy last-minute schedule.

"It is a wonderful opportunity for the Association of Archivists as well. We are committed to preserving history in its real sense as best we can."

"Surely you must know that history cannot be preserved, Archivist." So Pak realized he was beginning to sound like his father.

"Spoken like a true Historian's son." Alice Drukker had a gleam of appreciation in her eyes. "Historians think that history can only be told and retold, but we Archivists have to think differently. We are committed watchdogs. We turn our critical faculties on the Histories and evaluate them as to skill and accuracy. We are the critics. We like to think there is some absolute."

"A foolish concept," So Pak offered gently. Despite himself, he liked this woman. Alice Drukker had formidable credentials. She was the leading authority on twenty-first century legends. She had a rich background of European culture and had a real appreciation for Historians themselves. He had read her writings. She shared his father's belief, that it was important to understand the unspoken bias of each Historian before one could really understand the work of the man himself and had started a school of Histocrit based upon the theory. It was a courageous stance to take, in light of the Japanese views on the work of the Historians themselves. The Academy had an almost occult view of aesthetics and Drukker's view of historical bias was a refreshing counterpoint to the Academy's views that all a good Historian needed to produce a monumental work were tarot cards and a couple of handsful of fresh entrails.

Unfortunately, none of this changed the fact that Drukker was a scholar, whose last new work in the field had appeared almost twenty years ago. Certainly the longevity drugs worked physical wonders these days, but how resilient was she mentally? How could a scholar who wasn't used to off-world expeditions ever hope to be able to endure the physical demands?

So Pak shrugged his doubts away. The Japanese would never make such an obvious mistake. They weren't accustomed to sending a scholar out anywhere, much less to an old mining probe. They must be certain enough of the woman's mental and physical survival.

"I have always admired your father's work," She rose suddenly and stood, oddly awkward, before him. "In any case, I know you must have thousands of final details to take care of. I stopped by because I wanted to meet you personally before we lifted off. Academics can be problematic at best and I wanted to ensure we started out on the right foot."

So Pak appreciated her honesty. It was refreshing to meet an Academic who was direct in dealing with other people, someone who, however inconveniently, came to the point. Perhaps it was his background which made him susceptible. He had grown up in an atmosphere of one thing being turned into another on such a regular basis that one began to doubt the reality of anything on any kind of permanent level. Sometimes he had felt he was living in the house of an Alchemist, rather than a Historian. An Alchemist who metamorphosed truth.

"I think," Ms. Drukker added, "that the reason I was assigned to your probe was because, aside from the historical event itself, they assumed you would be sensitive to the needs of an Academician. It is not often that a probe captain is the son of a Historian."

So Pak lowered his eyes out of respect for the insight and nodded.

"Personally," she added, "I consider it an honor. This mining incident has always fascinated me and I have always been surprised it wasn't assigned to another Historian after Historian Conglaugh's unfortunate treatment."

So Pak raised his eyebrows in surprise.

"Historian Conglaugh used the entire incident as a vehicle for his own regional views and never told the story properly or gave the victims of the expeditions a chance to tell their own tale through him, superimposing his own views on them instead. What he managed to produce was a New Allegory, not an honest History. We can certainly understand his rebellious intent at the time. What he wanted was a history of a cattle raid or something equally archaic and what the Japanese assigned him was the off-world mining expedition. It was a simple case of the wrong man at the wrong time. Historian Conglaugh was determined to be an early martyr, so to speak. But it has been said that it is the Early Christian who gets the fattest lion. It is never a good idea to be a pioneer in thought or action."

Alice Drukker looked pointedly at So Pak, as if to

tell him she hoped he had no such foolish ideas himself. Foolish views which could endanger the success of the probe and the lives of them all. Her visit was also meant as a warning. She was serious. She would do her best to stop him should any hidden purposes or agendas endanger her ability to ferret out the truth.

Perhaps, So Pak thought, he was reading more into her statements than necessary. But the warning was clearly there and, even had he not spent his life around Historians and Academicians, he would have known that Alice Drukker was laying her cards out on the table. This was not a woman who had any trouble seeing beyond the vagaries of life and the sometimes mixed motivations of individuals.

So Pak rose and reached over the desk to shake the woman's hand. "I shall enjoy having you on board," he said.

"Perhaps. We shall see." Too honest to respond differently, she turned to go. As she walked out of the office, So Pak couldn't help but notice how her dignified, navy-suited figure brought a momentary order and mental discipline to the chaos of his office.

Ten minutes later, his next appointment arrived. So Pak half-rose from behind the desk and gestured to the chair before him. "Please sit down."

The young man sprawled in the chair in front of the desk, resting his elbows on the flimsy armrests. His energy overpowered not only the chair, but also the office itself. He had the loose-limbed attitude of all Americans who, to So Pak's mind, never really settled on a manner of sitting because they rarely expected to be sitting in one place for long. Even now, he looked as though the slightest interruption could catapult him out of his seat.

"Hi," the young man said, "I'm Michael Savage.

The Union sent me down. Said there was a job. I'm talking The American Navigators.''

So Pak nodded. The Japanese had assigned him a still-faced tech officer whose picture seemed to say he no longer expected much from life. Sitting before him was the Moscovite's American counterpart.

Michael Savage had Sinn Fein tattooed on his forearm. His pale blue eyes were wide and honest and an old knife scar ran from his lip to the base of his chin. It was the type of scar acquired fighting on the docks with regulation laser blades. Another scar, probably left by an ice pick, marked his right temple. There was an angry hickey where his T-shirt grazed his collarbone. So Pak only hoped Savage could manage navigating the heavens with less incident than he seemed to manage navigating the street.

''Welcome on board.'' If it wasn't completely true, it was the diplomatic thing to say.

But diplomacy was lost on Savage. He glanced at So Pak with a look that seemed to say, ''Cut the bullshit.''

So Pak tried another tack. ''Why don't you tell me a little about yourself?'' He was going through the motions; unions were unions.

''I'm six-five, one hundred eighty-five pounds. I'm twenty-five years old and have been flying missions since I was twelve. I lied about my age,'' he explained cheerfully. ''I do my job. I'm good at what I do. I inherited my union book, I come from a family of navigators.''

So Pak sighed imperceptibly in relief. At least the man was qualified.

''Don't particularly matter where your ship is going,'' Savage added. ''I'll get it there.''

So Pak didn't doubt it for a moment. ''Anything

else?'' He felt foolish. Savage was who he was, no amount of talking would add information. The Japanese had given him a break this time. Savage leaned toward him, resting his elbows on his knees and clasping his hands in front of him. ''When do we leave?''

''Four days from now. Will there be anything you require?''

''I could use an updated map of the Pleiades if you have any lying around, not that they've changed much in the last four hundred years. And a computac. I seem to have lost mine since I've been on planet.''

Probably sold it to finance some adventure or other, So Pak thought. Nevertheless, he nodded politely. ''Please submit a list of requirements to Operations Officer Chosyam Kim,'' he suggested. ''The sooner the better.'' It was not an easy task to find a computac at this late date, but if anyone could do it, it was Chosyam.

Savage nodded and grinned. He seemed relieved the interview was over. ''See you at 11:00, then, Captain,'' Savage said with respect. ''We'll make sure your godforsaken tub makes it to your filthy star in no time.''

''Planet, Officer,'' So Pak corrected.

''Whatever you say, sir.'' With that, Savage was on his feet and out of the room. It was only seconds later that So Pak heard him arguing heatedly with Chosyam in the outer office. Apparently, the sprinkler system was in order.

So Pak leaned back in his chair and tried to plan his next moves. His last appointment was in two hours. He had a great deal to do in the meantime. Despite himself, and all of the work pressing for attention, So Pak felt a rising bubble of excitement in his solar plexus. After all these years, it was really about to happen. So Pak, no matter what surprises the Japanese had in store for him, no matter that he knew a tendency to overexcitement could easily cause mistakes, was eager to lift off. He took several deep breaths, sternly reminding himself that excesses of emotion did not lead to clear thinking.

He sat completely still in his bodyform chair, performing the breathing exercises developed by the Historians to unite the right and left hemispheres of the brain and activate the central cortex. When he felt totally calm and mentally balanced, he opened his eyes and switched on the computer screen.

Multicolored static flashed onto the screen. Despite his newly acquired peace and alertness, So Pak couldn't help sighing. Why couldn't they have updated equipment in Newark? It was the busiest and most badly equipped Port Authority on the continent. Every year it got worse. Every year there were rumors of the relocation of passenger and commercial transport. Every year Newark rose again from the ashes like a squalid, grease-locked phoenix.

So Pak waited until the screen settled down. He punched in the program and waited for the assigned crew listings to show. No matter how much freedom the Japanese allowed, it was all illusion. The crucial members of the crew had been handpicked by Iwaski. So Pak spaced past Drukker's name.

ADRIAN KATZ. Pilot. Born 2056 in Tel Aviv. Served with distinction in the Israeli Army. Both parents live in newly colonized Antarctica Greenfield settlement. One sister, deceased. Exporter of exotic fruits and vegetables from 2072–2078 while studying Technological Philosophy at night. Graduated, 2078. Sapphoro. 2073–2083 agricultural technologist. Some knowledge of botany and agriculture and genetic alteration. In 2083, became pilot of FLEXNET. Off-planet three years. One of three survivors of expedition. Immediately requested another off-planet placement.

The computer then listed the probes, thirty-two in all, none very important and most of the status quo variety. Status quo probes scouted outer planets for the natural resources depleted on Earth nearly a century ago during the near destruction of the ozone layer. At the last minute, scientists had managed to seed a cover, but Earth's ecosystem was almost completely devastated.

So Pak leaned back in his chair and considered the screen. A competent man to whom something had happened somewhere down the line. A man who didn't have many years of probe scouting left.

So Pak sighed. It wasn't his problem. He needn't dwell on what this man would do—a man obviously running away from something—once he could no longer be useful aboard the probe ships. Perhaps he would retire. He had probably saved some money; it was impossible to spend much money in the one or two days he seemed to have on Earth between probes.

Israelis were often left alone by the Japanese. Although there were occasional outbreaks of terrorism to demonstrate the dangers of nationalistic feeling. Israelis were allowed wide latitude in behavior, their country wielding power through its oil fields and luxury truck gardening market. Katz was not atypical, except for the fact he was unmarried, he never seemed to visit his parents, and his parents had chosen to colonize Greenfield. It looked as though the family had been fairly well-rooted in Tel Aviv. Something must have happened to make them pull up and move to Antarctica. Perhaps the death of their daughter. Once again, So Pak told himself it was not his affair. He was running through his crew roster, not making a character study for a History.

He flicked the entry key:

KENJII YAKAMOTO. Born 2072, Japanese Taiwan. Parents dead. Raised in Shinto orphanage. Graduated 2094 from Tokyo University, Primitive Probe Investigation Department. The computer listed probe expeditions and published articles. Kenjii had been busy. He had visited interesting, primitive probe sites and had a promising career in probe exploration. He seemed to have a unique ability to get to the heart of the matter, judging by the awards he had been handed. He seemed to take to disaster probes like a fish to water, perhaps because he had been raised in insurrectionist, Japanese-held Taiwan.

So Pak rejected Kenjii, but his request was turned down. It was his assumption that the clearance board had an Iwaski agent forming policy despite the pro-world Japanese conglomerate factions after Mr. Matsuda, the virtual warlord of Iwaski. Japanese corporations were like feudal kingdoms, jockeying for power with Iwaski foremost of them all, despite the efforts of those with environmental interests and humane tendencies. In any case, Kenjii could be anything. The one thing certain was that he was not what he appeared to be. He could be anything from a government operative to a bona fide double agent and he bore watching.

So Pak flipped through the files and brought up two or three reports, but he was desperately bored before he got through the abstracts. Kenjii seemed a self-important individual. There was no denying he had a clear logical mind, but sometimes the innovative conclusions at which he arrived didn't merit the cross-proof and detail which preceded them. For Kenjii's sake, So Pak could only hope age and distinction would mellow him and make him less fascinated with his own brilliance.

LAWRENCE BENDER. Born 2035, Shropshire, England. It was a stroke of luck, being assigned Bender. Perhaps the Japanese thought him too old to be of any real value. So Pak had respected the man's work as long as he had known him, he had a positive genius for ferreting out bits of relics down to the smallest detail and spending years puzzling out particularly difficult problems. A great deal of his knowledge had never been used in the Histories. Much of it was classified, locked away in storage archives. He was a quiet, methodical man with no Historical inclinations whatsoever. He had turned down several professorships and museum directorships in Europe to live quietly and simply and pursue his cataloging of artifacts. For whatever obscure reason it had happened, So Pak was thankful for the inclusion of Bender in the crew.

TOSHIO KURISAWA. Born Kyoto, 2025. Monastic studies, 2040–2055. Served as Director of the Council of Historical Arts, 2055–2065. Administrative Director, Iwaski Arts Sector, 2065–2070. Administrative Director, Iwaski Sacred Sector, 2070–2075. Resigned 2075 to pursue meditative practice. 2090, became Chaplain of Arca, Alien Rehab Unit, Bristol, Australia.

That made some sort of sense. The Zeta Reticulan system was the birth home of many of the earthbound aliens, forced to the planet because of disease. The largest Alien Rehab Unit was in Bristol, Australia. Toshio must be a very dedicated and self-sacrificing individual to have spent so much time working in alien rehab by choice. It was the modern equivalent of working with lepers at the turn of the twentieth century.

Few of the race of ZR2 aliens, the only aliens known to Earthlings, had survived the recent plagues and, under the interstellar treaty of 2073, ZR2 aliens were allowed to be sent to Earth to die, entitled to human care and a lighter breathable atmosphere to make their deaths more comfortable.

ZR2 aliens interacted extensively with humans in the middle of the twentieth century. Ship landings were sighted; they became frequent toward the end of the century, although they were first attributed only to crackpots and conspiracy theorists. Some psychiatrists explained them away as birth anxiety—the hairless, big-eyed aliens were said to be a sick society's mass hallucination of birth fantasy. People who claimed to have been taken aboard to be studied were carrying out a massive return-to-the-womb fantasy. And the thousands who claimed to have witnessed themselves lying under lights and facing the scrutiny of an alien medical staff, curious as to the workings of the human body and unsympathetic to the pain they inflicted, were said to be recalling an infant's manifest memories of obstetricians.

As it turned out, the psychiatrists were wrong. The race of aliens known as ZR2 were on a par with human development except for their medical sophistication. Their vast curiosity about living things had taken them through the solar system. They neutralized indigenous disease by ingesting and chemically changing the DNA structure, rendering many diseases harmless. But, in the last two decades, very few aliens, who since 2035 had been allowed to pass and even to marry humans (some of them scarcely discernible from their human hosts), had been surviving recent plagues. No one knew why. It was as though their vast medical skills had failed them. But because of their contribution to intergalactic health, in 2073, an interstellar treaty was passed which allowed them permission to apply for residency status wherever they wished. Most of them chose Earth. In exchange, Earth got superior medical supervision, which it badly needed after the collapse of the health system in 2010, and, supposedly, received mineral deposits from the ZR2 planets, rich in uranium, plutonium, zinc, and boron.

Disease greatly distorted physical and mental facilities, but it was psychic fallout that was most troublesome to Earthlings. Iwaski, in particular, considered it socially dangerous. It encouraged speculation, independent thinking, and depression which an overpopulated planet like Earth could not afford.

Immediately before their demise, afflicted aliens began to Deathspeak to those around them—Deathspeaking being the equivalent of prophesying so accurately, it was almost as though the aliens, as they had once internalized and neutralized diseases, now internalized personalities and computed all combinations of fate and will, before giving frighteningly accurate and individual readings on anyone's future.

Undoubtedly, part of Toshio's motivation for requesting this probe was to see firsthand even this little piece of Zeta Reticuli. Perhaps he felt it would help him reach a better understanding of his former alien charges to see one of their home planets although, to So Pak's knowledge, they had never actually inhabited it.

EWHA THOMPSON. Ship's Doctor. A compuholo flashed on screen picturing a small and serious woman with the detached, minty quality of medical people. Her credentials were flawless, blending an excellent knowledge of Oriental and Occidental methods. But she was mixed breed, hunyurah. Her ancestors included an American GI and a Korean country girl, brought to America. Ewha had been assigned a series of second-class probes because of her outcast racial background.

Hunyurah were said to be unpredictable and violent, which So Pak thought had less to do with genetic strain than the ostracism in which they grew up. Ewha herself looked placid enough. As a victim of the system, she had probably chosen a helping profession in an effort to use her background constructively. So Pak felt a twinge of sympathy for the woman, and he quickly moved on to the outfitting procedures of the *Bushido*.

The floor plan read itself across the screen, echoing the floor plan tacked to the wall of So Pak's temporary office. Flashing red arrows indicated alterations that had been made to former interstellar carrier *Montcalm*, a minor heroic figure in the last Infrawar of '73. Chosyam had chosen the carrier, not for sentimental reasons—the *Montcalm* had barely performed three missions in the four-day war before being scrapped as obsolete—but because it converted power quickly and had an immense cargo bay, in which two landers now sat, greatly enlarged descendants of US Phantoms.

The *Bushido* had three decks. One and two held converted barracks which had been turned into private sleeping quarters, a mess hall, and war rooms that had been gutted, the walls torn down and made into laboratories. The forward end contained a three-story bridge with observation deck, elevator, and auxiliary engine and support systems. Below the second deck ran the centerline pod conducting energy to various maintenance systems throughout the ship. The third deck held a detaining bay, quarantine room, cargo bay, the nuclear fusion reactor, and the engine room.

There were a total of 12 propulsion units, six to each side. Computers converted energy from one system of the ship to the other, automatically regulating the flow of energy to the thrusters, life-support systems, and storage batteries in cargo bay. Propulsion unit operations and computers were located in the engine room.

Ship exits were bridge top and front, second and third decks port and starboard, through cargo bay and the weapons locker. Chosyam had chosen the beater fighter planes for their speed and maneuverability. They were essentially experimental aircraft to test a Tachyon Drive tunnel harness. The data link pods of the Daysun fighters had been disengaged from weapons storage and hooked up with comlinks to the *Bushido* and tracker ships, as well as monitoring and homing devices that could be attached to various scientists, specimens, and crew members. Whereabouts could be monitored at any given time, annoying to scientists used to working in solitary environments, but essential when exploring a desolate planet. Theoretically, Chosyam could launch live crew members (or any specimens or objects) to specific target areas.

He had torn out the weapons pods and pontoons and converted the area to living space, small lab areas, and a working medical emergency unit complete with laser operating facilities. When he was finished, he'd created two units large enough to house all members of the crew comfortably, even allowing them the luxury of individual privacy and research space.

All specifications had been carried out brilliantly, given the fiscal restrictions of outfitting a study probe according to probe requirements. It had been a blessed lucky event, the day Chosyam happened upon the *Bu-*

shido. Its mechanical systems were faultless, it had power, maneuverability and storage, all luxuries on a scientific ship. With the current interest rates as high as they were, the *Bushido* would have cost four times as much now as So Pak had originally paid. But then, neither the Japanese nor the German Federation were admitting to inflation.

He had, as well, been fortunate in his crew assignments. The Japanese did not appear to have set this up as a suicide mission. The only question was Kenjii. However, elements eventually found their own level. He had to believe that.

So Pak sighed and called up the more specific files to begin to double-check everything he could think of that had to do with outfitting the ship. He didn't get far. Chosyam popped his head around the door.

"Your appointment, sir."

So Pak looked up from his terminal to see a young woman standing respectfully before him, eyes lowered. She had been trained in a traditional Korean family. Her hands were folded before her as she waited quietly for him to tell her to sit down. But she was curious. Her lowered gaze did not prevent her from looking around the room as she waited.

"You may sit down. Please," So Pak gestured to the chair.

The young woman sat in a graceful fluid movement that was all of a piece. When she was seated, she stated, "I am here because you require a ship's biologist." Her voice rose prettily at the end of the sentence, forming a question. "My name is Yeshe Yoon. I have acted as biologist on three probes. It is unknown to the Japanese," here she broke tradition and gazed directly at So Pak, "but one of my ancestors was a miner aboard the Korean mining ship. I have personal reasons for wanting to be a part of this probe."

Having said all that, she lapsed into silence, waiting upon his decision.

So Pak was floundering. Carefully, he tried to formulate his response. "I appreciate your directness." Tradition demanded another type of behavior, mainly consisting of her response under his leading. "And your honesty," he added. Her eyes were very clear and her face completely impassive. So Pak caught himself thinking she reminded him of some sort of fruit. An apricot, perhaps. She had a delicately colored freshness about her. He stalled for time by looking at his watch. It was five o'clock, late in a day that had begun twelve hours ago for him. Perhaps he was just tired. His attention had begun to wander.

Dare he introduce a problem like this into his crew? Or was it really a problem? Certainly, only the traditional Korean mind would understand why she had to visit the site of her ancestor's death. The crew didn't have to know. But was it tempting fate to add this element into a precariously balanced but so far lucky probe? Perhaps he should take a chance.

"I know that you will want to think about this decision." Her voice was gentle, as though she understood his dilemma. "Unfortunately, I must say I can't wait for your decision."

He admired her persistence. To push was a delicate matter of balance, which she seemed to have mastered either through training or through inclination. Perhaps she knew that if he had time to think he would decide to hold to the conservative way.

He weighed the decision, realizing that time would not make a difference in his thinking. "Welcome to the crew." He needed to fill the position. Her insistence required direct response. "As a matter of form, I must look over your resumé and check your references but, if things are in order, you may be assured a position on the crew. Chosyam will inform you of details."

Once again, she became demure. "Thank you. My position at the Institute of Development requires that I stay fresh on fieldwork. I welcome the opportunity to leave the laboratory environment," she answered mechanically. *Too mechanically.* Something was wrong.

So Pak leafed through the small sheaf of papers in front of him. She had, he noticed, been instrumental in developing a new compact strain of seedless pomegranate, which would bear fruit year round. She had been on a balanced and varied series of probes, most of the planets much more interesting than Zeta Reticuli. It was not for So Pak to question her choice of planets. There was something disturbing here, although her credentials were quite in order. Perhaps he was merely unsettled by her resemblance to himself, a modern Korean straddling cultures and traditions willy-nilly, intent on solving riddles which sometimes blurred the personal and professional.

Maybe he was simply becoming oversensitive because he needed some rest. Reading between the lines was always a delicate matter. After a time, one's perceptions became muddled, inaccurate and sloppy. "Everything seems to be in order," he said.

She lowered her eyes, but not before he caught the look of relief on her face. She rose to her feet, made a small bow in parting, and walked out of the room.

He watched her leave, enchanted by her walk. There was something familiar in her movements, and yet they seemed as mysterious as a wooded path. But he had no time to think of her. As he worked through the flight tables and navigation paths, he felt peace and calmness stealing over him, born of working at a task that absorbed all his concentration. He was a man blessed. He had a good ship, stripped and tailormade to his needs, and if it was only equipped with the basics, well, the needs of the crew weren't extravagant. He was not captaining a luxury cruise for a wilderness adventure to an outplanet so inhospitable that the passengers retreated to the mother ship for their entire year of wilderness adventure.

His was the luckiest of probes, a scientific study of a lost colony. Money wasn't wasted on scientific probes often. Probes generally were designed to check up on existing colonies, more to report their progress to the Japanese than to ensure the safety of the alleged colonial protectorate. Or they were automated and unmanned, sent out for weather purposes. Or they were fact-finding missions, or following up a previous probe that had been on a find and deploy mission—in fast, out equally fast. And sometimes they were penalty assignments, designed to rid Iwaski of politically undesirable individuals. But his probe was an authorized study ship. He had off-planet clearance for as long as he wished. "You will be monitored," he reminded himself. He was, after all, still subject to the insanities of the duplicitous Iwaski Dictatorship. But his was not a penalty assignment. He had only to reach out his hand and clutch his freedom.

CHAPTER THREE

Several hours later, So Pak stepped out onto the Terminal Beltway. As the "fresh" air burned through his lungs, So Pak squinted at the blazing orange and purple fireball of the sun setting in the reddish brown sky. The sky over Newark was always reddish brown.

Striated clouds hung across the sun in the heat, like birds of prey in flight, wings hooked to catch the air currents, beaks tucked against their chests, perverse and beautiful. So Pak vowed to enjoy this sunset. There would be no sunsets where he was going.

Despite the heat, the Beltway was crowded with pedestrians, even though air quality warnings had been issued at least two hours before. No one in Newark gave a damn about the air quality.

The Beltway smelled of creosote, chemicals, fuel exhaust, and sweat. The greenspan on either side of the Beltway was engaged in a life-and-death struggle for survival. Vegetational watering had been banned and the last time it had rained was a month ago. Quonset huts identical to So Pak's office bordered the Beltway. They housed official and temporary offices for probes, trading company representatives, and Customs Clearance. There were chapels of every denomination, vid huts, commissary delis, and newsstands. The terminal homeless dotted the Beltway, arms outstretched, holding empty coffee cups or wax-coated Coke containers. Newark, it seemed, had the poor with her always.

Airport employees on breaks, baggage handlers, field-workers, and restless crew members between flights mingled with the quonset hut employees and the overflow city streetjive. Two black baggage handlers had set up a three-dimensional chessboard outside the Schiff Imports office and were staring at the board in fixed concentration as Spiderman, the Beltway chanter, played electronic keyboard not two feet away. Tonight his meditation music was overlaid by the rapid-fire beat of steel drums.

The air was densely packed with excitement, frustration, and a restlessness that fit So Pak's mood perfectly. He debated whether to head over to the vendor zone or, alternatively, to visit the bubble restaurant near the north Kleinhaupt Terminal. He decided on the bubble restaurant: it was closer to the bars and, although he was probably fooling himself, he liked to think it served a better quality of food than the Fish Bars.

The Kleinhaupt Terminal was located on the east side of the Interport Strip dubbed Space Square. Space Square couldn't have been larger than four thousand meters, boasting a statue of Astronaut Armstrong in the center. Every year, the Terminal Mayor promised to clean up the square. Every year, it got worse.

So Pak liked Space Square. The place pulsed with energy. Establishments ran interactive holo shows on the sidewalks to entice customers inside. Red, black, maroon, and yellow halolights flooded the walkways. There were geishas, hula dancers, silblondes, massage parlors, drinking clubs, animal pits, boys, girls, robos, comfort aides of every description, fantasy playgrounds, and martial arts exhibitions in which the contestants fought to death. Vigilante groups patrolled the area. Transit Cops cruised the streets in patrol cars and spincopters, turning a blind eye to the vendor wagons that sold drugs and weapons under the guise of frozefood sticks. Private car services and cyberslaves solicited business in parking lots.

At night, Space Square throbbed with violence and vice. For those who accidentally found themselves still there in the morning, the place was a gray, tattered, blasted out area littered with human flesh and garbage, populated by silent, gutted buildings and ghostly holos that jerked brokenly in the sunlight. Once night began, the magic started all over again. Space Square was a transformational illusion, a wonder even to its erotically perverse and jaded residents.

So Pak liked to sit in the bubble restaurant, have a few drinks and watch the street show while he ate a leisurely dinner. The bubble restaurant was adjacent to a transit tube that vomited people into the crowd at regular intervals. After dinner, So Pak often walked the streets until he was almost too tired to find his way back to the barracks to sleep.

Clouds boiled up against the sunset, looking like the ancient Korean dragons on his father's gateposts. Once So Pak had been told stories of the five beasts who stood for the four corners of the Earth: on the east, the blue dragon; on the west, the white tiger; on the south, the red phoenix; and on the north, the tortoise and the snake. As dusk fell, the cloud dragons turned more and more blue.

It had been Historian Han Woo Keum, who long ago remarked on the masterly swirling style of the beasts, painted on the inner walls of Korean tombs. Historian Keum contrasted the style with the "calm serenity" of Chinese painting. It was, in his opinion, an indication of the development of a distinctive Korean culture and the expression of a vigorous, aggressive, and outgoing people.

For centuries, Koreans had been far more aggressed against than aggressors. Invaded often, but hardly ever themselves the invaders, Historian Keum believed Koreans constituted the classic case of a people of spirit and individuality boxed in and battered this way and that by neighbors and an environment over which they had little or no control.

It was a country perpetually trounced by China and Japan, neither of which had any real ethnic or temperamental common ground with the native Koreans.

But that was the past. So Pak was beginning to think he had been too long away from his country. His brief visit home for his brother's funeral had been more a function of clan duty than a settling of his own personal relationship with his country. Sooner or later, anyone who left his country to make a new life elsewhere came to this point. The person he used to be must be reconciled with the person he had become.

There were times when So Pak no longer knew who he was: he had striven for so long to forget where he had come from that he had nearly succeeded. It was at times like these, and they generally fell, for some odd reason, at dusk, that the questions came back to haunt him. No matter how hard he tried, he never seemed able to answer the questions. Perhaps he wasn't asking the right ones. Who was he? What was Korea? Why did he care? In the year 2090, questions like these were construed as nationalistic, and nationalism had become a parody of itself. Even the probe, begun as a way to run far from himself and his problems, had become a Korean-Japanese mystery. Well, his mother liked to say that the world came round for everyone. Who was he to think he might be different?

The sun had set. Dusk gathered in Space Square, the soft light a fertile meadow for the wild, obscene orchid of commercial area business. So Pak stepped off the Beltway to pick his way through the three foot gutter that surrounded the east sector. He was halfway across when he heard the scream: a piercing wail of terror that rose above the street noise, musicians, and laser radios like a soprano solo in a classical requiem.

No one paid attention. No one paused to look for the source of terror and the scream rose again. So Pak sprinted across the gutter, stumbling over the curb and throwing out his hand to catch himself on the nearest halolamp post. He blinked and jerked his head around like some kind of mechanical tracker. The screams came from the bubble restaurant.

He elbowed his way along the walkway, choked with pedestrians, to a vacant spot beside the window of the restaurant, caught between what he saw inside and the specter of three Koreans running across in front of him, Snake Order tattoos stamped into their cheekbones. The tallest of the three looked at him with unseeing eyes and So Pak's pulse raced with dread.

He saw an electrician's van parked at the corner, the faces of the occupants like marsh flowers in a blackened bog. This was no simple hit in progress. The Snakers were as unpredictable as they were vengeful. Three years ago their leaders had been killed and the Snakers exposed for the cadre of sociopaths people liked to believe them to be. But there was more to them than that, they were one of the most secret of secret societies. Since that time, three years ago when Lo Fat, a half-Korean, half-Chinese politico had been gunned down by sublasers in the transit tube, nothing had been heard of them. There were rumors the Snake Order had been taken over by the Chinese. That they had disappeared underground. There were other rumors, too, but nothing substantial.

Carefully, despite the urgency he felt, So Pak picked up a vidphone from the booth nearest the windows and pretended to make a phone call as he looked inside, his face half-blocked by the vidphone shield.

His blood froze inside him. There were few people inside the restaurant, an oddity for this time of the day. Torn atmosphere nets hung from the ceiling, brushing the tips of the leaves of the tropical plants by the window. What looked to be a newly arrived alien sat at the counter, shoulders hunched, either indifferent or feigning indifference to the activity around him. A maintenance man made a show of pushing a broom around. This in itself was unusual. Cleaning floors was generally the job of broken, battered cyberslaves. To the left, So Pak could see shadowy activity by the front door, but the figures inside were temporarily lost in darkness. It seemed the halolights inside and outside the restaurant had been dimmed intentionally.

He walked to the next window and was rewarded with a somewhat better view for which he was anything but grateful. Several toppled chairs in the middle of the restaurant surrounded a young woman who was still screaming loudly enough to make herself heard from the walkway. Moments later, he saw the woman's bobbing head, surrounded by three crouched men who were, it seemed, taking turns punching her in the belly. As he watched, the woman broke away from the trio of heavily muscled Orientals and ran to the southwest corner of the room by the windows, kneeling down on the floor underneath a table, beating the floor with her fists.

Although her face was set in shadow, she bore an eerie resemblance to his brother's wife.

It seemed to him he watched her unrelieved dance for hours, an abstract ballet of systematic and choreographed torture. Her tormentors grabbed her, pulled her up and off the floor only to have her once again slither out of their reach, breaking away to kneel down in the corner and pummel the floor. Finally, So Pak focused his attention on the corner under the table and, when he did, he froze in shock. His fingers were keying in Emergency before his mind had fully registered what he was seeing. Stretched out on the tatami underneath a hydro-bred bamboo lay a Korean man, his face turned to the window. The man's head was oddly askew, his fingers tapping feebly on his chest. His eyes looked straight into So Pak's face for several minutes before blood began to bubble out of his tear ducts. The man was covered in blood. Blood smeared the inside of the window like a reddish brown wash. The man's breathing grew ragged as pain glazed his eyes. He raised his left hand from his chest and managed to stretch his arms toward So Pak and the glass. His fingers were taut with life for only seconds before they stiffened, streaking down the blood through the glass and leaving four finger tracks. He was dead. The patches of his clothing that weren't soaked in blood perfectly matched the color of the tatami.

"Confirm your location," the voice commanded from the vidphone. "Hello. Hello? Location, please?"

So Pak confirmed his location.

"Nature of complaint," the voice demanded.

"Violent crime. Gun wounds. The man is dead. Perhaps he might be revived?"

"Are you raving?" the voice queried.

"Perhaps . . ." So Pak's voice trailed off as he realized he was asking a vidphone operator to validate the death he had just witnessed.

"Scan, please."

"It's not finished. There are others."

"Scan, please."

Vidphone operators were trained to be literal-minded. So Pak obediently moved the scanner so the operator could see the restaurant and the dead Korean.

"Reporting number of bodies?"

Once again, the men pulled the woman up off the floor and began battering her. So Pak, impatient with the operator, furious at the assailants, sprinted to the front of the restaurant the handle of the vidphone dangling beside the booth, the tiny voice of the operator demanding the number of bodies out of thin air.

He got to the front door of the restaurant just as the two electricians arrived. One of them, wearing a union helmet, was bashing in the face of an Oriental by the door. Although he was kicking valiantly, the Oriental looked to be receiving the worst of the blows. The other electrician was inside, hacking off the ear of a wiry attacker who had been strangled with a length of copper wire.

Three kitchen employees were huddled by the thermo-fryer. One was burned so badly he was no longer identifiably human though he was still standing. He stepped away, his body in shock as strings of gray flesh melted into the cloth of his uniform and dripped into a greasy puddle on the floor like gum left too long in the sun. The man's body was completely flailed by heat. Red muscle tissue bubbled, blistered, and burst into liquid lymph and he melted as he stood, long past screaming through his open, lipless mouth. As So Pak watched, his chin split open, the raw skull white and clean beneath the boiling mess of his face. He fell to the floor.

In seconds, So Pak was around the corner pulling the smaller of the two men off of the woman who was now crouched on the ground, her head between her knees, taking the full force of their blows on her back. The maintenance man still pushed the broom mechanically. There was something wrong with him, some mental deficiency. Perhaps it had allowed him to remain unmolested.

The alien turned, snapping his head around, his eyes snakelike and cold. The scene had long ago tumbled into a tapestry of unrelieved horror, but So Pak had no time for that now. He grabbed the Korean by the collar of his coat and, with a quick three-fingered jab below the man's left ear, knocked the man out for the moment. So Pak kicked him soundly in the kidneys on his way to the splayed out position he finally assumed on the floor. The remaining attacker, he hauled off of the young woman, heaving him across the table. The table tipped over, the man slid toward the glass windows, spun through the air, corkscrewing over the body, and crashed through the glass to the walkway outside.

So Pak reached for the woman, but she was as expert in dodging his grasp as she had been her attackers'. He felt the slide of skin against skin, the quick cable of muscle, and she was up and gone in one quick movement. He glimpsed the back of her head, the silken sweep of hair shining purple against the atmosphere net and then she was gone, swallowed up in the crowd outside.

Moments later, the emergency floatcar arrived. A pair of Hispanic medics climbed out of the car and they and their assistants swarmed over the area. In the cleanup, no one noticed the remaining Snaker pull a knife out of his belt, wedge it between the slats of the table legs, and roll into it, killing himself.

It hardly mattered. Two Snakers had survived, enough for the Transit Cops to track down, take away, and interrogate. Not that they'd find out anything. The two electricians went over to the bar and helped themselves to a chemical beer apiece as the emergency crew began piling the fryer victim, the gunshot victim, and the suicide into thermal body bags.

"Massive cleanup," a sad-eyed Hispanic commented to So Pak. "You the guy who called?"

So Pak nodded.

"Nice try, but a little late, pal. Course," he said, narrowing his eyes and taking a closer look at So Pak's face, "stopping this thing might not have been a priority, huh? What about the woman? Report said something about an Oriental, right?"

So Pak nodded again, irritated by the mosquitolike voice of the man who was standing uncomfortably close to him. He was thinking of the woman. How she could run out of the restaurant after a beating like that was beyond his understanding. She was tougher than she looked, but he couldn't shake the familiar chords she struck in his mind: her resemblance to the meek and self-effacing wife of his brother chilled his blood.

"So, where's she at?" the medic's assistant probed.

"I don't know." So Pak felt useless.

The medic shrugged. "Well, I know how that is. Women know these things."

"What things?" He was surprised at the medic's Botanica mentality.

"Only reason I know of to run is if a person were expecting something like this. Probably didn't want to be tied into Snaker murders. Probably'd have to stay in Newark for the rest of her life which, way she's going, wouldn't be all that long. But even if she managed to stay alive, takes forever to investigate those ritual killings.''

So Pak looked at the man's face. His skin was gray and grainy. ''What ritual killings?''

''There's been a lot of Snaker murders in the sector lately. No one can figure out what's going on, but one thing's clear. Snakers want something. Only what that is, no one can figure out yet. You're Korean, aren't you?''

''Yes,'' So Pak said wearily.

''Well, the Snakers are giving your people a bad name in the sector.''

They stood together, watching the medic crew load the bodies into the floatcar. The man's voice turned sad. ''Everyone comes over here, hauling their wars with them. Like there's not enough wars going on over here already. It's a country of violence run over by mercs, assassins, stupid-ass sect murderers. And you listen to me.'' So Pak started as the man jabbed a skinny little finger into his chest. ''Things are just going from bad to worse. Used to be they could keep a lid on things like this, but you think they do that now? No way. And don't you let anyone tell you any different 'cause that ain't reality. Reality's a horse pill.''

With that, he picked up his unopened medic's bag and walked out of the restaurant toward the floatcar. So Pak stood aimlessly watching the floatcar drive away and, a few seconds later, he followed, leaving the two electricians behind him in the restaurant drinking for free, the maintenance man still sweeping the floor, and the alien hunched over the counter looking at his hands.

So Pak followed the walkway, hardly noticing where

he was going. His knuckles stung and throbbed. Unconsciously, he brought his hand up to his mouth and sucked the knuckles of his fist. His second knuckle wobbled against his tongue, flattening at the pressure. It was broken. He must find some ice, but where was he to look in this godforsaken hellhole? Plenty of ice back there at the restaurant, but there was no way he was going back there again. The place was probably overrun with Transit Cops. The pain of his busted knuckle was great but no greater than the pain in his heart at the thought of Koreans battling Koreans when everywhere they were treated by the Japanese as subhuman.

Space Square was boisterous, but the distraction of the night stalls held no attraction for So Pak. He scanned the horizon for the moon, but all he could see were clouds, their shapes shifting as they crossed the sky.

Against his will, So Pak found himself remembering the beauty of the night sky as seen from the window of his father's library years ago when he was still a child.

A wave of homesickness swept over him; homesickness for the peace and order of his homeland where his father had spent years of his existence studying chaos without emotion until it molded itself unwillingly into Histories; his father humming tunelessly to himself as he worked, chanting late into the night. It had been a time of simple remedies for sleeplessness; a book of poems could provide haunting answers to unspoken mysteries.

It was there in his father's library that So Pak taught himself to be fearless. Had his father known, he would not have permitted it. His father permitted it only because he did not know what his son was doing. Fear, like pain, his father believed to be necessary to survival; a warning mechanism that something was wrong. The man who felt no pain possessed a body that would rot away without his knowledge. The man who felt no fear was a fool and his life could disappear before him in foolishness and ignorance of obvious danger.

So Pak stared at his feet, moving his body along the walkway, trying desperately to explore the ragged edges of a fear he could not feel but knew he should be feeling in the face of his role as witness to the Snaker murders. But no matter he tried, he could feel nothing but surprise at surviving and the wonder at how quickly a world could turn upside down and inside out. In minutes, the bubble restaurant, which had given him many hours of peace and quiet contemplation, had become a stage of senseless death on which three people with nothing in common had met their end.

He cradled his split knuckle against his chest and rubbed his fingers with his uninjured hand, in a subconscious attempt to press the pain back into his body. The smell of thermo-fried flesh hung thick in his nostrils. It would be days before he could get the smell out of his mind, many baths would not get it out of his body. But worst of all was the sight of the woman's face, bent toward him from the window as he stood outside gripping the vidphone, the paleness of it like the ghost of an answer. There was something he had missed, some singular fact that he had observed that would make the pieces of a puzzle come together, something he had overlooked that would unlock a rush of sensations and, finally, make him understand. It couldn't have been Miss Yoon. If she were politically active, the Japanese would never give her permission to leave the planet and yet they had.

But even without her involvement, the killings had none of the marks of ritual murder. There were no red strings tied to the bodies in warning, no snake symbols cut into the flesh of the man's forehead. It was rumored that Snakers prided themselves on exquisite ritualism and there had been none of that. The man's eyes had not been plucked out and placed in his palms, his feet had not been tied together and embedded with crushed glass while he was still alive. He still had his shoes on.

The Snakers were not Koreans from the Southwest, as the Koreans in the restaurant appeared to be. They were Northern Koreans, a throwback to the sowan, a Confucian private school which appeared on the yangban country estates early in the Yi Dynasty which had lasted, So Pak once found from going through the Forbidden Histories, from 1392–1910. The Yi genealogical table was filled with notations about the rulers and male heirs to the thrones that read: Deposed, Abdicated, Poisoned, Killed.

In the last years of the Koryo Dynasty, one notable early sowan was set up by an official who quit public life rather than continue to condone what he regarded to be the contravention of Confucian ethics in the assumption of power by the new Yi rulers.

From the sowan, there emerged a cadre of young scholar bureaucrats who rode to power in their association with a young king, plunging, with his sanction into a reform program—only to be undone by their mentor's premature death and replacement by the most reprobate ruler in Korean history.

Prince Yonsan, the most wicked of rulers, found himself impotent from excess and sent to India for what were to become Korea's first snakes. He heard that keeping a basket of them under the bed would prove to be a sexual restorative. After his reign, Confucian influenced slipped, leaving the sowan as little more than a marshaling ground on which shattered or displaced factions could re-form and new ones take shape.

There were no Histories of this segment of Korean history, just the illegal oral tales passed down from generation to generation until the sowan developed into fearless fighters, heroes with a mythological ability to survive against all odds to right the world's wrongs, at least within the borders of the small clan-ruled, war-torn country that was Korea.

The Snake Sect, twentieth-century terrorists, claimed their roots in the sowan, collectives of scholars and bureaucrats whose emotional tendency toward violence had been schooled in a Chinese system of interminable reason and logic. But what had the medic meant, referring to the rebirth of the Snake Sect? How long had this been going on? What kind of parameters were being worked out within Korean politics? So Pak worried at the problem like a terrier with a rat in its teeth until, finally, his logic prevailed and he brought himself up short. Why did this concern him? What did it matter that the Snake Sect was active once again, when it held no allegiance to even the oral ritualism it had once possessed? Why was he making it his concern? He had been merely a bystander at the scene of a violent crime. He was allowing his imagination to become more overly involved than was wise. He should not be wasting valuable energy on wild flights of surmise and ancient historical references. It was imperative he focus his mind more stringently. He must take better care of himself. This incident was an indication that he was allowing his discipline to wear down. No longer were his priorities controlling his thinking. The fact of the matter was, terrorist activity in Newark was to be expected; it would be odd if he'd witnessed nothing during his stay here. And if the terrorists of the moment happened to be Korean, what of it? He was not put on this earth to unravel every Korean mystery that fell across his path.

What remained important about this incident was the fact that it demonstrated a flagging of his internal concentration, nothing more, nothing less. He was allowing outside events to distract him. That must not continue. Focus was of overriding importance. If he lost focus, he would fall short. His mission would be a pointless exercise. He must remind himself at all times that he was not a Historian. He had repudiated the path. History was nothing more than twisted shreds of observation, lies manufactured by whatever power was in momentary control. History, thanks to the Japanese, held no allegiance to truth, let alone fact; and there were no keys to understanding in the fabricated stories meant to explain past events. History was merely a mental reassurance, inferring that perhaps because we existed in the past as a society and structure, we would continue to do so in the future.

In any case, he could not afford to let theory or curiosity trap him. What was important was to focus his energy on the matter at hand, to take care of himself and his crew in the most fundamental of ways. He must find ice for his hand, food for his stomach, sleep for his mental health. That was what he had to do. He could not be sidetracked by concerns that had nothing to do with him.

By the time So Pak looked up to orient himself to

his surroundings, he was all the way to the corner of Tonkin and Whitehall. He must have been wandering in circles. A wide stretch of halolight blazed into the darkness before him, giving way to the Kleinhaupt Terminal. Tiny men, barely a mile away in orange reflecto suits, drove ground machines off-loading baggage. Their efforts, thanks to the great distance that separated them, seemed to have little more meaning than that of an ant dragging the carcass of a bee across a stone wall.

So Pak headed down Tonkin, a street known for its illicit musical entertainment. Tonkin housed the most prolific profusion of jazz clubs in the entire Western sector. The first time So Pak had come to Newark he had visited Tonkin Street only to find himself surprised at the smallness of the street, the tininess of the great clubs themselves, the gray film that seemed to cover everything. The clubs were often located in basement rooms reached by flights of stairs below the walkway. It was difficult to hear, the walls were thin, music leaked through from club to club. Somehow from the stories, So Pak had pictured the Newark jazz clubs as giant halls dotting a bleak and windswept plain.

Throughout the world, it was illegal to listen to jazz. The approved music was the controlled environmental music developed at the end of the twentieth century from meditative New Age schools. According to the Bylaws of the Iwaski Dictatorship, the purpose of music was to render its listeners calm and composed. Jazz, because of its tendency to incite individuality, was banned throughout the world despite the fact that the Japanese and Germans had once been rabid fans of the art form. Jazz practitioners were hidden by the patrons of the art in secret hiding places and brought out to play the occasional concert before being whisked away again into hiding. Even with that, the lives of jazz musicians were not lengthy. There were frequent jazz assassinations, hushed up by the media. It was difficult to know whether a particularly prominent musician were alive or dead.

A codicil in the Arts Laws, in addition to the Bylaws, banned jazz as an unprofitable art form. Perhaps that was why authorities did not crack down on it in the Transit Areas. Now, due to a great extent to its illegality, Transit Area clubs made a great deal of money. There was not much in Space Square that could not be translated into liquid currency. If the clubs didn't make money, they wouldn't still be there.

Tonkin was a notoriously ill-lit street; the halos shattered, the walkways littered with waste. A pool of light swept across the alley into which two homeless people scurried as So Pak passed. Tonkin Street was infamous for its dead junkies and for its inclusion in many a gripping city holo scene, the names of the jazz clubs carefully blacked out and renamed. But the holos were never faithful to the street. Depending on the subject matter, actors stepped out of Tonkin Street into Grand Hotels, city complexes, or hanging environments that were no longer seen in Manhattan, much less anywhere near Tonkin proper.

One or two robos walked the streets, showing no enthusiasm for their patrols. Small knots of people, faces shrouded in shadow, hurried into the basement clubs. So Pak heard the beat of a spincopter and the crack of laughter, nervous and shrill. A patrol car cruised by but didn't stop, its smoked windows impervious to bullets and sight. Two silhouettes in peaked hats were as much as So Pak could make out in the front seat and when the car turned left on Tonkin, he lost even that.

So Pak passed the first two clubs and walked into The High Hat. He was greeted politely enough by a bouncer and held in a plasto-paneled room where he was checked before being let into the club. The High Hat, like all other basement clubs, was small and dark. There was a long circular bar in the middle of the room around which patrons sat and two rows of tiny tables along each wall. The trio itself was crammed onto a small stage in the corner in violation of the cabaret laws, which allowed only one synthesizer and one musician onstage at all times.

So Pak looked around the dark smoky bar for a place to sit. The club was crowded, it was difficult to walk between the tables, let alone find a seat, but finally So Pak took a seat at the bar and ordered a single malt scotch from the harassed, unsmiling bartender, who regarded his customers sullenly from lowered eyebrows. The band started what must have been their second set of the evening and the noise in the bar settled down to an acceptable level.

The musicians were surprisingly old, having so far escaped all attempts at both assassination and youth rebuilding. At the drums, the Island musician danced over the skins with a sweet smile on his face and a nasty twist to his wrist. The pianist was white. He had no legs and So Pak was at a loss as to how he controlled the pedals until he saw the synthesizer hooked up to the man's forearms. The bassist was, uncharacteristically, white and his bass was the oldest one So Pak had ever seen. He listened to the band. They were good, and he was deep into a drum solo of "Lush Life" when the individual next to him spilled beer on his arm. In itself, it seemed an accident until the man started to make a major production of wiping it off with the fibernapkins stacked by the bowl of dried kelp on the bar.

So Pak tried to wave the man away, but he would have nothing of it.

"Hey," the stranger muttered. "I'm sorry. So you believe I'm sorry."

"It's fine," So Pak insisted. But the man kept nudging him until So Pak turned around in irritation and looked into the cold eyes of an alien. "Just drink your beer," he suggested. There was no other place to sit, So Pak noted as he took another quick inventory of the room. The bar seemed more crowded, if it were possible, than when he first walked into the club. There were corporate executives out slumming for the night, Anglo machinists, Chinese traders, Blacks, a faint smattering of disoriented-looking aliens. All of them were following the music intently but for a table of rowdy Americans in the back who were having an argument about football. So Pak stared into his drink and hoped the alien wouldn't get too conversational. Things seemed to be fine. The alien, having satisfied himself that So Pak's arm was bone dry, lapsed into silence. So Pak turned his attention to the music.

It was a new composition, rare in these days, particularly in a Transit club. Despite their skirting illegalities to hear the music, jazz fans were by and large traditionalists. They liked the old tunes and hated to have to listen to new material. But there was something about this piece that caught everyone's attention. For one thing, it was good. So Pak settled into the river of sound and let it flow around him, wrapping him up in a current, his mind drifting with the notes, devoid of any thought or speculation. It was, he realized, exactly what he needed. He thought too much.

But his reverie didn't last long. He felt a needlelike poke in his back as the alien leaned closer to his ear. Despite himself and his revulsion training, So Pak's flesh crawled. The alien's voice sounded a little off, as though human speech were difficult for it. The most unsettling thing about aliens, So Pak found, was the fact that they had learned to imitate humans admirably except for the fact that they seemed never to get the details exactly right. There was always something a little odd, a little off, something sensed rather than actually perceived that was unsettling no matter how much time one spent around the creatures.

"You should be careful with those around you," the alien began, determined to be heard. "You have the look of death about your aura and your vibrations are not high enough. You must raise your vibrational level."

So Pak politely pulled himself away, but the alien was insistent and would have none of it.

"Listen to me," it hissed. "I know."

But So Pak couldn't bring himself to listen despite the fact that he had, it seemed, no choice. The alien was bent on his enlightenment and its strange-smelling chlorophyll-like breath was close and irritating. "I know you have no curiosity about your future, but I must tell you."

"Please," So Pak continued to attempt to be polite and respectful, for this was an old one, but it was becoming increasingly difficult. The alien's small, nearly transparent fingers fluttered across the surface of the bar. It didn't, So Pak suddenly understood, have long to live.

"Yes, that's right," the alien confirmed sadly. "I

was sent here to die like the rest of my kind. There are many of us dying. Not all of us are recognizable as what we are. We are not strangers to death. They send us here to share and die, thinking it a great honor. It is not a great honor, it is a great ignominy."

So Pak stiffened. Yes, he had heard that. He had heard many things but considered them largely superstition. Somehow he had the luck to fall in with an alien who had managed to not only get himself drunk, but had also commenced Deathspeaking simultaneously. So Pak cursed his luck and bit his tongue until he could control his exasperation. "I wish to hear the music," he finally attempted, politely. "It is important for me to remember the way these songs sound. I am going off-world soon."

"Of course." The alien nodded. "There is confusion all about you."

Aliens near death were telepathic, or at least that was what people said. Some relegated it as alien lore, folktale, or superstition; whatever it was, So Pak knew this was an alien bent single-mindedly on Deathspeaking. He sighed and attempted to clear his mind. He imagined he was at the bottom of a clear, still pond, so dark and deep nothing could be read in its depths.

Finally, he determined not to let himself become seduced or charmed by anything the alien might say. Alien prophecy, based on telepathic impulses from the subject, was so personalized, answering to human loneliness so intensely, that it was difficult to ignore.

"Don't do that," the alien protested. "It will make no difference as to what I say and know, it will simply render the process more painful and require that the process take longer."

"Why aren't you in quarantine?" So Pak surprised even himself at the strident irritation in his voice. He refused to allow himself any more good deeds for the day. Due to the results of his activities earlier in the evening, he was beginning to believe the adage that no good deed went unpunished. It was asking too much to be strapped with an alien, and a Deathspeaking one, at that. He was too tired. He would not allow himself to feel pity.

"I see you for a strong and compassionate man," the alien whispered. Its voice was oddly metallic, inconsistent when read as human. "Off-planet you will find what you are searching for, to no one's great advantage. Your crew will perhaps succumb to madness and strife, and I do not know if you will disperse the clouds of darkness surrounding you." The alien coughed. Thin phosphorescent spittle sprayed onto the bar in front of them.

He cleared his throat and sighed deeply to clear his lungs. Something like breath rattled in his chest and he whistled as he spoke. "Your curiosity will be satisfied, of that you can be sure. You are a very curious man. Perhaps more curious than you are willing to accept."

The alien was going to die on him, So Pak could feel it. He suddenly found himself with a headache so blinding, that the air around the musicians became filled with brilliant colors, their bodies, however, remained only the vaguest of darkened blurs. So Pak downed his scotch, paid in yen, and, evading the alien's soft grasp, slid off the bar stool. He walked purposefully toward the door of the club, toward the exit sign that shone red in the darkness. He was determined to resist the gentle thoughts probing his brain like the fingers of a surgeon, searching insistently. For what? He closed the door behind him.

The bouncer stood with his back to So Pak, hands

clasped behind him. "Sir," So Pak informed him, "you've got a Deathspeaking alien in there. He needs help. He seems to be dying."

The bouncer looked at So Pak with cold eyes and So Pak recognized the fact that the bouncer was alien as well. "Just thought you'd like to know," he added apologetically.

He hurried outside into the mess of Tonkin Street, which was infinitely better in all of its crabbed seediness than the closeness of the bar and the reek of sickness emanating from the alien's body. Halfway down Tonkin, he had almost lost the headache and, briefly, So Pak thought of trying another club. But it seemed events were proving he'd played out his luck for the day. At the corner of Tonkin he hailed a floatcar, counting himself lucky when one braked to a stop in front of him and a silent, surly driver got out to open the door. He was lucky on two counts: his driver was decidedly human and he was most certainly not prone to conversation.

"Nanday Barracks," So Pak said as he settled back into the safe, enclosed leather interior of the floatcar.

"Certainly."

Once he arrived back at the barracks, he planned to have some miso sent up to his room with rice and green tea. It wasn't the dinner he had envisioned earlier, but it was at least nutritious.

In the back of the floatcar, So Pak resolved to become more disciplined. He would get lots of sleep and put the night out of his mind. It was still early enough for him to get a good seven hours. He could count himself lucky. He would have gone mad listening to the alien's metallic prophesying, spinning his future out like some kind of cheap sensapalm reader on the Whitehall strip. It was, after all, his own fault. He had allowed himself too many flights of imagination at the end of a long working day. That kind of mental attitude could be remedied easily enough.

By the time the floatcar driver pulled up in front of Nanday Barracks, So Pak had managed to achieve a functional but wobbly peace of mind, despite the irritating requisite meditation music filling the cab.

CHAPTER FOUR

Mr. Matsuda was a tiny, dessicated Japanese elder with a shock of white hair and the telltale sign of fanatical fire lurking behind his eyes. People said a lot of things about Mr. Matsuda in quickened, hushed tones, but none of it was true. The truth was carefully hidden, buried deeply by Mr. Matsuda himself long ago.

Mr. Matsuda sat at the head of the table. His back was very straight. His hands were folded in front of him, not placed upon the table like the hands of many of his associates. He was not listening. He was carefully regarding the council members before him, all of whom sat at the polished teak table wearing black suits, white shirts, and black ties. Each man wore two pieces of jewelry: a small gold Iwaski lapel button on the left lapel, and a gold Rolex, placed just below the wristbone on the right wrist. Only Mr. Tomita was left-handed.

Set in front of each man was a computer notebook and a gold laser flickpen. The conference table around which they were positioned dwarfed the cavernous room. The room was paneled in reclaimed oak paneling, lifted, no doubt, from at least twenty-five or more Irish manor halls. In the center of the table was placed a traditional arrangement of white orchids. Each orchid was immense and pure white, with no touch of blemish or color. Ancient but barely worn Oriental carpets covered the floor. Flow lights were tastefully hidden around the room.

Just yesterday, Mr. Matsuda had brought in Master Li at great expense from Mainland China to Feng Shui the room. Mr. Matsuda knew something was awry. He did not know what. He believed that the efforts of Master Li, adept at the art of room arrangement and placement of energy flow would aid him in his search for the source of the disharmony. Mr. Matsuda carefully watched the faces and gestures of the eight men before him. He had no doubt in the world that one of these men would betray himself; if not today, then at another time in this room. The energy of one of these men was not in harmony with the energy of the whole. And Mr. Matsuda believed in the harmony of the whole. He had achieved his position as First Chairman of the Iwaski Dictatorship through patience, waiting, and moving when the time was ripe. His had not been a studied rise to power. He was natural in all that he did. He had handpicked the men seated before him after much difficulty: they were all brilliant, gifted, astute men dedicated to the continued prosperity of Iwaski. All but Mr. Tomita and Mr. Seto had been with him since he had risen to power almost forty years ago. Mr. Matsuda knew he was not acting as an old man, prone to nervous suggestion and strange thoughts. He had detected a change some months ago and had carefully studied the situation. He had remained perfectly impartial. He would allow the situation to reveal itself. He had set the trap, all that remained was for the quarry to step into it. With some intelligence and experience, the prey could warily escape for some time but, eventually, with patience and the right conditions, it would be caught.

Mr. Matsuda collected his thoughts. He opened his agenda and waited for the others to follow his lead. This was a standard meeting, nothing more. Behind Mr. Matsuda, the conference room windows gave onto a view of the bay, sunlit and evocative. Nevertheless, no one's attention strayed.

"There are several items on the agenda which demand our attention today," Mr. Seto began. As Chairman, Mr. Seto led the discussions for Mr. Matsuda. His reactions were so perfectly timed that he knew each nuance of Mr. Matsuda's voice and physical movements. Mr. Matsuda, on the whole, found Mr. Seto indispensable but irritating.

"To begin, we will consider the alien problem." Mr. Seto nodded to Mr. Ishioka, Minister of the Alternate Life-forms Rehab Program. Mr. Ishioka blinked twice, looked around the table, and began his report. A thin line of sweat tracked down the side of his face through his sideburns. This, Mr. Matsuda disregarded. Heavy perspiration was the sign of a passionate nature and although one should avoid passion because it led to error, Mr. Ishioka was of a choleric temperament, unused to having to address the council. His was a junior role which allowed him time to grow into the position. Many First Chairmen had begun on the council in Mr. Ishioka's capacity.

"I would like to inform the assembled council members that the Committee on Outcast Life-forms has registered a complaint with the following alien communities regarding alien dumping on our planet." The committee to which he referred was a subcommittee of the Rehab Program, a volatile sector both politically and emotionally. In lieu of reading the complaint or the names of all the alien committees to which it had been submitted, Mr. Ishioka pressed the keyboard set into the armrest of his chair and the information appeared on the giant compuscreen to the left of the table. The complaint was short and standard in its demands. The alien communities flowed across the screen, listed by rank and level of cooperation in the past.

"Although we have, as you know, granted alien burial rights in conjunction with the Republic of New Germany who, as you are all well aware, is more sensitive to the problem than we are, it is our decided opinion that something must be done. We can no longer allow unregistered alien dumping, particularly at the Transit Ports. As we all know, we cannot tolerate disturbances in a population that has risen to 780 individuals per square meter in urban areas and 100 in undesignated suburban areas. Alien dumping causes disturbance in the population. We are all aware of the phenomenon of Deathspeak and its effects on the more superstitious members of the planet. It encourages individual speculation, concern with self-patterning, and an obsession with individual survival that is contrary to the progress of the whole. It is, I admit, to my discredit that marginal Deathspeak was allowed when we first permitted aliens to be buried here. All forms of Deathspeaking will be reported to Alien Centers and dealt with in the most extreme manner necessary. The Republic of New Germany has agreed to cooperate with us in this matter. Deathspeakers will only share knowledge through appropriate channels at appropriate locations. This knowledge will be stored in Deathspeak programs, to be referred to when circumstances dictate. Otherwise, this material will not be available for public use."

Mr. Ishioka paused to take a deep breath before he continued. "We have set up new quotas for alien dumping. It is my wish to bow to Mr. Matsuda's greater knowledge in this department. We have sent the necessary reports and only await his recommendation."

Mr. Matsuda nodded. He was pleased. Mr. Ishioka had fulfilled his duty well. The next step would be development of an alien disposal unit—a step toward which he was heading. Mr. Ishioka had acted wisely in bringing up the matter before the council before acting rashly on his own. Rash action led only to reaction. Mr. Matsuda must give clearance to the members of the Republic of New Germany cooperating with Mr. Ishioka on this matter. And the matter would take some thought: the alien question was an emotional one that fired the imagination of the people. One had to be extremely careful. It would be much easier if Deathspeak didn't have the reputation of being so unerringly accurate. The population at large still hadn't gotten over the twentieth century mythology that stated aliens were somehow more knowledgeable, more technically advanced, more enlightened than human beings. A view which had been romanticized by governments covering up the existence of alien presences on the planet. There were politicians who had hoped that, making the alien issue more open would destroy the mystic element of their behavior but so far it had not worked. Man was persistent in believing forces outside himself knew more than he did. Mr. Matsuda was not an unbeliever when it came to master plans, but he believed that master plans were best created by human beings, not outside agents. Mr. Matsuda did not expect to discover a real solution, short-term policies were the best anyone could expect to enforce. The situation was completely in flux; it could turn into anything at any time.

Mr. Seto backed up Mr. Ishioka's report by reading incidents of alien activity and their effects upon the population at large. Although there were many more than Mr. Matsuda thought possible, he did not register surprise. Trouble was, there was no way of killing them. They had to die on their own. And the alien colonies, ostensibly set up under the most humanitarian pretext, actually functioned as a means to contain the creatures in given areas so any possible inflicted damage was limited.

It was a simple enough matter. If Mr. Seto's figures were correct, there were many more aliens than there were alien colonies. And, it seemed, the population was not terrified enough of their effects on human survival, both in burgeoning numbers and in psychological effects. Mr. Matsuda resolved to have a meeting with Mr. Tomita: this was a matter for Historians and the assorted Historical Arts. Something could be accomplished through a History perhaps, to put people off the insufferable sympathy they had for other dying life-forms. Mr. Matsuda quietly awaited Mr. Seto's termination of the alien discussion. He was not disappointed in Mr. Seto's efficiency. Mr. Seto cut off Mr. Ishioka in midsentence. Although it was a mild loss of face, Mr. Ishioka remained calm as Mr. Seto addressed the next item on the agenda—simple clearance of departing probes.

Transport was the department of Mr. Kajii, a singularly thin and quiet man with a photographic memory. His voice was rich and well-modulated. Even if his manner was studied, it was a pleasure listening to his presentations, layer upon layer of complicated information laid upon itself until a brilliant piecework burst upon the consciousness of the audience.

Seventeenth hundred probes were scheduled to depart

in the next two weeks, most of the probes routine. Four hundred were investigatory probes given special humanitarian clearance, and charged with locating and bringing back samples of various natural resources—gases, minerals, microscopic fauna that could proliferate quickly and economically to an ecologically beleaguered planet. On the whole, probes were far from economical and it was a blanket policy to stringently limit unnecessary probes and interstellar travel. In addition, general sentiment at Iwaski held that it was not a good idea to have individuals wandering off-planet on their own, discovering things without control. Mr. Matsuda, however, had found probes to be beneficial in occupying the energies of individuals who possessed rebellious tendencies.

If they ran into trouble, it generally threatened the welfare of the probe. They were watched by communication and military ships. It was more economical than a penal colony, and drastic mistakes could be dealt with by mercs, reports citing the serious risks of traveling off-planet as the cause of death with no trace.

Mr. Kajii systematically reviewed the probe list until Mr. Matsuda's interest was piqued by mention of the *Bushido*.

Mr. Seto, alert to Mr. Matsuda's responses, requested, "Please give us a little background on the *Bushido*." Despite himself, Mr. Seto's face registered disgust at the unfortunate name of the ship.

At the mention of So Pak's name, Mr. Matsuda's memory was refreshed and he wished he could allow himself the luxury of a small smile. The Paks were a great clan of Historians and, before that, of literati. So Pak was the last living son. A disobedient son. It had been a simple matter to take care of the young man's brother who, surprisingly, was beginning to show brilliance. It was Mr. Matsuda's experience that brilliance eventually accompanied obedience.

Mr. Matsuda himself greatly enjoyed reading the Histories of Historian Pak. In fact, Historian Pak was Mr. Matsuda's favorite Historical Artist. Mr. Matsuda suspected he was a great one. Had anyone in the Historical Arts been allowed Master Status, it would most certainly have been Historian Pak. Out of respect for the man and his work, Mr. Matsuda had allowed him a full fifteen-minute closed phone interview during which Historian Pak pleaded respectfully that his son not be allowed to pursue his plans to explore the ancient mining expedition.

As a father himself, Mr. Matsuda sympathized. But he told Historian Pak in no uncertain terms that his son would be allowed to do as he wished. The area surrounding Zeta Reticuli was dangerous, not much was known of conditions there. Historian Pak knew then that his son was being sent off to die. Mr. Matsuda only hoped that Historian Pak would come to understand the wisdom of this decision in his later years. It was rare in this day and age that the sons of gifted parents became as great as their fathers and Mr. Matsuda, aside from getting rid of another potentially problematic member of the Pak clan, wished Historian Pak to understand the great gesture of respect that had been offered him: he, the father, would stand at the magnificent apex of the entire clan of gifted storytellers with none to surpass him.

Meanwhile, Mr. Seto was continuing to put Mr. Kajii through the routine questions of procedure regarding the space probes. Investigative probes were supported by auxiliary ships which kept on the progress of the operation. They formed two functions, backup and watchdog.

Mr. Kajii graciously informed them all that in addition to standard auxiliary ships, the *Bushido* would be accompanied by tracer ships: a communication vehicle and a patrol ship.

"And the crew?" Mr. Seto asked.

Mr. Kajii's generally great implacability and calm remained unbroken. "The teams will wear trackers at all times. It is standard procedure. Quite simple, really."

"The crew has been approved," Mr. Seto established, not willing to let the subject of the *Bushido* go because he still felt awareness of Mr. Matsuda's interest.

Mr. Kajii nodded, a sharp little bow of assertion. "Naturally." He looked around the table. "The itinerary has been set and cleared. The families of the crew members have been informed that, should the ship or anyone on the ship take independent action, the family members of the individuals in the crew will be disciplined as well as those involved in the probe."

"What of the information brought back by the probe?" Mr. Seto inquired politely.

"It will be sent to the library to await a new History."

Mr. Matsuda watched the shifting light on the faces of the men before him. Always the Japanese had understood the importance of eradication of all political and cultural activities in the control of nationalistic fervor. Since the hot, humid day in August of 1910, when the last Korean ruler of the Yi Dynasty signed a treaty officially annexing Korea to Japan with colonial status, the Japanese had been editing history. All major Korean language newspapers were closed; many writers and editors were imprisoned. Nearly all existing history texts were confiscated and burned and the

Japanese, while discouraging public gatherings and keeping a careful eye on theaters for expression of anti-Japanese sentiment, embarked on a program to rewrite the history of Korea.

Mr. Seto, who had exhausted all possible questioning of Mr. Kajii, glanced at Mr. Matsuda, who waved him on through the meeting with a barely perceptible flick of his fingers.

There was a brief economic report from Mr. Yamamata before the meeting was adjourned. Mr. Matsuda sat at the conference table silently as his ministers bowed in respect before their departure.

He had discovered nothing. Another meeting must be called soon, to provide an opportunity to allow the Feng Shui to work on his men. Perhaps there would be news of the *Bushido*. And there was the Korean question to discuss. In the meantime, he had follow-up work from this meeting to see to. There were numerous reports to read and the alien question to meditate upon. Perhaps he would schedule himself three hours more of work before going to the corporate baths. He could then work several hours at home before retiring at an early hour. Mr. Matsuda decided to make himself largely unavailable for the next couple of days. He resolved to have information on the progress of the *Bushido* relayed to his home office by compuprompter. He sensed that the situation, as well as being a pleasant distracting entertainment of sorts, would bear watching.

As he dismissed Mr. Seto, the last of his cabinet to leave, Mr. Matsuda allowed himself a smile of anticipation.

So Pak sat in the steaming quonset hut wondering blackly if the heat were just another Japanese plot to control revolutionary probes such as the one on which he was about to embark. Environmental control had broken down all along the Beltway due to a freak electrical storm the night before and So Pak's uniform was soaked with sweat. Despite the inconvenience, he was satisfied and content. Chosyam had managed to complete his assigned tasks without creating trouble and had shown a measurable degree of responsibility. His crew had been approved, his itinerary cleared, construction on the ship completed. It was as though some Biblical angel had descended from heaven and moved across the face of the waters to clear the way.

Mr. Seto punched in the security clearance code and accessed the airway shuttle to Building Block 46. He was exhausted. He had just begun his night. Aside from the work that still had to be cleaned up for Mr. Matsuda's breakfast meeting tomorrow morning, he had to take care of his own reports, read the reports of the twenty-five people who were responsible to him, and check in with his contacts.

Mr. Seto rubbed his eyes with the heels of his hands and, when that didn't relieve his eyestrain, he got out of his shuttle seat and went into the restroom. He splashed water onto his face and wet a paper towel with cold water and pressed it to the back of his neck. When he reached for another towel to wipe off his face, he stared at himself in the mirror, his hair in wet points around his face, moisture clinging to his eyelashes. He shook his head. Water spattered onto the mirror and dripped down into the sink. For a moment, he stared at the bathroom walls, letting it all go, enjoying an immense release just by blanking out and unfocusing his eyes for a moment. His life had been completely different since he'd hit upon the truth face to face. He checked his watch. It was time for checkpoint.

Mr. Seto reached into his pocket and pulled out a small wire which he ran around the inside of the bathroom door and the light fixtures. Bug sensitive, it flashed off and on, but the orange detection light didn't activate. Mr. Seto pulled a flat pocket vidphone out of his inside breast pocket and dialed Quan.

"Yes." By the look of it, Quan was having a rough night.

"Two points."

"Fire away."

"Iwaski is taking steps to develop an alien disposal unit."

Quan nodded. "That correlates with other information we've received from the Alien Rights and Environmental Protection People. Right around Florida, is it?"

"No known location."

"See what you can find."

"Tell Marcus at Freierhaumpt that any information the *Bushido* probe manages to dig up at the off-planet mining site is to be sent straight to the Library."

"Lock up?"

"Looks like they don't intend to release the information."

"I thought Iwaski sent a probe out there to check on whether or not the site was clean before they even gave Pak permission and clearance. He came up with nothing."

"He must have come up with something, or they wouldn't be sending it to the Library."

"I wonder what's up there."

"Hard to tell. Matsuda seems to think it's under

control. At least that's how he's acting. Something's bothering him though.''

''Something should be bothering him. He's single-handedly responsible for stripping the last chance we really had for an environmental turnaround. A planet of 50 billion and not even a century of resources.''

''Let's not waste time moaning over secom channels.''

''Well, whatever it is, get your hands on a copy and we'll circulate it through Intercorp. The snake. The man's a snake. We have it all, terraforming, people who want to get off-planet. We might at least have started real colonies by now, not just those luxury off-planet things. Ridiculous waste of resources and information. And alien dumping; I'm the first to offer them asylum. They have improved our medical knowledge immeasurably, but why do they want to come here to die? And how can we continue to allow it?''

''Iwaski has broken every Alien Treaty since they started negotiating for the Eastern Conglomerate.''

''And the Eastern Conglomerate is run like a Shinto alliance. Every corporation is a little feudal protectorate, and these are our allies, wouldn't you know.'' Quan complained.

He was interrupted by a voice with a thick German accent. ''Please, Mr. Lee, if you would be so kind as to refrain from using the secom channel to air personal opinions?''

''Yes, sir.'' Quan was all business.

''Thank you, Mr. Lee. And you, Mr. Seto, must have more important things to do than gossip with Mr. Lee over a barely secured com channel.''

Mr. Seto bowed his head, clicked off the report channel, and pocketed his transmitter. Then he left the restroom and returned to his seat where he opened the top of his compupak and began to work. He had twenty minutes before his next meeting and, if he was lucky, he could get through at least fifteen reports by the time he landed.

Yesterday, when So Pak visited the airfield, he felt a hard, quick flash of pride as he stood before his ship, thinking that, through his efforts, he had come a long way in breaking from his family and doing something which, however small, would bring hard facts back to the computers of the Historians. He would have been horrified to know that his Biblical angel was none other than Mr. Matsuda himself and that anything brought back was to be locked away in the Library of Probe Findings. As it was, So Pak regarded the completion of his preparations as a well-earned reward for two years of horrifying dedication. A singular triumph of his own few others would find any interest in understanding.

He had almost forgotten the incident at the bubble restaurant. It no longer seemed important except as a macabre incident in his life; an occult outburst of violence following uncannily closely after the accidental death of his brother. The ominous associations that had plagued him the next day had, in the long run, been no more significant than the effects of a short-lived illness. He had recovered his dedication and sense of purpose. There were more urgent things to consider than the haunting face of the victimized woman who had so quickly disappeared into the crowd. Soon he would be far from Newark, freed from its gaudy outbursts of violence. One had to expect that sort of thing in a Transit Port. It was not necessary to take an event like that too seriously, to read meanings and omens into things that weren't there.

So Pak had fought flights of imagination all of his life. Sometimes, however, his imagination had created opportunity. Had he not been able to let his mind wander freely, he would not be about to take off to explore a mining disaster that had caught very little of the imagination of the public at large.

Since boyhood, So Pak had been fascinated by the story of the mining disaster off Zeta Reticuli. The first time he had come across the newspaper clipping must have been when he was about eight. He remembered everything about that day. His father had been living in Seoul and it was summer. His mother had been frantically organizing last-minute preparations for a trip to the mountains. The entryway of the house was piled high with bundles. So Pak could hear his mother's shrill voice exhorting the children to find something to amuse themselves, reminding them that a shrimp is often crushed in the battle of whales. The heat and his mother's voice were oppressive. His brothers and sisters were fighting in the hallway. His sister had just begun to howl in full force when Kim took her cricket cage and let her cricket free, reasoning that it was only by chance the creature would survive since the servants would undoubtedly forget to feed it.

So Pak fled into the forbidden country of his father's study, not wanting to be around when his mother finally lost her temper and began smacking children and berating servants. He knew his mother's moods. She was like a brooding sea which could suddenly be provoked to hurricane force for no apparent reason. Once it ran its course, it became calm again. But the effects of the storm often remained and So Pak had been smacked often enough that he had learned to disappear when she began telling the story of the shrimp.

No one was ever allowed in Historian Pak's study, particularly while he was gone. But he had been gone for so long this time that So Pak's mother's discipline had become lax. The study was still and quiet. As long as So Pak remembered, it had always been the same. For one thing, the study smelled of his father: of the exported stubby cigarettes he smoked, of the smell of sandalwood that clung to him and everything he touched, of the dry acid scent of his skin which reminded So Pak of the exotic aroma of the peel of citrus when he sat in his father's lap and pretended he was sitting in a human chair, his head pressed tightly against his father's chest.

At first, So Pak began coming to his father's study to sit and be near him when he was gone to Seoul, or to Japan, or to the Republic of New Germany. He sat in his father's chair and talked to him, convinced that his father heard and understood. It was later that he taught himself to access his father's computer. By the age of eight, his father's computer was the most interesting thing in the world to So Pak, filled with true stories of the most vicious and bloody variety, the kind of stories of flesh and blood human beings who were constantly living with the threat of losing both, that no one ever got to read about satisfactorily enough in the Histories and no one ever told at school in either the History or Ancestral Events classes.

On that day, after he had first made sure there was a rousing, lengthy argument going on in the hallway outside, So Pak sat down at the computer and began accessing random information. His fingers whirled past entries of farming statistics and weather patterns for the year 2055. He lingered longer at the air disasters: freak weather patterns had caused numerous weather disasters that year.

So Pak smiled as he remembered the long-sleeved shirt, too large for him, that he had been ordered to grow into by his exasperated mother. He had tried to obey, growing a lot that summer, lying in bed at night wanting to cry because his arms and legs ached with a dull pain deep in the bone. However, he had not grown enough to fit into the shirt. The sleeves caught on the computer keys and So Pak was trying to figure out how to space back past where the loose sleeves had dragged him when the story flashed on the screen.

The entry was starred with his father's notes, mostly having to do with questions about the authenticity of the report. All his requests for more information had been denied. In 2055, a Japanese and a Korean mining crew, acting independently, had been engaged in a race to claim mineral rights on a nameless planet off Zeta Reticuli. Although Japan had the economic upper hand, it seemed Korea was winning the race for technological development. The two mining expeditions landed on the planet weeks apart. There were group pictures of each crew, taken in the Transit Port before lift-off. So Pak bent over the screen, trying to read a grainy individuality into each of the faces. Everyone looked hopeful, excited, and young. So Pak had spent a lot of time studying that picture, thinking that most of the miners were not much older than he. The looming shapes of the ships behind them were old, blunt-nosed designs, impossibly romantic, like the drawings of ships in his storybooks. In his excitement, So Pak touched the computer screen thoughtlessly: his fingers would leave smudges and his mother would know he had been there. He rubbed the screen with the sleeve of his shirt, hoping he didn't put scratches on it.

There were several subprograms of entries. One large article announced the ships' departures in Korean and Japanese. The article contained a lot of technical jargon So Pak couldn't understand. Naturally, the old files were difficult to read. People used a lot of flowery technical language that didn't mean much and was hard to puzzle out. So Pak read the article slowly and repeatedly until he could manage to make it out.

It seemed that, at the outset, the Korean ship was faced with technical problems. It left the Transit Port two days later than the Japanese ship. Once on planet, despite the fact that Japan was again at war with Korea, the two ships set up camp within kilometers of each other. For several months, things seemed to be progressing as planned, then, suddenly, the Japanese began sending back messages, incomplete reports and unintelligible pleas for help. Two Japanese scouts set out "bravely" to seek aid from the Korean camp. They discovered all the members of the Korean probe were dead. A handful had died in their bunks, the rest had wandered far from camp in miserable groups of four or five men. Whatever they had been looking for, they didn't find before death discovered them. The reported cause of death was a meaningless technical term impossible for So Pak to decipher: the pictures of the bodies were clear enough. It was obvious that these men had died in utter agony.

After the discovery of the dead Korean crew, the Japanese straggled back to their own ship without bothering to track down the remaining missing crew members. The Japanese themselves were skeletal, a blurred picture from a Korean paper recorded barely twenty-five emaciated men with a common and fundamental insanity lurking behind their eyes. Cannibalism was inferred. So Paks' eight-year-old eyes widened and a cold thrill of adventure ran up his backbone. But there were no further references. Just one small entry which seemed to indicate that the Japanese, after visiting the Korean camp, radioed back an ultrasound mining technique which Iwaski immediately purchased from the government, which was so embroiled in war, they seemed glad to get rid of it to funnel the money into North Korea in the form of arms and ammo. The description of the ultrasound device was an unintelligible scramble of terms. When So Pak searched his father's files for more information, he found nothing.

This entry was followed by one or two news articles, so heavily censored they were rendered meaningless. So Pak had been bent over the computer, madly searching the files for at least enough information to satisfy his curiosity when his younger sister came running into the study. She was, So Pak remembered, wearing a red dress. Her stubby legs were bowed. Like most Korean children, she had been carried on her mother's back, her legs wrapped around her mother's waist until they had gradually bowed out. She ran up to So Pak and stuck her finger in his mouth and she had just turned to the door again when their mother came flying into the room. So Pak knew he was about to suffer severe consequences. Naturally, his mother caught him at his father's terminal but, what was even worse, he was with his sister. Worked up within minutes by the heat and disorganization of moving the household, she began a righteous raging. She pulled So Pak out of the chair and hit him so hard on the side of the head with the flat of her hand that So Pak was convinced she'd deafened him for life. Despite a summer filled with growing pains, So Pak was still small for eight and his mother had no trouble seizing him by the shoulders and throwing him around the room. His sister began to howl as though an army of warriors were after her and his mother never once stopped screaming. Although So Pak could never recall exactly what she said, he remembered thinking it strange she should be howling about his father rather than about him and his transgressions. After all, it hadn't been his father who had disobeyed.

When he had had enough of being flung into the wall, he tried to make his body as loose, light, and liquid as possible, thinking she could hurt him less if he made himself weigh nothing. But after several flights across the room, he realized that wasn't a solution and instead, curled himself up into a ball on the floor. Eventually, as he had known it would, her anger subsided, his little sister was calmed by the servants, and his mother resumed overseeing the household.

What happened next came as no surprise to So Pak. He was left at home alone for two sweltering weeks with the servants and utter boredom while his family went to the mountains. In retrospect, he wondered if his mother knew it was a ridiculous punishment. He had no recourse but to turn to the computer. He spent a fortnight dreaming, awake and asleep, of the mining expedition. He made up stories consciously and subconsciously of the people and faces he had seen on the computer screen. He came to understand that he hated all mystery.

As he grew older, he brought up the story on his father's computer many times, but each time, it seemed as though more and more of the story had disappeared from the files. The last time he remembered calling it up from his father's office, it was no more than a mere paragraph of explanation that had nothing to do with the young men So Pak saw pictured before him.

It was ironic when it turned up in his assignment pack from ReutersKino. So Pak had been working in

Germany for two years on a Japanese assignment in cooperation with the German European Federation. As the top Japanese subliminals expert, he had been sent overseas to teach seminars in subliminal programming to the media, most notably the German news media. Within months, he handpicked his students and taught them the basics of neurolinguistic programming, augmented by the work of Girondeux and Anselm. And all the time, he worked on programming German news stories that came through the stray lines. He'd take innocuous human interest stories and layer them so that when the reader finished with them, he was questioning the voice of the paper, questioning the holostories and the entertainment holos and wondering . . . It wasn't much, he certainly wasn't feeding anyone any information, but it was a beginning.

He had been careful what he taught his students, sitting in the small, fern-choked, paneled room on the third floor of the Academy, until he was quite sure of them. Then he taught them the real stuff: how to use language as well as images, how to position words with images and sound, how to run positive affirmations through merchandise advertisements, how to use syllables and sounds to weave a secondary language subtext for the multilingual. "Always remember," So Pak told his students, "the mind is like a large sponge. It retains everything. The human brain wastes nothing."

"Unethical," Anderson mumbled. Anderson was far too serious for his own good, his gray-green eyes clouded beneath heavy eyebrows and a shock of hair the color of buttercups in summer, a thatch of hair that did nothing to lighten his intense nature.

"The current government would answer that simply," So Pak said, "by telling you it is the protruding nail that wants a hammering."

Anderson scowled.

"Meaning it is essential for all individuals in a society to be the same in order for that society to run smoothly."

"Individuals in a society must respect social authority." Ingralls quoted from the subliminal creed.

So Pak remembered the looks on the faces of his students: absolute and total despair. Except for Treel, in the back of the room, who was positively gloating over the thought of unlimited power no farther away than his keyboard.

"What of societies that have no authority?"

"What society?"

"Societies in which authority suddenly fails, or is taken over by revolution."

"Societies with no common language can have no organic authority and cannot hold. They foster fascist states and totalitarian governments, whose authority must erode and dissipate after great damage is done."

Anderson broke in, "Any society that doesn't share a common story cannot share an ethic and therefore will give rise to artificially structured authority instead?"

"Something like that." So Pak looked Anderson straight in the eyes. "Of course, subliminals are unethical. But they can be used to seed information, to make people question. And those with strong truth systems, or sense of self, while they may question information will eventually only use those questions to prove themselves."

"Oh, really," Treel said.

It had been that year that So Pak had run across the Zeta Reticulan mining story in his assignment pack from ReutersKino. It was a classic subliminal work and, when So Pak retrieved and worked through it, he was shocked and amazed at the layers in operation. He was beginning to understand why it had disappeared from the Historians' Archives.

He had the sense that someone specific was responsible for the layering: some German or European, who was stirring up interest and questions about the mining expedition and just what had occurred there.

There were speculations about a Japanese company using something intrinsic about the mining expedition to rise to the top in a Japan which, at that time, was torn by feuding corporations headed by presidents and CEOs who resembled nothing more than the old Shinto warlords. There were environmental themes familiar to So Pak from certain German/Japanese factions, companies banded together into an oddly militant ecological position. But most interesting and confusing of all were the transcripts of messages from the Korean and Japanese camps themselves which to So Pak, although he had little time to thoroughly decode them, seemed like DNA helixes of information, messages turning on themselves and spiraling out into unintelligibility.

The more So Pak studied the tapes, the more obvious it became to him that, if he didn't get Japanese clearance for the probe, he might be able to expect German clearance. Certainly they had some kind of interest in the outcome of such a project. It was only much later, about the time he had begun to organize the probe, that So Pak understood he had not been given the assignment pack by chance.

So Pak stood up abruptly. He was getting nothing constructive done, sitting here dragging himself through the past.

"Sir," Chosyam stood in the doorway. Physical sensations seemed to flood into So Pak, thick limpid heat pushing itself around his face, his sweat-soaked shirt, the hardness of the scanty patch of bare quonset floor underneath his feet. Chosyam, So Pak noted, was taking the heat badly as well. His face was flushed, his flight suit fit his body like peeling molded putty. So Pak wondered how it was possible for cloth to take on that blurry gray liquid texture.

Chosyam pulled at his shirt collar and hitched up his belt. His clothing shifted momentarily, only to settle once again back to the confines of his body. He had something to say, "Important news, sir."

So Pak toyed with one of the infernal glo-pens.

"Transit control called just now, sir."

"And what is it that they want?"

"That's what I'm trying to tell you, sir. They have sent over the port officials."

"The papers are on your desk, Chosyam. I put them there yesterday after we completed the last of the forms." The customs papers had almost blinded him. One hundred and twenty-five pages, all of which must be signed, notarized, and in perfect order before any ship took off.

"That's just it, sir, they seem to be misplaced."

"Misplaced?"

"What I mean to say is, I gave them back to you."

"Then they're in this office, aren't they?" So Pak looked around him at the piles of roach-infested data. "Where?"

"We'll find them." Bleakly, Chosyam began to dig through the nearest stack of papers until his face lit up. It seemed a miracle when he hauled a thick yellow plastic envelope out of the pile to the left of the door.

He waved the file before him triumphantly before disappearing out to his own desk in the outer office.

So Pak sighed, grateful that Chosyam always seemed to be able to find things. Once he sat down at his desk, he began to work through the pile of papers by his right arm. It was barely ten minutes later that Chosyam was back at the door, trying unsuccessfully to hold back the two Japanese officials long enough to formally announce their presence. But the two officials sailed into the room, coolly disregarding protocol.

The senior official, who introduced himself as Mr. Tienshan, took the opportunity to sit in the room's only unoccupied chair. Chosyam and the assisting official, stood.

"Captain," Mr. Tienshan said with a bare nod of greeting, "I assume, of course, that the necessary papers are in order."

"Of course." So Pak nodded to Chosyam, who hauled the folder back into the office from the outer reception area. He handed the documents to So Pak, who transferred them to Mr. Tienshan. A full minute passed as Mr. Tienshan reached inside his pockets for a pair of wire-rimmed glasses, affixed them to his ears, and settled them on his nose. He then picked up the file and began to read. Past experience had enabled him to juggle the bulk of pages with the grace of a card dealer.

After several silent moments, Mr. Tienshan cleared his throat. "I see we have some difficulties here." He peered intently at the pages before him.

Once again, So Pak sighed, this time inaudibly. He reached for the prepared envelope at the side of his desk. The envelope contained 2,000 yen. He slipped the envelope into the nearest empty file folder embossed with the Iwaski crest and walked over to the seated Japanese. With his back to the remaining official and Chosyam, So Pak turned his attention to the open files in Mr. Tienshan's lap.

"Perhaps we have neglected to add the proper citizenship papers?" he suggested, slipping the new folder into the file.

Mr. Tienshan opened the envelope and peered into it with practiced eyes. A hint of annoyance, feigned expressly for So Pak's benefit, crossed his face. "It is rare," Mr. Tienshan began, "that Korean ship's papers are correct and in order. I trust that, next time, you will include all the information when requested upon arrival. Efficiency is a valuable quality in a ship's captain."

So Pak nodded. Chosyam was attempting to look disinterested, but Koreans transplanted to America had no talent for dissembling and an expansive grin threatened to break out and spread across his face. Fortunately, neither Mr. Tienshan nor his associate noticed. Mr. Tienshan was busy slipping the envelope into the inside pocket of his regulation jacket. When he had finished, he stood and performed the politeness of a small bow. "Since everything is in order, there will be no problem arranging your departure as scheduled. Please notify the Tower of your departure as quickly as possible." He looked around the room, allowing himself to show mild distaste.

"And please see to it that this disorder is taken care of and the room vacated by five o'clock this afternoon. Probe Captain Yurelli will be expected at eight thirty tomorrow morning and will need the office to arrange for his ship's departure." From his tone of voice, Mr. Tienshan made it plain that Captain Yurelli's probe was of much more importance than an ancient and forgotten mining disaster.

Once Chosyam had shown them out, more out of courtesy than any real worry they would lose themselves in the confines of a regulation quonset hut, he returned to So Pak's office.

So Pak looked at him as though requesting no comment, but Chosyam was not to be derailed. "Doesn't it seem odd that we are not being detained?"

"Not at all." So Pak was unconcerned. "If a probe does not operate with efficiency at its inception, what hope will there be that it will run smoothly at all?"

"That is superstition."

So Pak's patience was wearing thin. "There will be many things to question once we are on our way. Let us not use energy questioning things best left to the gods."

"All I know is, once my mother hears this, she will be lighting serial candles for me at the Buddhist temple in Chinatown."

"We have a lot more to do than sit around wondering what's on their minds."

Chosyam looked around the room. "You think we'll get these records moved today?"

"We'll have to, won't we? Get on the phone and call a floatcar. We will have to keep the storage house open late if necessary."

"We could take some of this with us."

"Where?"

"On the *Bushido*, sir."

"If something happens to the *Bushido*, it won't do us any good, will it?"

"No."

"Thank you. I do intend to leave some record of all this behind, no matter what." And with that, So Pak began going through stacks of papers.

* * *

Out on the Beltway, Mr. Tienshan and his associate marveled at the contents of the envelope. ''How could they have gotten so much money?'' the associate asked.

''Mr. Pak is the son of a famous Historian,'' Mr. Tienshan replied. ''What puzzles me is not the money but his lack of knowledge. He didn't have to pay us off, you know. His probe is underwritten by the German European Federation.''

CHAPTER FIVE

In less than forty-eight hours, So Pak was standing on the bridge, monitoring his crew. He had invested ten years of his life for this moment and now that he was off-planet in deep space thicker than the thought of velvet, the *Bushido* groaning internally in flight like an ice-locked lake in the dead of winter, all he could think about was Earth.

Savage hulked in front of him, curled against the vid screen navigation charts which ate up wall space like a virus gone wild. Savage dwarfed his sector with his hunter's energy. The deck was a jumble of cables, cul-de-sacs, open cisterns, and drainage tubes, all looming up at odd angles out of the darkness like fifteenth-century gargoyles. Dented, scarred chrome gleamed around the flight deck like the eyes of nocturnal creatures surprised by light.

Katz seemed to dance at the controls as though the ship itself gave him light. Outside, he was clumsy and bearish. Hooked up to the control panel, his movements were graceful, delicate, and precise, and So Pak had been absurdly grateful when Katz took in the details of the flight deck with no complaint.

Meanwhile, Potter was lurching around in her seat, talking nonstop into the com speaker with the communications officers of the tracker ships scheduled to accompany them three quarters of the way before veering off to the Pleiadian run and checking back toward the anticipated close of the mission. Now and then she'd toss back her hair or sprawl against the console, earning a glare from Savage, who responded by crouching so determinedly over his navigation table that it seemed he might manage to meld himself with his laptop.

So Pak tried to remain in the moment and concentrate his attention on what was before him but, like most things long anticipated, he found the actuality anticlimactic. And there was the other thing. Ever since the *Bushido* left Earth, So Pak had had no peace from his brother's memory. At night, his brother screamed at him in his dreams, striding relentlessly through So Pak's night hours until finally So Pak woke up sweating, sitting straight up in bed, his lips pressed firmly together in a futile attempt to keep himself from crying out. Last night he had awakened to find himself staring at the wall before him. He'd gotten out of bed, drunk a soma solution, and paced the tiny cabin like a panther in a cage, staring into the darkness and wondering if his brother's ghost was bent on chasing him down the galaxies.

During the day, at least at first, he'd hardly thought about his dreams. There had been so many details to attend to. But now that the ship's activities had become routine, So Pak's worries had caught up with him and Kim's ghost seemed to be putting on flesh rapidly enough to assume mortality at any moment. Only stress, So Pak told himself, that's all it was, and that was the whole of it, no more. Ghosts didn't take up residence on Earth, let alone in outer space. Discounting personal demons, of course.

He had thought that, had he grieved for his brother

more deeply, he might have circumvented all of this. Had he only worked out his grief over his brother's senseless death by sleeping on his grave, as was the custom, until he managed to pound down his brother's ghost into the earth beneath his body. For whatever reason, Kim Pak was not proving to have died as easily or as simply as he had lived. But then, in his more lucid moments, So Pak had to admit he didn't really know how his brother had lived. Certainly, except for an undeniable familiarity of person, his brother's ghost seemed nothing at all like the dutiful and placid son Kim Pak had been in life. Except, of course, for the righteous indignation he exhibited whenever people's rights were threatened and a certain lingering, tenacious belief in truth and justice.

The night before his brother's death, Kim and So Pak sat in Kim's spartan study drinking rice wine halfway through the night. For the rest of the night, they walked around the garden's reflecting pool, still drinking rice wine. It was perhaps only the fifth or sixth time in their lives the two had actually talked with each other and that night they parted company in a drunken fury. The next day, Kim was dead.

"And what makes you think the Japanese will allow you to find out anything on your bloody probe?" Kim asked. "What makes you think they aren't trying to get rid of you once they have gotten rid of me?"

The question had made no sense at the time. "Why would they bother?"

"Don't act so innocent, elder brother," Kim's voice held a bitterness So Pak had never heard before. "You know they consider you unfit for society. Although where they get that idea is beyond me, you have never been more in my experience than vomitously conservative."

"Me?"

Kim's eyes flashed in the darkness. "Oh, yes, and far more the elder brother than you will ever admit. Ironical, that." Kim raised the wine bottle and drank. They were standing beside the reflecting pool and Kim wobbled at the edge of the water before collapsing to his knees. He pushed the bottle away, tipping it over into the ornamental sand that was raked every morning. So Pak watched the dark stain of rice wine sink into the sand and disappear without a trace. Kim bent down on all fours and stared at himself in the pool. Then he buried his hands up to his wrists in the water and shoveled the liquid over his face. When he was finished, he shook like a dog. So Pak remembered beads of water flying from his brother's hair like unstrung pearls disappearing into the night.

Kim Pak sat back on his heels and peered into the pool as though he could, by will alone, force it to give up the future. "Idealism in your case, elder brother, is fatal. Perhaps idealism is always fatal. The Japanese don't have to kill you, you've joined the ranks of walking dead voluntarily." Kim turned his head to look at his brother, his expression scornful. "You disgust me."

"And why is that?"

"Because while you run off after your insignificant dreams, the rest of us have to pay. Did you ever think I might have more to do with my life than walk around in your discarded shoes? Did it ever occur to you that one of these days you might have to fulfill your own responsibilities? I have always cleaned up the debris you scattered in your mad rush to shatter rules at random. The colorful, adventuring older brother. It's time you know I won't always be here."

So Pak wondered once again if Kim had known of

his own death. If he had been trying to bring himself to warn them both that the number of his days was coming to an end. So Pak gripped the twisted guard rail Chosyam had gotten a deal on because it was irregular. He'd never know now.

So Pak remembered sinking to his heels, squatting in the damp summer night, watching his brother twist in the clutches of fate. "I didn't ask you to take up any of this. It was always your own choice."

Kim spun toward him, furious. "Nothing is ever one's own choice. Even when one believes one is choosing, it's a lie. You are nudged this way and that, events and people push you into dead alleys from which you can bolt only if you are quick enough. If you choose to stay, there's not much you can do to register displeasure. You can write on the walls, become catatonic . . ." his voice faded, "or you can revolt."

"Revolt is the last thing you'd do."

"Of course," Kim laughed, a harsh throat-ripping sound. "You call beating around the universe rebellion? When you have me to back you up and shadow your every move? You are still the first son and it is I who am disinherited," he said sorrowfully, staring over the still surface of the pond. "And I have said too much." Moments later, he'd grabbed the collar of So Pak's shirt, pulling his brother's face close to his. So Pak smelled rice wine, lack of sleep, and the musty odor of pond water. "You stupid, self-righteous fool. You don't know the half of it and, if I'm lucky, you won't. No matter what comes out."

So Pak tried to shove him away, but Kim was wiry and strong. The pond reflected the sky, the trees around the pool, and the two brothers locked together.

A slight breeze stirred the surface of the water and the image dissolved, reappeared, and dissolved again.

"You have some secret life I don't know about?" So Pak stared down into his brother's eyes. "You've lived in this village since childhood, enjoying your nice safe little life, married to a safe little wife of whom everyone approves, doing what Father tells you you must do while I'm out scrambling, trying to get people to understand there're things going on that need to be set right. What point is there in being a Historian? Histories aren't true and the stores aren't literature. It's pablum for people to swallow, all to keep them facing in the right direction."

Kim gave him a good shake. "It was your duty and you denied it. Your judgments are simplistic. You know little of the layers upon layers of secrecy required of those who choose to stay in one place. And for all your high ideals, what have you become? A subliminal programmer. Who could respect what you have become?"

"Duty?"

Kim snapped and grabbed the back of So Pak's neck in a wrestling hold. "Did you ever once think of anyone other than yourself? Did you ever once think of the life you sentenced me to?"

"It was your choice. I didn't sentence you to it. You chose it yourself, fashioned it yourself."

"In these times? Think again, big brother."

"Times of a world in transition."

Kim let him go. Kim could have snapped his neck. So Pak chose to read that moment as a gesture of dominance rather than one of real violence.

"And what would you know? You've been in America."

"America, the greatest of all democratic experiments is going the way of all democracies. A talking head once said, 'The strong grab power from the weak. Once the wealth of a democracy becomes evenly distributed, its owners become conservative. Once they become conservative, they get greedy and soft.' The American Dream has long since rotted out before everyone's eyes."

"Everyone throughout history considers himself to be living in times of chaos and transition. You should know better than to fling those terms around lightly. You are still a Historian's son, after all. You know," Kim said, shoving his hands into the pockets of his crumpled linen trousers, "your concepts lack a certain realism. Perhaps that is where you went wrong, always thinking things were one thing only and not other things as well. You think in surface concepts, gained from a lifetime spent traveling to new places, used to adjusting quickly to surface perceptions. Because you have not stayed in one place, you have not had to dig deeply within yourself for understanding." Kim spoke with the certainty and passion of a drunk. He swayed and caught his brother's shoulder to steady himself. "Still, you were stubborn. If not practical. Stubborn and solid as a great bloody wall. That you combined with a great ability to prevaricate."

So Pak couldn't remember how it was they'd started on this night. It was a new moon. The stars shone brighter without the moon there to wash them out. They would never understand each other. He knew then that it was too late. So Pak drank from his bottle of rice wine and passed it to his brother. Being a brother to Kim could have been so easy, but So Pak had never been able to make out how. Once Kim had been simple, wanting simple things from life. Denied that, by some perverse irony, he had become complex.

Kim flailed at the wine bottle and So Pak drew it back, cradling it to his chest. Kim had only really felt passionately about two things in So Pak's memory. One was an oversized teddy bear which a village bully had thrown into a shuttle transfer when So Pak was eleven and Kim was six. So Pak had never been able to forgive himself for not being able to beat up the bully or retrieve the stuffed bear. It was, to So Pak's knowledge, the last object in the world that Kim ever really cared about. He had moved on to ideas, perilous things to pin a world to, at best.

The first thing had been a pair of red sandals. Kim loved those red sandals and it took weeks for him to talk their mother into buying them for him.

"He'll have trouble with those shoes at school," the peddler warned her, screwing up his eyes in disapproval when So Pak's mother gave in and bought her son the shoes.

The peddler proved right. Every day, someone called Kim names because of the sandals. Every day he got into a fight. This lasted a month and a half, until he belted So Pak for taking on one of the red shoes battles himself. And to what end? The shoes wore out. Kim gained a reputation as a fighter. The shoes got thrown out in one of his mother's household purges and his mother simply explained the incident away in terms of anthropology.

"There's quite a bit of French in Koreans," she'd say, as though that really explained anything.

Kim turned on him, interrupting So Pak's drunken reverie. "I have been here by Father's side while you've been running around the world, first of all in the plush job you had. What were you? Corporate Functionary something or other?"

"I believe we've just been over this territory."

Kim nodded. "And there you were, traveling all over the world, visiting clubs at night, taking on women, drinking in front of fools. . . ."

So Pak shrugged. "Business."

"What business? What business actually got done in all those hours? I was breaking my brain trying to learn to do all the Histories correctly."

"It was the way we did things then. Everyone was hopeful."

"Everyone was stupid. There is no success without discipline. And you off pretending to be Japanese and getting the family into debt. But then, you were the first son, weren't you? The genius, as well. You were allowed faults. I, on the other hand, was allowed none. One wrong intonation in language and Father sulked for days. I behaved correctly and received no notice. And then you came home in disgrace."

So Pak remembered that day. It was the end of spring and a sweltering afternoon. The servants had served him a light supper and he had been ushered in to see his father. "Political reasons."

"What do you know about politics? It was all money," Kim snapped back. "Anyone with half a brain could have maneuvered himself out of that trap the Japanese set for you."

"Not the Japanese. Mr. Yamata."

"Yes, well, it's all very immaterial, isn't it? You squandered the family fortune. The results are not appreciably different, are they?"

Despite his unclear perceptions, So Pak turned wary. "What are you saying?"

Kim knelt by the reflecting pool and scrubbed his hair with his hands as though, with enough effort, he could rub the memories out of his brain. His eyes were hard. "At first, I refused to believe that you, my genius brother, could have been so stupid as to not see the pattern. You were always quicker at the patterns than I. I had to work to see them. They appeared for you. I must admit, you went down in my estimation after that. I no longer worshiped you when I realized it had evened out. My learning the patterns taught me to see them, you forgot everything you ever intuited.''

''I'm sorry.''

Kim looked at So Pak, betrayed. ''I worshiped you. That's why, at first, I didn't mind becoming Historian. I wanted to do it for you. I knew you would do important things for both of us. Things I couldn't quite manage. I was helping, you see. Helping you to change history. And then,'' Kim whispered. ''Well, after you come back, I began to watch you carefully. I realized you weren't as wise as I'd thought. First it made me afraid. I'd sacrificed everything, believing you would accomplish for both of us. For two years, I was impossibly unhappy. Then I discovered that in sacrificing for you, I had created the most perfect cover for myself.''

''Cover?''

''I could do almost anything. I was respectable. After all, those years of selflessness counted for something. No one watched me the way they watched you. I didn't draw attention to myself and I had attained the state of perfect invisibility. I decided you had, shall we say,'' Kim said sarcastically, ''unstintingly given of yourself to provide me with exactly what I needed. There was no reason to hate you anymore. There was only reason to tell you at some appropriate time how close I came to killing you.'' Kim stared at him clear-eyed. ''When I found my freedom, I could no longer love you.''

''We're both drunk. . . .''

"Oh, I have thought about this for years."

"I think we should call it a night." So Pak put a brotherly arm around Kim's shoulder and started to head him off toward the house. "You can tell me the rest tomorrow."

"Little by little, I began to use the opportunity. I built up the organization bit by bit, carefully, taking into account the smallest details. And why not? I had plenty of time." Kim's shoulders squared. "I discovered I had a talent of sorts."

"Certainly, you do."

"Don't patronize me," Kim was furious and threw off his brother's arm. "You have no idea what I'm talking about, do you? I had nothing to fear. You'd already disgraced the family."

"You're talking about the status you achieved as a Historian."

"Damn you to hell. I am not talking of Histories. I am talking of the present. Of action in the present. I am not a contemplative sort. History was a yoke I wore around my neck until I found a way to use it." Kim stumbled over the worn footpath south of the pond. His thoughts seemed to have been jolted along with his body. "And what of Wei? Could you not at least fulfill one small obligation by marrying her? We are childless, as you well know."

"Wei is Chinese."

"And in the face of everything else, do you think that matters? You are quite blind, and what's more, you will spend your life going everywhere but where you are needed."

"And where is that?"

"Right here." Kim began coughing, a sure sign he was fighting himself no matter how vehement he sounded. As long as So Pak could remember, his brother had coughing fits. It was like a form of nervous stutter. So Pak handed Kim the bottle, and this time Kim drank. "I wanted to trust you so I could tell you more."

So Pak was stung. "Trust me? I speak to no one."

"Not that kind of trust. Maybe you are the worst kind of visionary, the one who does not see what is right before him."

"And what are you?"

Kim stopped walking. "I am nothing. I am one in a sea of faces assembled on this earth like the sand on the shore. Just one more grain with its petty hurts and grievances. If I have created anything that will live on beyond me, it won't be a History. I do not dare to think it will make a difference. But I did what I could. Which is more, I think, than anyone will say of all your off-world probing."

"I am sorry, but I had hoped at least you'd understand."

"I understand nothing. Our worlds are mutually alien. There is no commonality. We are both equally fools." With that, Kim ran, crashing off into the trees. So Pak wished he had followed him to keep him from death. But he had let Kim go. To the day of his own death he would wish he hadn't. It was the next morning at ten o'clock that Kim had been found strangled in the poacher's rig, a death no better than that of a wild boar's.

People talked, as they always did. There was no game on the Pak estate; it had been hunted clean years before. There were only a handful of poachers in the entire province and those kept mostly to the rivers. There was no reason for a trap, unless the game intended was one of the Pak family. People said the trap had been set for So Pak, that his brother, as he had done so often before in life, found himself in So Pak's stead. Only this time, he died in So Pak's place. So Pak, even then, was not convinced. But perhaps that was guilt. He had never been able to tell Kim the things he wanted to tell him. The dream of his excursion to America. His hopes for the expedition. The fact that he loved him. It was gone, washed away, in the not unreasonable daily expectation of having another day. But the next day never came and now Kim's badly informed ghost, lacking half of the facts, was bent on tracking So Pak down amid the stars, determined to make him suffer the way Kim himself had suffered throughout his lifetime. Of all the things So Pak remembered, the most poignant was his brother's faultless calligraphy. Kim's calligraphy was perfect, even when he was drunk. Kim had been holding a calligraphy brush when they found his body. They said he was drunk and there was no reason for him to be holding a brush at all. So Pak knew that it wasn't so. . . .

If they had been on-planet, it would have been October, Ewha thought, the world washed in crisp, cool air, the early morning light clear and rich as molten bronze. She was restless. She was always restless in autumn and even though she was cooped up in this tin can, hurtling through space, her restlessness wasn't disappearing. Oddly enough, it was getting worse. Being cooped up with the crew made her even more curious and hypersensitive. Unsettling things were happening all around her. She could feel her skin opening up to intrigue like a flower to the sun. She knew the ship carried something that was not quite right. Sometimes the presentiment came so strongly that she thought she might burst. And then she would caution herself, prescribe discipline and meditation and, like a good patient, obey her doctor despite the fact that she didn't want to meditate. She was superstitiously afraid of what she might discover if she let her mind roam. She didn't want to curb her curiosity or restlessness and she wanted someone to tell her what was going on because she was beginning to understand that something was going on on this mission. She determined to make it her business to find out what. And once Ewha swore to herself to satisfy her curiosity, she nearly always did. If she really thought about it, she would have admitted she became a doctor in the first place to counteract her fascination with secrets. The most interesting things in life were the secrets, even if after they were disclosed, a person wished them secrets still. Ewha sat in sick bay staring at her newly arranged shelf of medicinals, knowing they would never be enough if the crew truly ran into trouble. She stretched her neck, snapping it to the left to crack it, even as she resolved to pay closer attention to the conversation going on around her, although she could frankly care less about the opinions of Jaffee—for example—on anything.

"Something has gone wrong with the Glahdj fertility drugs."

"That's news?" Drukker asked.

"I heard rumors a week before we left Earth," Yeshe said. Ewha wished she could have half the composure Yeshe exhibited; the woman's face bore a round, placid contentment usually confined to pregnant women. "There's something to the stories."

"And," Jaffee tossed out, "they say the Snakers are now leaderless. News drops have it that their leader was secretly assassinated and the organization is without direction. Makes you glad you're not on Earth, doesn't it?"

No one said anything.

"Scuttlebut has it Snaker directives are building up for a major show of strength in urban areas."

"What urban areas?" Ewha asked scornfully. "Newark?"

"Newark, Pittsburgh, Philadelphia, Los Angeles, Seattle, Banff."

"I'm sorry, but you can't expect me to take the Snakers seriously," Ewha told Jaffee. "They're just a splinter partisan group whose sole aim is to bolster Korean nationalism. Nationalism is an eighteenth century concept, that resurfaces when the world spins out of control. It's not going to help anybody glomming together with a bunch fo strangers just because we all theoretically swarmed in from the same country a hundred years ago. Like genetic and historical value supersedes everything else. It's the present, we've got to deal with."

Jaffee shrugged, secretly delighted. "Hey, I'm just reporting the news."

In that moment, Ewha understood Jaffee completely. The key to her character was that she was no more, and no less, than a thin thread of communications wire, stretched taut around the world, collecting information and reporting it to others. What others did with this information, providing they reacted in some way, was of no concern to Jaffee. Neither was registering facts or applying them to her own life.

"Please, what of the fertility drugs?" Yeshe asked politely.

"Babies are being born with multi-dysfunctional organic dupes—arms and legs, fingers, and stuff. Fucking kids look like roaches."

Yeshe had been composing a poem on the surgery table. Stricken by compassion, she dropped the brush on the surgery floor. She reached under the table to get it. Despite the foul light of the examining lamp, her skin was like a blush rose.

"Truth's too much for you?" Jaffee demanded.

"They rushed testing on synthetic hormones last year," Drukker said. She had been reading a book on the history of Western art, her finger stuck in a page on Rembrandt. "There was a study written up in the medical journals. No one did a thing about it. But then, who could expect anything different? People never change. Look what happened with the aliens."

"Yes?" Yeshe asked expectantly.

"Oh, and there goes the bleeding heart," Jaffee spat in disgust. "All ears over the plight of the filthy aliens. Geez."

Drukker pursed her lips and looked at Yeshe over the tops of her glasses. "You don't think that we allow aliens to die on Earth out of the kindness of our hearts, do you? Because we humans are such decent creatures, full of compassion for those in pain?"

" 'Course not. A lot of them are half-breeds."

Ewha glanced scornfully at Jaffee.

Drukker turned to Yeshe. "In any case, we live in a world that tolerates waste above all else. A world that will mutate its young rather than tolerate one single wasted bottle of medication. So explain to me how it is that we will allow aliens, strange flesh, the solace of the blue planet on which to die and the questionable comforts of its indigenous life-form?"

"Because," Jaffee said practically, "They have nowhere else to go. They can't die on their own planet, they're contaminants. They have to go somewhere."

"Why Earth?" Drukker insisted.

Jaffee rolled her eyes. "Nowhere else is appropriate. Aliens have been banned by Referendum everywhere else. And neither Neptune nor Jupiter can support them. Besides, like I said before, it's hard to tell whether they're human or what. . . ."

"And that leaves only Earth." Drukker continued.

"Of course not, but . . ."

"But Earth is the only place they can die with no danger to others, outside of Deathspeak, of course, but no physical danger."

"Well, yes."

"And still we let the quarantine ships through at our ports? How do we really know it's safe?"

"It's a little late now, isn't it?" asked Yeshe. "If it's not safe, that is."

"I am only saying," Drukker pointed out, "that perhaps humans are guilty."

"Humans are responsible for the alien epidemic?" As ship's doctor, Ewha's interest was piqued.

"There are the journals that claim that a virus carried by humans . . ." Drukker began.

Ewha was impatient. "Medical journals are always going on about viruses carried by humans. And it is mostly speculation."

". . . to the Pleiades, where they were spread by physical contact."

Ewha nodded. "The smallpox on the army blankets syndrome?"

"Certainly, the principle is correct."

"I don't remember the white man feeling badly enough to make any real reparations." Ewha looked more closely at Drukker. "You're saying, then, that we caused this epidemic?"

"I'm not saying anything. What I'm suggesting is that someone should analyze the evidence. Read what it is telling you."

Ewha tucked her hands behind her head and

stretched out lazily. "What that has to do with us or with anything occurring on this mission is beyond me."

Drukker smiled and her face, despite the smile, was tired and worn. "That's what missions are for, aren't they?" she said, before turning back to her book on Rembrandt, to the light and dark chiaroscuro, the washer woman picked out of the crowd to represent beauty of form and transcendence. "I find the most unproductive thing is, like the Buddhists say, idiot compassion. It weakens response and helps no one."

As the weeks went on, the ship fell into its own rhythms and routines as everyone settled into carrying out specific functions. The crew had become a perfect body: Jaffee was the ears and mouth, Savage the eyes, Katz the legs, and So Pak the brains of the operation. The others waited until they landed, keeping their parts of the organism in shape, knowing that once they landed at the target objective, they would want support from Jaffee, Savage and Katz, while they went about the investigative work. They were an odd group, half flight techies, half academics and researchers, their commander haunted by his own demon, an unexpected ghost brother who followed him off-planet and proved to be much harder to lose than real life flesh and blood. And it was unrealistic to expect that of those on board, they were all who they pretended to be, especially considering the fact that this was a Japanese approved mission manned by a Korean commander and underwritten by the German European Federation.

The techies were busy night and day maintaining equipment when they weren't operating their stations. Chosyam had done an excellent job getting the ship outfitted and equipped, but it remained a low budget operation and it was part of the routine for Jaffee to turn up at dinner with com cables to splice together, or Savage to sit down with a screwdriver and his quadrant. After ten days, the ship took on a trapped, cluttered quality. Confined completely to the ship, the younger members became tense. Savage paced the flight deck, Chosyam spent long hours pounding the air in the exercise pod, Jaffee talked faster and moved around the ship as though looking for emergency exits before they landed. Drukker, Katz, Kenjii, Bender, and Toshio contented themselves with their books and notebooks. But even Lawrence Bender admitted on more than one occasion to missing his walks. Ewha surprised herself by wanting to put her fist through a window just to breathe something other than recycled air. Yeshe stared off into space for hours on the observation deck or tucked her feet underneath her at mealtimes and gazed off into the wall as though determined to bore her way to freedom with the use of her eyes alone.

A month and a half after lifting off, they sat in the mess, a steamy, cavernous room battered by noises from the ship's engines. It had once been weapons storage and its high ceilings and doomsday graffiti in impossible places (once the only places within the former crew's reach) did nothing to encourage a positive attitude. Jaffee dug around in her freeze-dried ragout without much interest. It had been a slow news day and the tracer ships were dropping behind to pick up an escort for another couple of weeks, southeast of the *Bushido*'s course. Jaffee was going to miss the com officers, although she couldn't say she'd miss the military ship that made her feel like the Japanese fleet was breathing down her neck every time she activated her radio. "So what did they have to tell you before they left? What last parting words?'' Chosyam asked Jaffee, wolfing down his macrobiotic noodles.

''They are depicting a sluggish economy for the new year. The World Patent Office is investigating Iroha Trading,'' Jaffee began, but her heart wasn't in it.

''About time,'' Katz said in approval.

''So what's the problem?'' Savage clapped Jaffee on the back. ''Drifting alone in a big, bad world, are we?''

Potter wriggled her shoulder out from under his arm and scowled at him.

''Japan has always been a patent minefield,'' Bender said from the other end of the table as though Jaffee's news had just arrived there. He was too far from Jaffee and Savage to take note of their games.

Bender was right, So Pak thought. The Japanese not only patented technological processes, but steps in the process, beginning with superconductivity, until there wasn't a technological process left in the world whose use in a country other than Japan didn't demand some sort of license fees from the company or country which wanted to use a specific technology. And, what was worse, the triviality of Japanese patents allowed competitors to be hemmed in, forcing them to grant licenses to large amounts of their own technology in exchange for the right to use small portions of Japanese technology.

''They will investigate and find nothing,'' Kenjii, who looked far younger than his years, had learned to master the impassive expression, perhaps as compensation. Impassive but for his lips, which were compressed into a thin slash across his face. ''It is a poorly managed corporation that has not learned to cover its tracks.''

This earned him a surprised look from Bender.

"There is not a corporation in the world that can cover its tracks completely," Ewha argued calmly.

Savage, completely bored by the discussion, took a helping of Chosyam's noodles and lost himself in eating, his eyes clear blue and dreaming. His face took on the look seen on young men in bars on wet afternoons, staring out of windows at the street after a couple of pints of draft, not speaking, dreamily concocting solutions meant to affect the universe at large.

"And that's it, then, for the news?" Drukker asked efficiently, sipping at yet another of her endless cups of tea.

"Well, my sources say . . ."

"You call that flying utility sink out there a source?" Savage demanded, for which he earned a laser-sharp glance from Jaffee.

"They are saying," she continued, not skipping a beat, "that the Snakers and Ronin Historians have united into a terrorist group called Terror Two. According to the flying utility sink, Tokyo transit tubes were bombed yesterday. Thousands of people are dead. It was declared a natural disaster. They still don't have an accurate death count. . . ."

Jaffee caught herself and put her hand gently on Toshio's arm. "I'm sorry, you have family there, don't you?"

Toshio said nothing. She was right. He had two children in Tokyo attending school. His arm tightened under Jaffee's hand until, finally, she let go.

"Snakers warned the Japanese government a month before the attack, but the Japanese thought it not worthwhile to warn passengers or to make the news public. Their official statement had something to do with the theory that if they took every terrorist threat seriously, no one would go anywhere on the Tokyo line. An action deemed detrimental to the good of the whole."

"Yes?" Ewha demanded.

"In the last few months, whenever terrorists have threatened strikes, the city has come to a complete halt. God knows, the Deathspeakers fuel enough civil unrest out there without having to consider Snaker civil disobedience," Kenjii said. He was rewarded by a look of disgust from Ewha and a curious glance from Yeshe. Cowed, he turned his concentration to drawing on his eating mat with the end of one of his chopsticks.

It has to be more than just arrogance, So Pak thought, that forced Kenjii to continue along those lines. "Korea has always been independent," he said flatly, bait to draw Kenjii out. But Kenjii said nothing.

"In a pig's eye." It was Chosyam muttering.

"How do they know it was Snakers?" Denisovich asked sanely. "It could have been anybody. Bloody unlikely a bunch of Snakers and Ronin Historians would manage to blow up anything, let alone a Tokyo tube train. Sounds to me like someone's decided it's up to the Snakers and Ronin to take the fall for some stupid bureaucratic error." It was good, common sense. But then, Denisovich was not So Pak's idea of someone troubled by anything he couldn't touch, feel, or reason out quickly. He sat at the corner of the table, his hand wrapped comfortably around his vodka bottle, at peace with the world, his face as healthy, tanned, and fit as though he'd been trudging through the Black Forest for a week instead of cooped up in the close quarters of a probe ship for over two and a half months. Denisovich did not worry about things that were not his concern.

"Bureaucratic errors always take the form of bombs going off on public transport," Kenjii said poisonlessly.

"Next they'll be blaming it all on jazz musicians," Denisovich said. "Would it be too much to ask you all to consider the problem logically?" he asked of no one in particular. "First of all, who's going to fund a bunch of Snakers who just decided to commence a program of worldwide terrorism? Second, what good are Ronin Historians in cross fire? In fact, tell me when the Ronin Historians last contributed a controversial work? Ten years ago, maybe? And what happened to the author? Suicide, right? All Ronin Historians manage to do with any consistency is kill themselves. And we're talking eventuality. Got a strong, overriding death wish, the lot of them. Besides, I don't know what's been happening to the Snakers in the last couple of years, but Ronin Historians are on the run. Last I heard, suspected Ronin were not being reissued food coupons. Not only individuals, mind you, entire families, not that there are a lot of Ronin with families, doesn't fit with the life patterning. Or, come to that, with a death wish. Still, that's a real kick in the teeth. No," Denisovich knocked back another gulp of synthetic grain-alcohol vodka, "as a literary movement, the Ronin have lost their hold over the imagination. Got their shit kicked out of them and gave up. And then, the Japanese were smart. Absorbed the Ronin Histories into the mainstream while there was still time. Watered-down versions, of course, the kind that can't do any real damage. After awhile, what the Ronin were saying no longer had any effect. Didn't they set up some special council?"

"That's right," Drukker jumped in, "The Council for Creative Response. Of which, I believe, Toshio was the honored director for a time."

"That was awhile ago," Toshio said mildly. "I was never acting director. I advised the director. At the time I was Director of the Council of the Historical Arts. Interesting days."

Of all the eyes turned to Toshio, only Bender's held amusement.

"Bunch of candy-assed intellectuals," Savage muttered.

Toshio regarded them mildly. "There is an interesting Chinese legend of the God of Medicine," he began, losing half his audience, perhaps intentionally, Ewha decided. "He had a red whip with which he customarily thrashed all herbs." Savage and Chosyam looked at each other, Savage crossing his arms over his chest until he looked like a wall with a head on it. Chosyam scowled at Toshio.

Their actions were not lost on Toshio, who chose to treat the two of them as immaterial, not only to the conversation, but to his world.

"Whenever the God of Medicine took out his red whip to beat an herb, it would reveal to him its true nature: whether it was hot or cold, how it was to be used, its degree of toxicity and effectiveness in treating disease. It was, in addition, his responsibility to taste each herb. Now, his body was transparent for this very purpose. He tasted thousands of herbs a day and was poisoned many times in the course of twenty-four hours. But, with his transparent body, he could easily determine which part was affected and what he might do to set himself to rights. Some who tell this story suggest it was the bowel breaking weed that had so noxious an effect on his body that he could do nothing to counter its effects, but it seems to me that he must have been killed while treating a monster sickness called the Hundred-Legged Vermin. As the story goes, each of the hundred legs grew into more and more vermin and that is what finally killed the God of Medicine.''

All except Jaffee, Savage, and Chosyam had listened politely enough, but only Bender and Drukker showed any real interest in the story, though for completely different reasons. Toshio behaved as though his entire audience were enthralled. He sipped his tea, rinsed his gums, and swallowed before continuing. ''Had he thought about the matter for several days before testing this noxious plant, it is my opinion he might have concluded that it would be a simple solution to inject each of the hundred legs within a specified time period, say twenty-four hours, and monitored its effects inside his body before continuing the experiment.''

So Pak appreciated the brilliance of Toshio's story. Drukker was looking at him with revulsion. The remains of the meal littered the table like the carnage of a small battle.

''Nice story, but what about the Snakers?'' Chosyam asked. He stared intently at Jaffee. Jaffee shrugged.

''Who knows about Snakers? The Japanese have decreed all reference to Snaker activity to be unofficial at best, severely limited, and have enforced screening of news of their activities. All references to Snakers have been cut out of news holos until the crisis is past.''

''Crisis?''

''I suppose Jaffee means the terrorist crisis.''

''Snakers are nothing but hopeless romantics, hopeless dreamers with nothing to substantiate their dream of independence.'' Yeshe, to everyone's surprise, spoke with rage. ''Most of them are not even Korean. They are the dregs of cities all over the world. Nationalists with no idea whatsoever of life in Korea as it is today. There isn't a Snaker alive who would live one moment in Korea.''

''They say their leader lives in Korea,'' Katz commented.

''Their leader is recently deceased.''

''Korea couldn't hold their leader without the Japanese knowing his identity,'' Kenjii argued.

''You don't know that,'' So Pak said.

Bender waved away their squabbles. ''It is the small countries, those that have managed a life that is still close to the earth, who have the best chance of surviving in these uncertain times. Countries whose people haven't forgotten how to live within the scope of the Earth's resources, countries which do not depend completely upon technology.'' He pulled his pipe out of his uniform pocket and began to stuff it with a strange, knobby herb not known to proliferate on Earth. ''Human beings have characteristically wiped out simpler more practical cultures by insidiously introducing technological developments.''

Drukker bent her head toward him, the uncertain light shining on her hair, which, even when pulled back and knotted on the top of her head, escaped in wisps around her face. ''May I understand you correctly? What you are saying is that Korea has a better chance of survival because it is not yet as technical as Japan? What kind of revisionist bullshit is that?''

''Whenever human beings get too far away from Earth, their culture begins to suffer.'' Bender nodded.

''This makes me sick.'' Chosyam shook his head.

''It all has to do with survival.''

Savage got up and left. He was closely followed by Katz. Jaffe tore down the hall port after them. Those still left in the dining room could hear the far off howls of laughter. Chosyam drummed his fingers on the table and watched. Toshio cleared off the section of the table in front of him and got down to work on a battery of performance charts as the talk began around him again.

Yeshe and Ewha observed them all. There had been something odd here, Ewha thought. Toshio was adept at feigning disinterest, Kenjii was more attentive than the conversation merited, and Bender seemed ill at ease, although as a traditionalist and intellectual, Bender was not out of character in backing a noble savage point of view, Ewha decided.

Yeshe had decided she disliked Kenjii and these abstract discussions, for that matter. She was a biologist. She believed in the ability of all living things to grow and transform cycles of death and rebirth. Her nature was relentlessly positive because she took to heart the rule of all organic matter: life came out of death. Seeds germinated because they died first. Old civilizations seeded themselves into the new. Things didn't remain the same. Perhaps that, more than any other reason, explained why she'd been determined to come on this probe. One of her ancestors had been a miner on the Korean ship and it was herself in him that she was searching for.

Meanwhile, Ewha got up slowly and slipped out of the room. She pressed the hallport buttons and made her way through the dark corridor, a jumble of wires and cross boxes branching off into service corridors like some great central nervous system. Chosyam had done a good job of outfitting the ship for practical considerations but aesthetics had not rated high, and Ewha knew he had no inkling that some people might be set on edge by having to shoot through deep space with wires dangling in front of their noses and industrial duct tape sticking to their flight suits every time they turned around. Sharpened sensitivities, highly tuned to diagnosis, could just as easily be rubbed raw. Sometimes, people could be too sensitive to live and Ewha tried to believe she was pragmatic enough to curb her own sensitivity. Sometimes, she felt chafed by life.

Ewha had her own theories about what had happened on Zeta Reticuli. It had been strengthened by Drukker's comments, despite the fact that Ewha seemed to take them with a grain of salt. What if there had been a virus, carried aboard the ship by humans, that had suddenly wiped out both crews? And what if the alien spotter ships then landed, discovered two camps full of viral miners, made contact, been unable to assist, taken off, and carried the virus to their own planet where it began systematically wiping out the entire population? And what if someone or something survived all of that? Enough for the aliens to be able to blackmail humans into allowing them to come to Earth to die? During the start of her career, Ewha had worked as an intern in an Alien Death Camp. She understood the progress of the disease and the toll it took upon its people. She also understood Toshio. Someone spending all those years under the Interstellar Treaty of 2073, working in alien rehab would have learned to think alien which was, Ewha was convinced, no different than thinking in any other culturally induced pattern. And sometimes the cultures and myths and heroic types overlapped. For instance, Toshio had to know of the overlap between Chinese and alien mythic figures to tell the story he had told tonight. There was a transparent Chinese god of medicine who could look within and heal himself. Aliens were reputed to be able to heal themselves of most diseases, with the notable exception of Deathspeak. Toshio knew that. He must also know that much alien medicine consisted of herbs and remedies set up to encourage the alien body to absorb poison and expel it as stabilized chemical matter. And aliens had been blamed for the deaths on Zeta Reticuli. For decades. Ewha remembered her childhood skiprope chants in which Deathspeak was not a mysterious alien plague visited upon humans. In Toshio's story, the God of Medicine had been fatally overcome by the Hundred-Legged Vermin. Which could be translated as loose political affiliations, perhaps not dangerous in themselves, but fatal in aggregate.

Ewha walked silently through the long hallport threading the ship's belly, her slippers kissing the iron strut floor as she passed. She was lost in thought. She hated loose ends with the dislike of a surgeon. And there was something unsolved here, larger than the day-to-day mysteries of human existence: life, death, love. Something nagged at her mind, some missing flash of insight that, could she but remember it, would cause everything to make sense. Ewha laughed and told herself to stop obsessing. If she kept on like this, the first thing she could expect when she stepped out of the ship was a fox spirit—foxes being associated in Japan with sickness, which Ewha considered odd, as the Japanese also thought of them as autonomous entities that moved in to possess a person whenever they felt like it. And anyway, there were enough obsessive types on this probe to staff an entire Investigative Branch.

Ewha slipped around the corner and headed for the sleeping area. She wanted to sit awhile and write down her thoughts before sleeping. Before Drukker showed up and began fussing around with her bedtime preparations. But as Ewha turned the corner of the hallport, the lights flickered and went off. Ewha hurried down the corridor toward the sample rooms. She had almost turned the corner when an electrical cord, not two feet in front of her, fell, lighting her up in a bluish-purple flare. Seconds later, electrical wires were shorting out all around her in bursts of sparky, ozone-laden air. The hallport floor rippled and Ewha was flung to the side of the corridor, grasping at the smooth cylindrical walls of the ship. It was like being lost in a sewer pipe, Ewha thought, remembering the underground sewers her brother had pushed her down in Milwaukee because, he said, it was her fault they called them hun-yurah at school. Of course, it wasn't. Her brother was as much a half-breed as she. But he looked more Caucasian than Ewha.

Ewha managed to scrape herself off the wall of the hallport and begin picking her way forward. Suddenly, she saw a running figure far ahead of her in the gloom. She broke into a run, but as fast as she was, she still had to dodge all of the hanging debris and she couldn't catch him. He darted in and out of the shadows, spun in a quick ninety-degree turn, and vanished down a sideport. The figure was male, of that Ewha was certain, but whether he was running toward something or running away from it, she had no idea. She slowed to pick her way between the live electrical wiring, wondering what could have happened, when she heard a horrible gurgling sound coming from behind the door to the private quarters on her left. Ewha eased open the door and, even with all of her medical training, she gasped. Denisovich lay spread-eagled on the floor, his throat slashed open, his windpipe hanging from a vertical slash in his chest. The last thing he saw before he died was her face, framed in the doorway of his room. Then his eyes clouded over and he died. Blood haloed his head like a rusty blessing. As Ewha closed his eyelids with the palm of her hand she thought she heard a small, tinny voice speaking Russian. She looked around her to see a wrist radio partially hidden in the half-open bottom drawer of Denisovich's desk. Instinctively, she grabbed for the radio, but it was palmate sensitive and couldn't read the imprint of her hand. The radio went off, its frequency lost, and Ewha was left gazing at an icon, hanging over Denisovich's bed in the murky darkness of his room.

Ewha shivered and blamed her superstitious feeling on the close quarters of the ship and its effect on a group of people who found themselves jammed together in a confined space after learning to value spending great amounts of time alone. The Japanese believed people who died violently or in acute distress were likely to become ghosts. In extreme cases, an unhappy ghost could become a harmful god. Denisovich's death, Ewha could not stop herself from speculating, looked to have been unhappy indeed.

CHAPTER SIX

They buried him the next day in a body cylinder in deep space. Their faces were pale and still, less from grief than from the knowledge that the murderer was still among them. So Pak held a Russian Orthodox service in the common room which lasted the required forty minutes, during which time the crew members who wished to could pay their respects by attending, sitting on hard black unfold chairs, staring at a black and merciless body cylinder containing Denisovich's body, a body cylinder that looked like a warhead, devoid of decoration except for *BUSHIDO*, written in half-inch script on the left side. Half-inch print did not seem to be enough to stand as the only identifying mark on a body capsule that would spend several epochs floating in space. That was the unspoken opinion of both Ewha and Yeshe, although neither of them could have possibly known how closely their thoughts resembled each other. Or their rationales, for that matter. And both simultaneously came to the decision that they couldn't waste a great deal of time wondering about it, having been trained to think scientifically.

There was more confusion than grief evident on the faces of the mourners. After all, no one had really known Denisovich well. He was shy, well-mannered, good-humored, and nondescript. He didn't attract notice. He didn't appear to have secrets. He was another space lifer like all the rest of them except for the academics on board, and the lifers knew the stats. Twenty percent fatalities on routine flights, nonmonitored. Up to sixty-five percent on probes and ships flying interstellar trade routes. Safety had never been a concern of Iwaski. The only astonishing thing about Denisovich's death was that it had happened to Denisovich. He was a loner who had kept too much to himself to have made any enemies.

They ranged themselves in a ragged row several feet away from So Pak, who was reading the service out of the Captain's book. Ewha studied them all, mechanically diagnosing stress and fatigue. The tidal inflections of So Pak's voice blended with the sounds of the engines, the soft, hissing of the maintenance and life-support systems, the heartbeat of the ship.

"Poor bugger," Ewha heard Savage whisper to Chosyam, "not to mention the rest of us."

Chosyam was a stone.

"I mean, I seen a lot, but the guy's throat was torn out."

Chosyam jammed Savage in the arm, an attempt at shutting him up.

"It's street stuff. No class, no respect, nothing. Captain's got his first body. It's some kind of strange dance is on. Probably figured spanky clean probe like this, I'm talking from the intention point of view, understand my point, all that study, a lost expedition stuff—what's that about anyway—keep him immune from reality. Whatever."

Odd that the trackers disappeared less than eight hours before the murder, Ewha thought, but then it was best to think of it as merely coincidental. Across the room, hands behind her back, Yeshe was the only one listening to So Pak. Although there was a gulf of distance between her own American-mutt upbringing and Yeshe's Korean trad background which, among the upper classes was particularly reactionary, Ewha was beginning to perceive Yeshe as an ally. To what end, she wasn't sure. Yeshe wouldn't have murdered Denisovich. And Chosyam was on his own course, Ewha decided, playing the clown to cover his subversive activities, or charging ahead foolishly despite advice against youthful folly. Whatever demons raged within Savage could be put to death by work. Katz was absent. Drukker was, Ewha suspected, unstable. Toshio, calmness personified, and Kenjii, looking uncharacteristically jumpy, stood side by side thinking God knew what. Bender was not in attendance. He'd walked by, smoking his pipe, and, when told he could not smoke during the service, he'd left amicably enough. There was something a little odd about Bender, but Ewha couldn't put her finger on it.

So Pak raised his eyes and looked at them all. It was a challenge and one Ewha didn't know if they were up to meeting, depending upon what else happened on this mission. She looked at them all again. It came to her that Chosyam was undoubtedly targeted to die.

The service completed, there was a moment of silence during which Yeshe could be heard chanting softly. And though they were all stalling, there was nothing to do but to hook the body cylinder up to the disposal unit. Most of the crew had been witnesses to death in space many times before. They were professionals and, if they hadn't made their peace with death, they'd negotiated through the rituals before.

As the crew drifted out of the room, Ewha made her way to So Pak.

"I'm sorry," she said.

"Yes." Up close, she could see the hollowness in his eyes.

"Is there anything I can do?"

"I don't think so. Remember as much as you can about the death scene."

Ewha nodded. "My report is almost complete."

"Thank you, Doctor. I shall expect it."

She placed her hand on his arm and gave it a small squeeze, not out of affection, just enough to suggest he was not alone.

Ewha went to the observation deck. Chosyam was already there, prickly with anger. They stood side by side and watched as the cylinder was released from the air lock and spun off into space, Ewha's throat ached at the loneliness of the cylinder disappearing. She became aware of Jaffe muttering away at the com console, notifying the distant trackers of Denisovich's death and burial.

It was a Thursday when Mr. Matsuda heard the news, relayed by satellite to his boardroom from the tracker ships, which had been monitoring all the *Bushido*'s communications. Mr. Matsuda was sitting alone at the conference table when he got the call. His forehead which, due to the stresses and strains of recent business dealings, had become habitually marred by two vertical lines, one on either side of his eyebrows above the bridge of his nose, now straightened and cleared until his skin became as smooth as a baby's. Mr. Matsuda was very happy.

He called the Office Girl, who came into the room and bowed. "Please," Mr. Matsuda gestured, handing the Office Girl a bit of paper with a vidphone number scribbled on it. "Put this call through for me."

The Office Girl took the number. She had skin like

the first spring cherry blossoms, skin so transparent that Mr. Matsuda often felt the need to touch it, although he restrained himself. He picked up a cigar. She clipped the end for him and waited to light it before trying to reach his party on the vidphone. Then she bowed and turned the vidphone over to him, sweetly and silently leaving the room, closing the double teak doors behind her. Mr. Matsuda sat up much straighter and bent forward so his image would fill the vidphone screen. Mr. Matsuda stared out the conference room window at the great aquamarine expanse of the bay.

The Office Girl returned, bowing and smiling, to announce his next meeting, but Mr. Matsuda waved her away. She hid her surprise. She had never known Mr. Matsuda to delay a meeting.

Historian Pak rubbed his eyes, pushed his chair away from his compuscreen, and picked up the telephone. Though the rest of the house had vidphone units, he had indulged himself by keeping this one old-fashioned device in an otherwise modern office. Where was his house boy and why wasn't he answering the phone? For that matter, why was he the only one in the house who ever heard the thing ring in the first place? He swiveled his chair to look out over the meditation garden, shriveling away in the autumn. No, not shriveling exactly, drying, in the process seeming to shrink to half of its original size. Fall and winter were a process of contraction, Historian Pak decided. First the trees shrank, preparing the landscape for the snows of winter, which made the world silent, close, and small. Manageable and sometimes comforting. In order to prevent eyestrain, Historian Pak took every opportunity when he was working to ease his eyes by looking at his garden. Unfortunately, thoughts drifted in unbidden.

"I trust your health is good," Mr. Matsuda said respectfully.

"Quite good," Historian Pak answered.

"There is a Japanese tale of the great Monster Slayer," Mr. Matsuda began.

"Surely you did not call me to tell me stories," Historian Pak chided, listening to Mr. Matsuda inhale his cigar as he tried to buy himself time to think. Historian Pak's head was thick from working all morning and he couldn't clear his mind as quickly as he would have liked. He grabbed the arm of his leather chair, hoping his son was still alive. Why else would Matsuda be concerning himself with him? "I salute your knowledge of the old ways," Historian Pak said. "It was my impression that the old tales were forbidden."

Mr. Matsuda chuckled. "And so they are. But surely at our advanced age, we old ones have earned the right to tell old tales."

"Let me quote you when my next History comes up for censorship," Historian Pak said wryly.

"Might I remind you that it is your government that has banned our infinite wisdom?" Mr. Matsuda said.

"Quite right."

"I stand corrected. However, I use the old tales to instruct and entertain."

"Why else does anyone tell any sort of tale?"

"There are those, I believe, of the decadent schools, who believe in art for its own self."

The man was a fool, Historian Pak thought. And Historian Pak didn't suffer mortals gladly, much less fools. He chose to say nothing in return in the hope that Mr. Matsuda would rush to fill the silence. After inhaling once again, Mr. Matsuda did as Historian Pak thought he might, he began to tell the story in a quiet monotone. The man spoke like a snake, Historian Pak observed to himself, even as he wearily submitted to the story.

"You have heard of Japan's great archer."

"Yes," Historian Pak answered. "Most correctly, it is China's great archer who has been moved to Japanese culture."

This, Mr. Matsuda chose to ignore. "After his first task, which was to shoot down the ten meddlesome sons who refused to be orderly and ran wildly through the sky, causing great havoc, which brought great light to the Earth but also great disorder, the Great Archer was dispatched to slay the monsters caused by the sparks from the death of the ten sons. We will dispense with the story of the creation of the giant rock that evaporates seawater and explains why, even though all the waters of all the rivers and streams empty into the sea, the sea never overflows."

"Certainly, one must edit one's own tales," Historian Pak said promptly.

A note of displeasure crept into Mr. Matsuda's voice, but he continued, "The Great Archer went on to slay fierce and harmful monsters that plagued the world at that time. The most destructive beast was a monster with a dragon's head, a tiger's paws, and the cry of a baby. This beast came from a celestial line. His ancestors were gods, whose reputations had been destroyed by two other gods. It was said that he made his fortune feeding on human flesh and that he had taken the lives of many, but in actuality, he was a disobedient son who pretended obedience in order to cause violence and oppression to the great order of the universe. Fierce and cunning as he was, the Great Archer killed him with a single arrow and he was mourned by his family as a dutiful and obedient son, which he was not."

Historian Pak trembled with rage. "My son is dead, his memory unassaulted and untroubled. Leave his memory with me. It is said . . ." but Historian Pak bit off his words before he said too much. After all, words were most effective when used judiciously. He stood and walked away from his desk. "The cause of my son's death was not accident. I do not know how or why he died, only that he has been taken from me before he, too, could give me sons. I will not allow his memory to be stolen from me as well."

Mr. Matsuda smiled. It was like playing a game of Go. "Next, the Great Archer went into the fields of the South, Land of the Red Phoenix, to kill the monster of the sharpened teeth. This monster had the head of a beast on the body of a human being. He fought with a weapon that was no more than a set of teeth itself, five or six feet in length. Knowing he needed more in order to do battle with the Great Archer, Sharp Teeth used a shield to protect himself. He was still no match for the Great Archer, who dispatched the monster promptly with a new bow and arrow given him by his superiors. What this story means," Mr. Matsuda said, leaving nothing to art, "is that every effort to keep your son in the interstellar port of Newark was to no avail. He managed to bribe the customs officials there and consequently evaded all efforts to keep him grounded. I am sorry, sir, to have to inform you of the failure of our plan."

Historian Pak waited. He had been informed of the failure of the plan to ground So Pak weeks ago. He knew Mr. Matsuda was not calling for this reason. There was something else. He must meditate upon the story of the Great Archer although its meaning was obvious. Kim had been assassinated. Something had gone wrong with So Pak's crew.

"A Russian named Denisovich was murdered on your son's ship." Mr. Matsuda savored every moment of announcing this distasteful news. "Your son will be investigated for allowing such a thing to happen on a simple probe mission."

Historian Pak didn't answer.

"It doesn't speak well for his control of the crew or for his administrative ability. He did, however, report the incident to the tracker ships. This will be taken into account in his favor. With any luck, once he has been cleared, if he can be cleared of this charge, he may return home. It is unlikely he will be able to leave for many months. Unlikely, because he will be put under arrest. In deference to you, your home will be his prison."

Historian Pak still said nothing.

"I am telling you this out of the greatest respect," Mr. Matsuda's voice changed. "It is natural for a man to love his son. It is also natural for a man to respect another man's work. I, who have the utmost respect for your work, must tell you it is my goal to have you, the pinnacle of the Historians, outlive your son in great glory. I am not a heartless individual. I appreciate quality, and the dilution of quality is to be avoided at all costs."

Unfortunately, Historian Pak could keep silent no longer. For all his wisdom, he was subject to that frankness from which he found it difficult to restrain himself in times of stress. "Are you telling me, sir, that you have had one of my sons assassinated and are about to murder the other?"

But while Historian Pak was frank, Mr. Matsuda was conciliatory. Mr. Matsuda inhaled and waited a polite interval to show his respect. "There is your best interest to consider," Mr. Matsuda said. "And there are many more installments of the legend of the Great Archer. It is quite a long story. Good-bye, Historian Pak. I must leave you with my great respect." He skipped a beat and added, "My wife has planned a small soiree. We had hoped you might be in attendance to read from your work in progress. I shall await your reply."

"Mr. Matsuda, I am afraid that the story of the Great Archer is originally a Chinese cycle tale. But I do have a Japanese story for you." The sun blazed through the branches of Historian Pak's cherry tree, blazed onto the bare, strong bark, turning it gold and black against the encroaching evening. Historian Pak wondered at the karma that set two old men to telling each other the old stories in a world in which the stories were banned and neither of the old men cared to live.

Historian Pak looked carefully at the tree, "There was a very old monk who lived at the Golden Peak. In those days, the senior monk of the abbey was appointed and this one had been a monk longer than any of his colleagues.

"For many years, the monk who was to succeed the head monk wished his superior would die, but the man was in excellent health and not about to give up his life. At every birthday, he seemed to renew his strength and by the time he was eighty, he was healthier than he had been at sixty. At seventy, his successor knew all too well that he was not nearly as strong as the old monk.

" 'I could actually die and never become abbot,' the successor moaned. 'And I can't have him murdered. Someone would find out.'

"After much thinking, the monk decided to poison the abbot. Naturally, he was afraid of what the Buddha might do, but the temptation was too great. He began to think of what kind of poison to use. After thinking about this for many months, he decided upon a mushroom called The Great Beyond because that's where it sent those with the temerity to taste it. It was sure to kill anyone who ate it. He would gather plenty of Great Beyonds, make an incredibly savory dish of them, and feed them to the abbot as ordinary mushrooms. That would take care of him in short order. 'And then I'll be abbot,' the soon-to-be new abbot gloated.

"Well, it was fall, and the monk went straight off by himself into the mountains, gathered lots of Great Beyonds and brought them back at dusk to his hut. He cut them up in a pot, seasoned them nicely, and made them into an attractive stew. The new day had hardly dawned when he sent a disciple over to the abbot. The abbott arrived in due time, leaning on his cane.

" 'Yesterday I was given some beautiful mushroom,' the successor explained. 'So I made a stew of them and thought you should have some. It's when you're old that you appreciate delicacies like this.'

"The abbot nodded, smiled, and sat down. His host made rice, warmed the Great Beyond stew and set it before his superior. The abbot ate heartily as the host ate a bowl of mushrooms he had prepared separately.

"They ended their meal with a hot drink. 'Well, that's it,' thought the successor, who waited anxiously for the old boy to start going mad with his last headache on Earth. But nothing happened. It was very odd. Until the abbot's toothless mouth broke out in a grin. 'Best batch of Great Beyonds I ever tasted!' he declared.

"Being an abbot, he had known all along. The successor stole speechlessly from the room while the abbot went home. The abbot had enjoyed Great Beyonds for many years, though, of course, the successor had not known this, and he had never been poisoned by them. The whole plan had gone wrong." Historian Pak fell silent.

"I see," Mr. Matsuda said indifferently. "Quite an innovative individual." There was a pause and then Mr. Matsuda said, "I hope to see you at the soiree. Let me get the date and time for you. If you notify my secretary, we will send a limo to the airport to pick you up. I must discontinue our conversation, I have a meeting to attend to." He cut the connection.

Historian Pak was furious at Mr. Matsuda's inferences and, worse, at his invitation, which was less of an invitation than a demand that he appear. Historian Pak found it nothing but annoying to travel to Japan and endure every indignity at the hands of the man who was systematically killing off his sons. Mr. Matsuda wished him to know who was in charge of his life, who had a foot on his neck and the neck of his only surviving son. There was much to think about. Mr. Matsuda had come to the conclusion that both of Historian Pak's sons were a threat. One had been subsequently dispatched, but Mr. Matsuda did not feel this was enough.

The cherry tree outside Historian Pak's window stood mute against the horizon as Historian Pak stilled his mind. Ten minutes later, he decided on offensive tactics, one tactic in particular in which Korean politicos had become particular masters, and one which Historian Pak was well-equipped to perform—the rumor. If Mr. Matsuda insisted on his personal appearance at some absurd soiree, what better place to begin rumor-mongering?

* * *

Zeta Reticuli is found on the farthest edge of the Pleiades, three hundred light-years from Earth. It reflects forty-four percent light and is flattened at the poles. It has two moons, two suns, one of which rises and sets three hours before the other, much more distant sun, and eleven major currents. The currents striate its surface. The pull of its moons, which control the surface currents, cause periodic sandstorms on the planet. Zeta Reticuli is an environment of gas and rock, beaten into a concentration of minerals by the pressure of the pounding winds and the heaving, liquid mass underneath its mineral-rich crust. It is a perfect planet for mining.

In the late twentieth century, Zeta Reticuli was said to be inhabited by a society of spiritually evolved aliens who waited to walk humankind into the next level of consciousness, thereby opening the way to the next highest dimension once the physical matter of the human beings in question had been refined. Diet, meditation, and certain exercises were said to further the refining process.

Granted, many people had simply disappeared during the twentieth century, but whether that was a result of the high crime rates or of alien advice was now impossible to prove. Most people believed the former. Certainly, no natives had been found on Zeta Reticuli, at least no aliens indigenous to the planet. Many had used the planet as a stopping off point on their way through the Pleiades, and it was inhabitable enough, if one didn't mind the monotonous landscape and the sand and sulfur enriched air so thick that lungs rebelled and contracted until one became used to it. Human beings had come to understand that the Pleiadians were no more advanced or spiritually evolved than they themselves, just different. And, except for Deathspeaking, no more psychically aware than the average human.

Storms rose violently and quickly upon the planet's surface, moving in bands around the lower atmosphere. They effectively moved entire oceans of sand from one side of a land mass to the other in one or two Reticulan days. For this reason, So Pak would have a difficult time in trying to pinpoint landmarks denoting the exact locations of the Japanese and Korean mining camps. They were going to be hell to find, but Chosyam had the foresight to include a jimmied ultrasound surface tracker that sent back computer photos to the mainframe located in the ship. He had also equipped the ship with laser wands that operated like the old dowsing wands and detected Earth-originated material on other planets.

There was a great deal of rock on Zeta Reticuli as well, which could prove to be a godsend as the rock outcroppings, although daunting, did not change or move across the planet's surface like the sand. Little was known of animal life. The miners of the expedition did not have much to say on the subject. The *Bushido* set orbit coordinates and, in what would have been the autumn of 2095, the crew prepared to land. There was a lot of butt-slapping and equipment-stealing and other good-humored high jinks on board when So Pak announced landing at 0300 hours. He walked into the common room and, Chosyam in attendance, stood at the head of the table. There was immediate silence.

"We will be disembarking on the planet at 0300 hours."

The crew and academicians cheered.

"Pilot Katz and Com Officer Jaffee will remain on board. The rest of you will take your places in the two landers in the cargo hold. Please remember that the cargo hold has no life-support systems and can be reached only by air lock. Wear suits and helmets and oxygen wires."

Everyone but Com Officer Jaffe beamed.

"Let me at them Daysun Bandits," Savage pumped the air around him with his fists. The Daysun Bandits were gutted and rebuilt fighter planes, famous for their maneuverability.

"I believe your job is navigation, Officer Savage," So Pak said mildly.

" 'Course it is." Savage sank his head onto the table in front of him.

No one was late. At 0300 hours, they were all there and accounted for. With Katz holding the *Bushido* in orbit and guiding the tracer lines, *Arachne* and *Lips III,* the two beater fighters that had been expanded and outfitted as complete mobile units with quarters, a small sick bay, and laboratory stations, touched down on the surface of Zeta Reticuli as planned, despite landing in the middle of a windstorm strong enough to send *Lips III* skidding across the surface of the plain like a stone skipping across a calm lake. Chosyam and So Pak sat in the observation bay of the *Arachne,* Chosyam shuddering with every strain of the ship. It wasn't the landing that concerned him, it was hoping the lander would stop before it blew halfway across the planet. Chosyam hadn't made allowances for the fact that Daysun Bandits used pop-out drag chutes, or BAK4 portarrest recovery system emergonets. The landing jets wailed like the carnivorous Mother of the West, Goddess of insatiable disease, calamity, and killing.

From *Arachne*'s sick bay, Ewha looked through the shield window and clenched her jaw at the effort it would take just to maintain sick bay sterility amid the endless swirl of copper colored sand, glinting red in the sunlight. She could see Toshio and Kenjii in the observation bay located in the nose of *Lips III*, and smiled at their atmosphere suits and helmets, which they hadn't taken off yet. She walked closer to the window and saw that the sand wasn't sand at all, but small crystals that looked like flying specks of purite. Ewha wondered how sharp-edged they were. The manuals said they were capable of embedding themselves in the skin and tearing at it from the inside like tiny retractable arrowheads. Savage was pounding on the navigation console. "Dammit all, Jaffe, you're wrong."

"I am not wrong," came Jaffe's voice from the comlink. "I'm never wrong about location siting."

"We are not 1500 kilometers from the mining site, fool."

"And why not?"

"Because I feel it in my bones and navigation is genetic."

"So is stupidity in my book," replied Jaffe.

"Besides, I can see domes right over there."

"Jaffe," Katz broke in, "radio confirmed landing. And coordinates, please."

"You want to give me some coordinates, fool?"

Savage rattled off numbers, signed off, and pulled himself out of the blisterpod. He sauntered over to Ewha. He put his hand on her shoulder and squeezed her collarbone. "Nice country out there."

The suns burned down.

"Disengage from landing stations," So Pak's voice came out over the com speaker. They moved through the necessary checks, swiftly and efficiently. Savage was grinning from ear to ear. "In no time at all we'll be out there digging up that good stuff."

* * *

In the days that followed, they moved fast, erecting a life dome, setting up support systems and coordinate lines to the excavation sites. On the third day, they gathered in the mess of the *Arachne* to screen the scout roboholos. It was the first time they had been assembled together since Denisovich's funeral and the landing and even the excitement of the holos couldn't dissipate an undercurrent of uneasiness and suspicion.

Chosyam, Bender, Savage, and Drukker arrived together from *Lips III.* With Denisovich gone, the bulk of operations fell to Chosyam and Savage. It was Chosyam's responsibility to relay information and administer supply flow between the *Bushido,* the landers, and the dome. Drukker was to coordinate documentation and findings from the two camps, Bender to go on site to the Japanese camp and classify information.

The remainder of the crew was gathered on the *Arachne.* All shared the life-support camp space, where the working labs were located. Finalized results were transferred to the labs aboard the landers and any pertinent hard exhibits would eventually be transferred to the *Bushido* under Chosyam's direction and stored in the cargo bay.

Toshio, Kenjii, and Yeshe were assigned to the Korean site, with Toshio responsible for any alien tracings, a secondary mission of the *Bushido* that So Pak kept carefully under his control. As it turned out, the Korean mining camp was a makeshift one, buried under two feet of sand and a thick crust of mineralized skin from some long ago disruption that had heaved the broken crust of the planet's surface over the camp itself. They could make out shapes of intact tents, carefully layered with mineral deposits and then fossilized by the planet's heat. The Korean ship had the look of an exploration probe rather than a full range mining cruiser. An odd fact, unless the Koreans meant to rely on a tremendous amount of technology which, everyone knew, the country hadn't possessed at the time. There were only about seventy-five men all told that could have fit on a ship of that size on the best of runs. The ship was so old it could have been displayed in an air museum. Ships like that had long since ceased to appear in American beater junkyards. It was rare for anyone to have the chance to run across one so perfectly preserved in working order. So Pak regretted that Denisovich had not the opportunity to explore the ship himself. He would have spent endless hours uncovering operational conditions aboard such a craft.

One hundred yards from the Korean camp was the remains of the Japanese ship, wrecked upon impact. It seemed the crew had spent some time trying to piece the ship back together again but had not succeeded. There were odd additions to the hold and engines. The Japanese camp was much larger and better laid out than the Korean camp. And its miners had evidently begun to excavate a primitive strip line, which stood between the Japanese and the Korean camps. To the right of the Japanese camp was a wild area marked out with eighteen holes, suggesting the miners had constructed a golf course. Other than that, there were no signs that either camp had taken their stay on the planet with anything less than the utmost seriousness. It was a sad and chilling testament to the fact that adventuring was not what it was cracked up to be. At least that was Ewha's take on the situation. But then, she reminded herself, she was looking at this from the point of view of a ship's doctor not that of a professional. Miners did not go off-planet expecting entertainment.

Chosyam fine-tuned the ultrasound receiver, which

controlled the three-legged probe that was crawling over the wreckage and sending back pictures. They could see mining tools, crockery and food stores, and a row of bodies ossified by the climate, neatly laid out by the promontory which marked the edge of the strip mine. The probe camera swirled and shot, images coming to them in milliseconds

"More from the Japanese camp?" Chosyam asked.

"No, that's fine for the moment. Now let's take a closer look at the Korean camp," So Pak decided. "That is, unless anyone has any particular questions now."

Whatever suspicions had been present at the beginning of the briefing were quickly dissipating under the curiosity of the crew. Perhaps curiosity was a much underestimated quality in human beings, Ewha thought to herself.

Steadily, the probe picked its way across the mining pit and climbed the other side tenaciously. There were no piled bodies on the Korean side. But there was evidence its inhabitants had fled. The Korean ship seemed to have been in perfect working order and, however quickly and for whatever reason its men had deserted, they left behind them a perfect working camp, as though they expected to return again, if only to board ship and head home. But all of the *Bushido* crew had learned not to make hasty assumptions about what they found on probe sites.

When the probe screen finally blacked out, Bender leaned back and lit his pipe. "It's years of work."

"Yes," Kenjii agreed, humbled in the face of this discovery.

"As you know, we do not have years," So Pak reminded them. "We can only hope to excavate the most important areas and leave them cataloged and in good condition for other probes, should someone else decide to build on our work."

"It is an opportunity for first-rate scholarship," Toshio said respectfully. "It is excellent that the Japanese gave Drukker and Bender clearance. It will be through their superior experience that we will give honor to this discovery."

His comment made Ewha look over at Drukker. When she did, she noticed Drukker was pale and looked unwell. Ewha decided that at the first opportunity she would give the woman a physical. It was important for the survival of the group. Not only would they need her expertise, but her physical presence could be important should something happen. They could not lose too many and still hope to make it home in any kind of decent shape. So Pak spoke and his tone was almost reverent. "The excavation proves to be a challenge to us all. We must proceed slowly and be as thorough as possible in processing the data. We must spend adequate time in land analyses and send reports that are as complete and as well-thought out as possible to the com ship on a biweekly basis. There will be no room for promoting pet theories. We must behave as scientists."

Everyone agreed. Kenjii, Drukker, Toshio, and Bender were nodding. Kenjii and Toshio were sorting through the photographs before them. Kenjii was comparing the mining sites to sketches taken from the Kyoto archives.

"As there is not a great deal of vegetation to study, Yeshe will put her talents at the disposal of Mr. Bender and will be available to Toshio and Kenjii," So Pak said, smiling at Miss Yoon. She was sifting through a handful of the mineral crust scraped from the shalelike surface of the sandswept area at the ship's port. At the mention of her name she looked up at So Pak and blushed under his scrutiny.

Unbidden, the scene at Newark came to So Pak's mind, the woman beaten by Snakers, her face like a calla lily for a moment in front of him before she fled into the night. His nightmarish memory was shattered by Toshio's voice.

"I suppose we can rule out the expectation of any survivors wandering on the planet," Toshio said abruptly.

Ewha was surprised at the sadness in his voice; she had thought he would have learned to distance himself during his work in ADC.

So Pak deliberated for a moment before answering. "It seems safe to assume there are no survivor colonies," he agreed.

"You don't expect us to search the whole bleeding planet for survivors?" Savage demanded, outraged.

"It might give you something to do," Toshio said mildly.

"I've got enough to do with Denisovich gone," Savage complained.

"Most likely," So Pak agreed without sympathy.

"With the climate as unpredictable as it is, I want maximum communication set up on all sites," he continued. "It is not the windy season, and the sites have been swept clean by the last storm, but we must proceed with all caution."

The others nodded agreement.

"Test your com equipment before you leave and clean it once again when you return to the ship. Under no circumstances will anyone go off alone. If I have to tie you to each other, that's what I'll do."

"If we do, on the off chance, encounter survivors it

will be best to leave them alone,'' Toshio commented, some odd rote memory kicking off his instincts.

''An odd thing for a humanitarian to say,'' Ewha suggested. ''Survivors have been found in the oddest places, Alpha Centauri, for example.''

''And we know what happened to them,'' Kenjii replied. ''Shuttled back to Earth in a ship designed from the start to implode once it hit Earth's atmosphere. An accident, I believed they called it.''

''Yes,'' Ewha said. ''But what can you expect from a society that deliberately cut off communications to probes suspected of sustaining survivors?''

''They were expected to die or survive without aid,'' Katz said, his face hard. ''Not much different from Earth, when you come to think about it.''

Drukker raised her head, her eyes flashing. ''I do sincerely hope you are not referring to the German agreement for MIAs.''

Katz slapped himself on the forehead with the palm of his hand. ''How insensitive of me.''

''It was Japanese policy,'' Ewha intervened. ''As was the decision to filter any survivor stories through the Historical Arts before allowing general release in the news.''

''Unapproved leaking immediately debunked and ridiculed by the media,'' Toshio added.

Drukker's face was the color of the underside of some nocturnal marsh plant. Her eyes had darkened to jet. ''Orientals should not have the authority to investigate German probe ships.''

''I did not volunteer for the job, my dear,'' Toshio answered mildly. ''As I recall, I was sent because of my alien expertise by order of one of your own Chancellors.''

''Come off it, all of you,'' Savage cut into the discussion. "Ancient history. We all know why space probes, including this one, exist at all. It has nothing to do with information. Or your bloody careers booting ideas about the frigging galaxy, which is about all I see you doing. The real reason for space probes, in case any of you dorkheads haven't noticed, is to rid the planet of undesirables. Prison ships, that's all probes are. Going to nowhere. What do you expect the Japanese," he nodded to Drukker, "to do? Monitor the bloody things?"

"I'm sure your views are somewhat extreme," Kenjii said haughtily.

"Extreme, my ass. Just one of you tell me who it is on this frying pan parked in the sandbox here, or what on this planet is so damned important to the Japanese?"

No one answered.

"There you have it, then." He settled back smugly, having made his point. "Don't you kid yourselves we have any value. None of us'd be here if we did."

"Well, there's the lifers," Toshio began.

"Right. And just what makes a person a lifer? Don't see them collecting retirement money, do you?"

"I am sure there is no reason for considering Yeshe, for example, an undesirable," Ewha began reasonably.

"I should say not," Savage agreed, his eyes softening for an instant before his face hardened into a leer. "But we don't know what the girl's been up to."

So Pak felt his anger rising. "This is not the time for speculation on the fate of the probe," he said, forcing himself to speak without emotion.

"Fair enough," Savage agreed. "But it burns me to see the lot of you sitting there like God, deciding how you are going to tell the story of the lads out there when the fact of the matter is, you're in worse shape than the lot of them. They at least had legitimate reasons for being here. You got shipped out."

A deathly quiet fell over the group.

"There's not one of us isn't a public embarrassment," Savage continued mercilessly.

"It is difficult to go through life without becoming a public embarrassment to someone over something," Yeshe said gently.

Savage looked at her and bit back his words. "Bunch of intellectos," he muttered. "You think all of you are better than the working man. You think we're stupid. Well, let me tell you something just to address the brain trust here. We see what's in front of our noses while you're so busy looking down the road, you forget all about the car that just hit you." He glared around the table. "And you haven't forgotten the most important part of all, have you? The part about any of us stepping out of line. It isn't our asses on the line alone, is it? They go after our families, don't they?"

"May I ask you a question?" So Pak broke in.

"We're all of us a walking human tragedy. Investigative Permission, what's that? Permission to self-destruct."

"So what are you doing here?" So Pak asked.

Savage rubbed his chin. "Let's see. I was thirsting for adventure's what it was. And there's precious little to be had in Newark, grounded for two years. And that fool Conglaugh, the bleeding Welshman himself." Savage was silent a moment. "I guess I have a confession to make. They put his History in a comic book, you know. I loved that comic book. Had it for six years. Even slept with it until the colors came out in the sheets. Finally my mother in her infinite wisdom threw it on the fire in front of my eyes when I was fourteen years old and I swore I'd make her regret it when I had my own life.''

''Local confession?'' Ewha asked sardonically.

''Yeah, well, no problem.'' Savage shut up and stared at the wall. But he had single-handedly destroyed the excitement of the crew and left them open to the ghost of Denisovich. Yeshe shivered. Kenjii busied himself with studying the tabletop and Toshio, despite his practiced detachment, looked uncomfortable.

''All's I can say is it's a good thing we buried that poor sod in deep space,'' Savage added finally.

''Will you shut up?'' Drukker demanded.

Savage turned on her, ''Filthy Saxon.''

''We proceed in pairs to the assigned excavation sites.'' So Pak said. ''Chosyam will monitor transmissions to Jaffe. Ewha and Toshio will select bodies and do autopsies. And please,'' he added, ''keep it to a minimum. Bender will catalog the Japanese site, Kenjii the Korean site. Drukker will work as liaison and bring appropriate documentation back to the ship for me to go through. Is that clearly understood?''

The group nodded.

Ewha dug around underneath her chair and pulled out a bottle of sake. ''Shall we celebrate?''

Yeshe went to the lab for a burner and container to heat the sake. Drukker made a trip to the mess for glasses. Fifteen minutes later, they'd loosened up. Some of the excitement returned and the expectation was back.

Even with the wires and cables and bared electronics announcing Chosyam's decorative powers run amok, the ship, Ewha decided, was a pleasant enough place to be. The little group drew closer, warmed by the sake, which burned down their throats and filled their bodies with warmth. And the one thing they'd noticed was there was little enough warmth on this planet when the suns went down. Ewha turned on the lasertape machine and Savage pulled out the Earth tapes. Chosyam cleared away the tables and, on the tiny dance floor, Yeshe danced with Savage who, as it turned out, was a terrific dancer.

In the corner of the room, So Pak stood with Ewha and Toshio, discussing plans for the next day.

"It could have been worse," Ewha said, refilling So Pak's sake cup.

"Meaning?"

"There could have been nothing left when we got here. Or it could have all been buried under sand." She shook her head, "I know all about the blasters, but digging out would still have slowed us down considerably."

So Pak nodded. "Then we would have been sure Savage was right."

"And who's to say he hasn't gotten a bit of the truth and skewed it up?" Ewha asked.

"Do you know what I think about that?"

"Can't imagine." Ewha had no idea of what So Pak thought important.

"I don't actually give a shit if the entire World Office booted us off-planet. I'm exactly where I want to be." He thought for a moment of telling her about the subliminals, but shook off the idea. For one thing, it would take too long to explain. For another, he wanted more information before he jumped to conclusions.

"Oh?" Ewha looked at him curiously. "You and Savage both."

So Pak's face suddenly looked vulnerable and Ewha found herself wanting to break open his reserve, an odd thing for her. The unfortunate thing about being medical officer was seeing the most self-contained people's reserves break down. Anyone trained in the medical arts saw human nature at its worst. That knowledge crept out at the most inconvenient times and tended to make doctors who were the least sensitive fight to keep their distance.

"You could just be obsessed," she suggested, more coldly than she meant.

"Perhaps," he admitted. "But where does obsession leave off and one's life work begin?"

"If you are asking me to express an opinion, I think the difference is that one's life work is what one understands one accomplished looking back on life."

"And what do you suppose you will say about yourself from that perspective?" So Pak asked, rather personally, Ewha thought, for him.

She tried to answer honestly, "I don't know. That I observed and healed when I could. At least, I hope that's what I have to say. But then, one must allow for change."

"The Japanese have many stories illustrating change," So Pak said.

"I was raised American. I don't even know the Korean stories, much less the Japanese."

"Korean stories are full of lost love. Love for women, love of lost opportunities," So Pak's eyes followed Yeshe around the dance floor.

"Oh?"

"Lost love and longing. We enjoy sadness, crying for lost peace and beauty."

"Perhaps it is compensation?"

"For?"

"My mother questioned any existence of peacefulness or beauty in the Korean spirit," Ewha said, choking back a chuckle.

"On the other hand, the Japanese have many stories about surprises."

"Not entirely the same thing." Ewha's attention began to wander. What she wanted to question So Pak about was obsession. And in particular, his. After all, he was in charge of the expedition and expeditions, like corporations, took on the personalities of their leaders. And there was something about this man, no matter how controlled he appeared to be, that made Ewha want to know the truth. Or at least made her understand there was some truth here she did not know. Maybe it was her American upbringing, but Ewha liked to think of herself as someone who could look unflinchingly into the face of truth. Perhaps that was only another lie.

She turned from So Pak and looked across the room, trying to present a persona that might be construed as unthreatening. "Something drives you."

So Pak thought of his brother's ghost and said nothing.

"What is it?" Ewha believed direct questions were best. The only way to find anything out was to ask.

So Pak thought of the ways language became twisted into subliminals and remained silent. How was he to answer her? Should he answer her? Would an answer presume some kind of intimacy?

But it was only the ship's doctor he was talking to. And doctors, no matter what function they performed, got to know it all, sooner or later. They considered it professional baggage, he supposed. There was nothing he could tell her that would surprise her. And it would be a relief to talk. He would have preferred a perfect stranger, but sometimes you had to take what you could get.

He cleared his throat. "Two things haunt me."

"Only two."

"Both of them, oddly enough, tied to events which occurred just before the ship took off."

Ewha waited.

"One is self-explanatory. The death of my brother, Kim."

Whatever Ewha had been waiting for could be no worse than this. She almost dropped her sake cup, which slipped through her fingers as though it had a will of its own. "Kim Pak?"

"You know of his Histories?" So Pak seemed amused.

"He's a Historian?" Ewha was even more shocked, but she told herself it made sense."

"Of course, he's a Historian."

"There were rumors of the death of the leader of the Snake Order before we left Earth. I didn't know enough to give credence to them. I am very sorry."

So Pak took her arm, pulling her around to face him. "What are you saying?"

"Kim Pak? Lives in a small rural village in Korea with his father, Historian Pak? A quiet life. In the mountains by the northern border. A Historian by profession?" Ewha thought a moment and shook her head. "It makes sense."

"What else would he be?" And Ewha heard the bitterness in So Pak's voice. "I left the family, refusing to take on the tradition. He decided upon the honorable course of action."

Ewha thought quickly. She would have to tell him. "Your brother," she said, gazing levelly at the *Bushido*'s commander, "is the leader of the central division of the Snakers, a Korean terrorist group dedicated to Korean independence. The movement began fifteen years ago under the guise of the Japanese crime syndicate. Since then it has grown to encompass Russian dissidents, American-born Koreans, who are perhaps the most nationalistic of all and send money for the movement's support, several well-known jazz musicians, quite a few Ronin Historians, and Japanese and Pakistani emigrees to America. In short," she added bluntly, "your brother is the brains behind the nationalist uprising."

"My brother," So Pak said, with decorum, "is dead. He was buried before we left."

"Then Savage was right," Ewha whispered.

"Savage."

"We have been sent off-world to certain death."

"Accomplishing what?"

"Don't be naive." There was nothing to lose so she continued. "You are about to tell me you are chased through the stars by the death of your brother, but you have made it very clear you don't even know who the man was. Or what power he wielded. And now he's dead. Perhaps they mean to kill you. . . ."

"He died in a poacher's trap," So Pak's voice was mechanical. "Caught. An accident. There have been poachers on our family land since time immemorial."

"The Japanese do not poach."

So Pak said nothing. He couldn't refute her. It made too many things clear. Still, what was important about all of this was that he had never known his brother nor told him he loved him. And she did not know the whole story. It was not a doomed expedition despite Denisovich's murder.

"And the other?"

"Of no importance. Something I saw the night before we left. In Space Square. A random act of violence. A cameo of cruelty. It means nothing save as a symbol."

"Indulge me." The world was a comfortless place. People needed to talk. And before she knew it, Ewha found herself making a conscious decision to get to know this man.

"I know little of the Snakers," he said. She turned away again, the right side of her face shadowed by darkness, her profile, caught in the light, resolute and determined. "And the event at the spaceport?" She prompted.

"I saw a man being murdered and a girl beaten by Snakers. They ran away before I could help her."

"Do you know what she looked like?"

"She looked like Yeshe."

"It wasn't Yeshe."

"Of course not. But every time I see her face, I remember."

"And your father?"

"My father?"

"What of him?"

"Does he know of my brother?"

She touched his arm in sympathy. "I'm sorry. If you want to talk, I'm here. But right now, I must go back to work." She shoved her hands into her pockets and grinned. "If that sounds conflicted, I suppose it is."

So Pak watched her small, square back as she walked out the door and disappeared into the hallport. He waited several minutes and left as well.

The corridor was narrow and cold and he shivered as ghosts descended upon him. Kim's ghost, he imagined, would be thin, velvety, and as sharp as a garotte.

CHAPTER SEVEN

Historian Pak stepped out on the heliport and brushed at his formal attire. He should have packed and flown in more comfortable clothing, but he hated luggage of any sort and, since he was being airlifted to the limo pool and driven to Mr. Matsuda's private residence by limo, the best he could get out of the deal was minimal haulage. He told himself it hardly mattered if he looked a bit wrinkled. His great age would help him get away with it. People would think he was eccentric. Although he told himself he wasn't as old as that yet, and if he ever managed to attain an age of that magnitude, one would hope he would have acquired some wisdom along the way. Historian Pak seemed to be getting it backward. The older he got, the more ignorant he felt.

The heliride was vigorous and windy. Historian Pak was glad enough to reach the limo. The chauffeur opened the door and took his bags. Historian Pak climbed inside and rested his head for a moment against the buttery leather seat.

He was lonely. The driver was a quarter of a city block away from him. Children could have played a rousing game of racketball in the back of the stretch limo. He turned to the window and thought longingly of his garden, misty and haunted this morning, the mist streaming down from the mountain at four-thirty before it settled into the valley like a whispered prayer. The trees had been still, their yellow, red, orange, and bronze leaves mixing, their glorious vibrancy smudged by the mist which softened the colors, and the whole punctuated by wet black tree trunks and branches.

The ride through the Tokyo streets was jammed with floatcars, limosines being used only for extremely formal or state occasions. The Ginza was packed with twentieth century vintage neon and people striving to relieve others of all their disposable income. Although Historian Pak had been looking forward to being in the city once again, he found that his interest had deserted him. He could not even be bothered to crane his neck to take in the activity on the street. Perhaps he was getting old. If it weren't for his personal hidden agenda, he wouldn't be attending Mr. Matsuda's soiree at all. Affairs of this sort were all identical. Only the seasons and faces changed. Mr. Matsuda required his presence to balance the guest list and to prove to his critics that he was a man of fine cultural understanding. Men of cultural understanding had the good of the people at heart and could be trusted. They could be trusted to believe at worst that people were a natural resource which could be turned to this or that. Mr. Matsuda counted upon Historian Pak's presence to disprove the truth: that Mr. Matsuda was someone not greatly bothered by the larger meaning of things or life.

Historian Pak was marching in obedient attendance on the man responsible for murdering both of his sons. The fact that one was still alive meant nothing. It was only a matter of time.

After the traffic jam in which Historian Pak's driver got into a violent argument with the driver of a floatcar, which required the chauffeur to get out of the car, bang rudely on the hood of the offending floatcar and make slashing movements at the helium bag under the floatcar with a bared martial arts knife, the limosine drove on. The disagreement had been settled to the driver's satisfaction and the dour-faced man smiled. His smile was frightening, and the experience seemed to have loosened his tongue. "Traffic is for shit. You notice it always balls up at the train and space stations?"

Historian Pak studied the interior of the limosine. The cherry paneling was veneer, and the observation shocked him. So little was real anymore. Even luxury was no longer genuine.

The driver glared at Historian Pak's implacable face reflected in the rearview mirror, but his eyes jumped away when the limo clattered through another of the fiber-filled potholes and the left front wheel sank up to the suspension in filthy glass shards. For his part, Historian Pak decided he definitely disliked the man's oily features.

But the obstacle course before the driver only served to make him more verbal. "Word's out, says it's Terror Two causing the jam-ups. All a sort of protest, like. Them Snakers don't know which way the wind blows and never have. And them Ronin Historians is always looking for things to write about, trying to make out things are worse than they are."

"Are you English?" asked Historian Pak.

"My parents were, sir. First they went to Hong Kong. They almost didn't make it out before the uprising. Came to the Tokyo slums and hung on for several years before they were caught by surprise and died. Wasn't a big adjustment. It was the East End, only everyone spoke Japanese."

"After the hunger riots." Historian Pak believed in the accuracy of primary sources, no matter what faulty emotional drivel primary sources insisted on retaining.

"Yes, sir. Weren't nothing left of the community, sir, not even the buildings." The limo headed down a wide, macadam street slicked with an icing of greenish oil, constant reminder of the acid rain and poisonous city air.

"I was lucky to get the job with Mr. Matsuda, I was, sir. At least I thought so at the time. They say I'm lucky in life. A great deal of potential, but that's an American way of thinking. 'Course, then it was an American told me that."

Historian Pak performed a series of soothing and relaxing exercises while the driver reminisced about the appealing energy and allure of the American fortune-tellers in the Newark area, most of which he attributed to their close approximation to the Deathspeakers.

"And when were you last in Newark?" Historian Pak asked.

"Couple months ago, sir. Mr. Matsuda was visiting and he likes to take his drivers. There was a shooting. I have to tell you, sir, the Snakers are very active in the Newark area. It was just after the assassination of their leader, naturally it made more incidents. I don't know what good it did." Again, the driver regarded Historian Pak intently in the rearview mirror. "The leader of the Snakers was just a lad killed in Korea on his parent's estate."

"Nothing new. Many sons are killed on their family's estate in Korea in these times," Historian Pak said, unable to keep the bitterness from his voice.

"Of course, sir," The limo driver knew when to

keep his place. ''Newark is in shambles, what with the Snakers and the musicians dying like they've been and the aliens perishing stockpiled in the city unable to get a decent burial like they were promised, not like I think they deserve it, but they were promised, weren't they? It's not right not to issue them the visas. And they weren't giving them visas, at least not to the ones what didn't have the tattoos on their hands.''

''Tattoos?''

''Identifying them as Deathspeakers, or about to Deathspeak, or whatever stage they needed to be at. There's progressing stages and there's the new resolutions saying the stages have to be tagged. More bureaucracy, as though we all didn't have enough of that already. It's lovely times we're living in.''

''Yes.'' Historian Pak rubbed his palms together quickly and held them over his eyes, feeling the deep body heat penetrate and relax his eyeballs. It was essential he be on his guard, for all he knew, Mr. Matsuda might assassinate him in Tokyo. But he was wily and he had survived this long, wiliness and survival being attributes his youngest son seemed to lack. Not for the first time, Historian Pak was grateful for the fact that the human brain did not diminish in capacity as it aged. He knew he would need every bit of wisdom accumulated over the years to match Mr. Matsuda. He wished he were a more physical man; sometimes his energy felt entirely trapped in his head, stalling, convulsing, doubling in and under itself until he felt as though his mind were strapped to a laser conductor.

His only weapon for combating Mr. Matsuda's business acumen and corporate power structure was his experience as a storyteller, which seemed to make for an uneven battle indeed. But if he had learned anything by now, it was that he could parlay his talent into effective rumor-mongering, and, if all conditions were right, he would catch Mr. Matsuda off-guard and gain a brief advantage. There was also his knowledge of the old stories, but that was only an intellectual surface game to be played with Mr. Matsuda as a fine old entertainment, chess being a good analogy. It was ridiculous to think that, in the aggregate, their stories meant anything at all in the greater context. Historian Pak found himself smiling. His wandering mind returned to the confines of the limo and to the custody of this strange-eyed guide escorting him through the Styx of Tokyo, whose streets were piled with the bodies of the homeless, vacant-eyed and starving. Not for the first time did Historian Pak wonder what great law of karma pitted him and Mr. Matsuda against each other, dinosaurian rivals in a war whose outcome was no longer relevant. For several moments he idly watched the driver's eyes, flickering in the mirror before him, alert for intersecting limos and floatcars, all ships of the night bearing goods and passengers to Hades.

The driver shifted furtively in his seat and a look of wariness crossed his face. Testing the safety of the ground before he began, he said, "They say the Deathspeakers are more numerous than they have ever been." The man licked his lips and his clenched knuckles shone white as bone in the darkness, riveted on the steering wheel. The disease has taken on a new symptom."

"Yes?"

"The fact is, the buggers are beginning to glow. I've seen it myself. The light just pours off their skin. You could stand one in a room in the dead of night and you'd have no need of flowlamps. It's a phosphorescent discharge. They say it's caused by their skin, in combination with the disease, activated by the atmosphere. The poor bastards are in agony with the cold fire upon them." He swallowed and a look of unaccustomed pain passed across his face. "Naturally, they look holy."

Bars of streetlight swept over Historian Pak's face in slatted neon shades. There had been stories about that, too, about what had actually caused the Deathspeakers to self-destruct. Some said the aliens had charitably internalized a virus they knew was fatal when it was first discovered in the outer reaches of the off-planet commercial concerns, in order to keep it from spreading throughout the galaxy. Thinking they could neutralize it within their systems, none were more surprised than they when the disease, to which they had first been biologically immune, turned virulent and mutated to kill only their own kind.

There were other rumors, of course. There was a school of thinking that claimed Deathspeakers were permitted to come to Earth to die under the auspices of humanitarian policy. But the real reason was the fact that the aliens' nitrogen-rich decomposed bodies were a rare treasure for the depleted planetary ground cover, and that the Japanese viewed any amount of psychological damage done by Deathspeaking to be well worth the ecological gains of nitrogen-rich soil.

The more heretical monks, of course, claimed that the aliens weren't dying at all, but were merely inconvenienced demons—inconvenienced because no one kept up or attended to the shrines any longer. If no one had any respect for the shrines, disorder could be expected to be unleashed throughout the countryside in the form of outraged demons, incomprehensible prophecies, and a dissatisfaction among the people, who had been tricked into believing there really were sentient beings from other planets when everyone knew they were only demons in various stages of frustration, engaged in paying for the results of their Earthly activities.

Historian Pak was amused at this explanation, until he suddenly remembered the story of the monk, Doko. Doko, who as stories had it, devoted himself to the lotus sutra, had been traveling one night when he came upon a distintegrating image of a road god, part-man, and part-horse, with the legs of the horse broken off. Doko did his best to restore the image and waited to see what would happen. What happened was that riders arrived quite shortly thereafter and an old man climbed up on the statue at the crossroads to ride with them. He didn't come back until dawn, but the moment he arrived, the old man came to Doko, where the monk stretched out under a tree, and announced himself to be the road god.

The old man informed Doko that the riders he had seen were gods of disease and it was the road god's job to clear the way for them. The interesting part of the story to Historian Pak's way of thinking was what came next. The road god asked the monk to stay and chant a sutra for him, hoping it would enable him to leave his suffering body and be reborn in the Land of Bliss. Doko, true to his word, chanted for three days and three nights. The fourth day, when the old man appeared again, he told Doko that, due to his compassion he would be taking on another body—as a follower of the Bodhisattva.

Surprisingly, but naturally enough, when Doko made a boat and laid the image on it, the boat sailed straight toward the south where the road god said he was to be reborn.

Those killed in particularly unearthly ways were said to become demons. Or those who had lived particularly worthless lives and for whom no one would say the lotus sutra, their being completely beyond the bounds of human compassion. As the limo pulled up before a large townhouse, Historian Pak found himself wondering if Mr. Matsuda ever contemplated the possibility of an afterlife. His ruminations were at an end.

Historian Pak, unescorted, walked toward the gates of the townhouse and surrendered himself up to this meeting that held so much importance. Suddenly, he was tired, weary to his bones, exhausted by social niceties and social interchange. It was all done with mirrors, social interaction, the man in power at a fleeting moment, expecting, because he was a man that his power would be eternal, even though he had replaced someone who had held power before him and had the most empirical of evidence that his stay would not last, either. Historian Pak suspected that long ago Mr. Matsuda had forgotten the rules of supplanting and overcoming, for he had placed himself outside it in a fragile circle of privilege. His mistake was in assuming Historian Pak was in an even finer, more distant orbit around what anyone might regard as objective truth.

As Historian Pak buttoned the second button of his evening jacket, he negotiated his way toward wide oak doors as forbidding and formal as the gates to his own death. He caught sight of the sun, washing the glass-encrusted skyscrapers with a peach light more delicate than the whisper of a woman's kimono in the night as she arrived to meet her lover, and wondered if this would prove his last sunset. Cursing himself for a fool with romantic notions of escape when one's life was anything but escape from itself no matter how hard one attempted sleight-of-hand, Historian Pak straightened his stooped shoulders and faced the doors, his features carefully worked into an expression of slight pleasure, in the event someone's intention should be to surprise him into betraying himself.

What anyone could now see, including the astonished limo driver, jolted into recognition at last, was the greatest living Historian, a man of whom it was claimed that his only desire was to live in total and absolute isolation. A man who never ventured into public view, a personage as rarely sighted as a thousand-year-old comet. On the surface, he appeared to be a slight Korean man who was balding and nearly blind, but his physical vitality was remarkable for a man of his age and sedentary occupation. He walked as though he were used to a lifetime of carrying himself about his world on powerful thighs that never once failed him. His shoulders were deceptive under his evening jacket, which had never really fit. They were, in actuality, the shoulders of a man used to going several rounds as a matter of course, of a man disappointed when there was no longer any apparent challenge. Punches had not stooped him nor clouded his eyes; it was the punches that kept the ravages of osteoporosis from his bones and his eyes were dissolving in the whites as though it were only a matter of time before he became a flesh and blood enigma, or maybe a demon after the Japanese fashion.

He was met at the door by a man fulfilling the function of servant, although it didn't take a great deal of observation to peg him for a bodyguard. He was tastelessly packing a hydraulic machine gun around which his suit jacket bulged in an annoying way. Ingratiatingly, the man cupped Historian Pak's elbow, ostensibly to help him across the threshold, but actually to take a quick inventory of body build and physical mass. Historian Pak breathed his last lungful of freedom and allowed himself to be ushered into the soiree by Mr. Matsuda's man.

Historian Pak abhorred social gatherings. He had always detested large crowds, particularly when the individuals had any remote connection to each other, a feeble explanation for the fact that they had chosen to all share the same room, or as in this case, suite of rooms.

In all of his sixty years, Historian Pak had not found humans in social groups to be at their best. Anonymous crowds were something entirely different. Here one could shine individually, be absorbed into anonymity, strike up short, intense relationships, express oneself completely or not as one wished without having to lug around the artificial cultivation of intimacy just because one happened to share the same occupation, or even worse, friends.

He hated social congress of any sort. As he stood at the top of the mahogany staircase waiting to be announced, looking down upon the sea of men and women in an uncomfortable though inarguably elegant black and white room in which the only color in the unrelieved palette was provided by the bright spots of women's dresses, he realized with the clarity that comes of age that he couldn't ever remember having been happy at any social gathering. What he could remember was not wanting to go in the first place, the hours before the event dragging on interminably because the event must be faced, not wanting to be there once he arrived, politely talking to people while feeling trapped, never having made it through a single such gathering in his entire recollection without leaving on some pretense part of the way through to walk around outside for a while at least once and often several times, never being able to leave any social event soon enough, and always feeling utterly exhausted and empty afterward as though his time had been squandered away.

This contemplation filled Historian Pak with an exceptional feeling of well-being and euphoria, even in the face of the soiree before him. It also served to give him an almost psychic understanding of his son So Pak, a nonverbalized, nonintellectualized, gut sympathy with the way the DNA of the family genes had been reassembled in So Pak to propel him to the stars in direct defiance of what other people thought important. For Historian Pak had come to understand that what he so disliked about social events was the way people postured as though they actually believed they were anything more than a skeleton upon which a little meat hung, the whole of it animated all too briefly by life. The thought that anyone was of any more importance than anyone else was purely a matter of pride, and wasn't it pride, the Victorian missionaries taught, that was the father of all other sins?

Historian Pak presented his invitation to the sour-faced attendant and was duly announced from the top of the stairs, amid the noise of the party. Faces turned toward him like water lilies on the surface of his meditation pond at his home in the mountains. Then he was walking down the stairs to a small flurry of formal bowing which his entrance caused.

He found himself surrounded by hawk-faced men and round-faced men, wise-looking women and women possessed of impossibly perfect flesh, talking and dancing below four two-storied chandeliers. Historian Pak made his way to the bar, almost obscured by four and a half foot wide arrangements of white flowered birds of paradise flung into obsidian vases with a trained and forced carelessness.

The bartender was of the new school, a telepath, or perhaps he was an alien tottering on the borders of Deathspeak. Historian Pak hardly cared, so thankful was he that he had been handed two fingers of scotch in Waterford crystal, and a matching tumbler of mineral water. He downed his scotch, tipped the bartender, and began his peregrination of the room with the tumbler of mineral water in his hand.

It was quite a party. Everyone was there, even one or two of the more respectable Ronins. Historian Pak wondered at the Japanese penchant for the bizarre, at their determination to set up ordered structures in order to break them later. A small jazz trio played listlessly in an ice-cold marble hall as though buried alive in their own mausoleum. He saw the reputedly most famous calligrapher in Japan standing at a leaded glass casement window staring morosely out at the Tokyo night sky, puce-colored from pollution and industrial wastes, a low cloud of chemical waste reflecting the neon colors of the lights of the Ginza back onto the street and eventually across the calligrapher's form.

There was the requisite assembly of artists for taste, politicians for power, society people for acceptance and status quo and, most of all, corporate representatives, warriors in the war of economics. Historian Pak knew why he was here and he was not happy about it, although assassination seemed to be a paranoid dream. He did not like his unspoken role as assenter to the activities of Mr. Matsuda and his corporation, or his nodding acceptance of the death of his youngest son and of the license to die of his eldest, shot off into space to die with his crew, obscuring the very information and the importance of the information he'd gone off to investigate under the cover of a completely new tragedy. Still, the game must be played.

Certainly, there were enough people here under auspices similar to his own—the artists, the Ronin, the jazz trio, and the two other attending Historians, their faces a miserable blur in the crowd—for any thinking and reasonably sophisticated person not to take any of it seriously. None of them could possibly be in agreement with Mr. Matsuda's policy which, as Historian Pak was beginning to remember, had been responsible for alien reparation in the first place.

Historian Pak found he had witlessly allowed himself to stand entirely alone in the middle of the parquet floor as he sipped his mineral water and tried to remember exactly what role it was that Mr. Matsuda had played. He must of necessity remember it entirely on his own, there was no help from resource material—it had been wiped—including the archives. It wasn't the first time Historian Pak regretted his decision not to file for a resident Deathspeaker. Much of their prognostication was useless drivel, but ocasionally, if well-handled and questioned carefully, they could access information such as this, hidden information suddenly essential. It was getting more and more difficult to write a decent History with half of the information and research codes accessed and the other half erased altogether.

Historian Pak wandered across the floor to a side alcove where he could observe the room without being obtrusive. But his refuge was soon invaded. A calm-looking, successful Japanese businessman was guiding a prosperous-looking German businessman toward his corner. After surreptitiously checking Historian Pak out and deciding he was no threat, the Japanese turned confidentially to the German.

"Yaohan is buying the diamond concerns in South Africa and selling off the smaller mines that are not equipped with the necessary technology."

"But the technology is old and dated. Its manufacturing companies are slipping on the market," the German protested. "It isn't cost effective."

The Japanese businessman looked straight into the German's eyes. "Let me tell you something. You know how Iwaski made its money? From technology. Stolen technology at that." He looked furtively around him, but Historian Pak surmised that business loyalties to German interests, whatever they were, far outweighed his corporate and national loyalties to Mr. Matsuda. Historian Pak looked for an Iwaski company pin on the man's lapel. He saw a small name tag. Historian Pak fumbled for his glasses. "Mr. Seto," the name tag read. Mr. Seto's fingers started to dance across the sleeve of the German engineer's jacket. "Götterdämmerung was my contact."

To Historian Pak's recollection, Götterdämmerung was a revolutionary German-Japanese conglomerate with ecological interests devoted to usurping Iwaski corporate power.

"That old technology was a ruse."

"Do you expect me to believe the word of an industrial spy?" The German cut him off cold.

"I happen to know for a fact that the diamond mines are not operating on dated technology. They have been operating for decades on stolen technology from an outdated mining disaster that occurred on Zeta Reticuli. Some nonsense mining expedition that was an execution voyage for everyone on board."

"The same mining techniques are being used in Northeast China and the Baltic Sea."

Mr. Seto shrugged to demonstrate that was not his

concern. "For its time it was a very advanced form of laser technology that mined and melted crushed diamonds by satellite. All it required was a South African agent to ship the goods to Japan."

The German looked far more interested in the tray of hors d'oeuvres circling the room.

With uncharacteristic frustration, Mr. Seto became unguarded. "What I am trying to tell you is that for decades, Iwaski has been melting down diamonds and shipping them overseas as fiberglass, melting that down again and using diamond film as the innovative coating on car windshields, knives, and so forth, all illegally." It was at this point that Mr. Seto came to his senses and studied the room with a more than cursory glance to make certain he had not been overheard. He saw the milky eyes of Historian Pak, magnified by glasses, regarding him, but dismissed the man as did many who believed quite irrationally that because a person was dim of sight they must be dim of hearing as well.

In the face of this revelation, Historian Pak wandered over to the nearest wall to think, stumbling over a broken champagne glass which he didn't see despite the sensorplants, perhaps because of the lack of attention he was giving to his surroundings as a whole. He had several hours before he had to function officially. What he wanted to do with them was run programs through his computer. Perhaps he would plead an emergency in the family and not stay at all.

He looked up, startled, into the eyes of Mr. Kajii, who stood before him, quietly taking in the sweep of the room and recording the details with his legendary photographic memory. After a moment of this, he advanced toward Historian Pak, hands outstretched. Putting his left hand on Historian Pak's shoulder, he began shaking hands with his right. Historian Pak was surprised by Mr. Kajii's gentle and sincere touch. But they didn't get an opportunity to speak. For the efficient Mr. Seiyoko, another Iwaski official, appeared from the softly lit marble hallway, the heels of his shoes clicking intrusively, too much so for good manners, and within minutes, Mr. Seiyoko had propelled Mr. Kajii away from any possible discussion with Historian Pak, one hand planted firmly inside Mr. Kajii's elbow at the acupuncture point.

This time, though alone, Historian Pak was in a position of strength thanks to the extraordinary revelation he had just overheard. His back was also to the wall. And if he chose, he could easily slip right out through the French doors and leave all of this behind him. A foolhardy thought, he knew, but the option of a way out, an escape, made all the difference. Historian Pak was suddenly delighted he had come. Even his eyesight seemed to have improved. It was bad luck that Mr. Kajii had been hauled away so perfunctorily. He would have liked to have talked with him about his newly discovered bit of information as well as to have begun to seed the rumor. After all, wasn't Mr. Kajii the representative of the Department of Transport?

Historian Pak sipped the remainder of his mineral water and deposited the tumbler on the silver tray of a fresh-faced cyborg, who smiled graciously and dipped the tray away from the bared shoulder of the cultural attaché from Indonesia.

A string quartet played Bach energetically and tirelessly but, because it was a good two hours into the soiree and the careful soufflé of food, ambiance, beauty, and gracious living was beginning to soften and suppurate gently around the edges, the Bach seemed to threaten violence. The best that could be expected was that the entire gathering would merely lose its focus. Indications were strong that it could become a disaster.

Two bottles of champagne had tipped over on a table to the side of the bar and a frothy puddle, dammed by a great mound of spilled foie gras was sinking into the priceless rug. Three businessmen from the Republic of New Germany were engaged in a heated discussion by the door. The jazz trio, for some unaccountable reason other than their own entertainment, was playing the blues. It had only been a few hours and already the guest list had separated into special interest groups. The artists were walking around with a great deal of attitude, pretending boredom with the luxury that had pulled them there in the first place. The businessmen were drunk and boisterous, the politicians trying to plant seeds of this and that here and there in order not to lose the night entirely as they began to leave to attend their next engagements. Members of the diplomatic corps were standing around looking worried. Historian Pak was relieved. It didn't look like the party could possible stretch through dinner. If he wanted to leave early without reading from his works, he would have to redeem the time. It was a party built on theory rather than true celebration.

Despite the influence of the trays of drugs and alcohol carried about by the perfectly behaved cyborgs, the faces of the guests were becoming sharper and more angular, lethal rather than round, comfortable, and friendly. Even the chandeliers had taken on a cold, pointed, sword-of-Damocles look. The women's jewelry had come to resemble weaponry rather than captured light meant to reflect the beauty of those it adorned.

Historian Pak pulled himself together. He was allowing his mind to wander and his intentions to become lost. Concentration was the rule of the day. Never lose an opportunity. That was important to a profitable life. On a positive note, with the party falling apart around him, people were more approachable. Historian Pak's practiced eye told him he could take care of business more quickly and imaginatively than he had at first thought possible.

Mr. Ishioka stood by the jazz trio, talking to an alien representative from the Alternate Life-forms Rehab Program. The Iwaski staff had been well-trained, and Mr. Ishioka, as he saw Historian Pak approach, greeted him warmly, introducing the guest alien as Dr. Lesch. They settled into a brief discussion of recent alien disorientation in the Death Camps and all agreed it was a difficult issue to deal with, before Dr. Lesch wandered sadly away.

"We are so pleased at your presence here," Mr. Ishioka told Historian Pak with genuine warmth and admiration in his voice. "It is a very great honor to be in attendance upon you."

"It is a pleasure to be here," Historian Pak lied warmly as he noticed Mr. Ishioka dabbing with his handkerchief at the sweat on his face. What Mr. Matsuda analyzed as a passionate and undependable nature struck Historian Pak as a personality capable of great feeling and deep compassion. Perhaps his task would be easier than he had anticipated, for he found himself actually liking the man. He regretted that Mr. Ishioka was perhaps not the necessary gossip he needed to spread his story, but he was the Director of Alien Rehab and the information would show up in his reports eventually. In addition, he was the natural person to approach for information that might clarify data turned up in general personal research. Frankly, Historian Pak would have seriously suspected his own story, but fame had to bear some compensation. So far he had found it most often to be a questionable commodity.

Mr. Ishioka glanced warmly and openly at him and the jazz trio began a sentimental and, most importantly, a quiet ballad that a person could talk over. In a profound and not unpleasant moment of identification, Historian Pak touched Mr. Ishioka gently on the shoulder.

"Just the man I was looking for," he admitted. "Frankly, I was hoping you would help me."

"Certainly."

Through the still impressive party glitter, Historian Pak saw Mr. Seiyoko making his way over to Mr. Ishioka. What Mr. Ishioka lacked in gossip-mongering, Mr. Seiyoko certainly compensated for.

"Ah," Historian Pak began again, "perhaps Mr. Seiyoko might be able to help as well. Is he previously engaged?"

"I don't believe he is. And I know he would be greatly honored to speak with you himself. He has a keen intellect and can perhaps answer questions which I cannot," Mr. Ishioka said, as he motioned Mr. Seiyoko over with a signal from his immense handkerchief. So incongruous was the gathering of the three men that several people stopped what they were doing to eavesdrop on the conversation.

"Historian Pak," Mr. Seiyoko bowed, a quick and energetic bending of the waist that combined graceful economy of motion with appropriate respect. The string quartet and jazz trio, both having risen in volume now that many of the invited guests had disappeared elsewhere, battled for attention while the premises took on the appearance of some well-proportioned and ancient library casually used and discarded by the most decadent of thrill-seekers. In short, Historian Pak delighted in the setting, which was more perfect than real life normally provided, for what he was about to perform.

"I mentioned briefly to Mr. Ishioka that I had run across a very puzzling bit of information in the data banks as I was researching my most recent History. I don't mind telling you that it puzzled me a great deal. I found no amount of logical explanation could solve the mystery for me and I must admit I was quite eager to attend at Mr. Matsuda's invitation because I knew I might perhaps be able to enlist the help of men with knowledge and experience such as yours."

Mr. Seiyoko tilted his head in acknowledgment of Historian Pak's appreciation. "And what is your question, sir?" he asked. "We shall be most happy to oblige you with any information you might need."

"It's a small point, having to do with the alien virus. . . ."

"Yes?" Mr. Ishioka, imagining this to fall within his province, asked the question although both men were attentive.

"Please understand the intent of my question," Historian Pak stated, casting about helplessly so they would understand his intention as a simple search for information, not an occasion to accuse or to jump to conclusions. "I am sure there must be an explanation for the confusion, but I am at a loss to conjecture what it might be. The fact is, I came across several entries referring to source papers dealing with a viral disease that was developed illegally by Iwaski late in the last century. The intention of its creation is not altogether clear. It doesn't seem to have been developed as a weapon or a means of warfare. The documents say that Iwaski tested this virus off-planet in an outpost mining community,'' Historian Pak took quick inventory of the two faces before him. What was most important was what he left unsaid. ''It was fatal to human populations but first tested on aliens. I'm not clear as to whether they were volunteers or not. In any case, the virus mutated. As you can guess, I am most interested in whether or not this information can be validated. Perhaps this might explain why members of our planet have been so hospitable to the disabused alien population.''

''It is a most interesting theory,'' Mr. Seiyoko stated.

It took all of Historian Pak's self-control not to break out into a victorious grin. He had sensed rather than seen Mr. Seiyoko and Mr. Ishioka exchange glances, which was all to the good. Already, their minds were racing to make the connection to Mr. Matsuda. In order to be really effective, he must dismiss himself before they actually gave him any information. Once they exchanged information they would, within a day or so, come to think he had wanted confirmation to avenge the death of his son, providing either one of them knew that his son had indeed been killed by the Iwaski Dictatorship at the direction of Mr. Matsuda. Once they began, particularly Mr. Ishioka, to understand the implication—that Mr. Matsuda had caused an entire alien population to be wiped out because the disease his corporation developed had been intended for human camps but had spread to aliens who were not, as they were supposed to, able to develop an antidote, initially meant to be used as a human vaccine. As it turned out, there was no need because this virus wasn't fatal to humans. It was, however, perhaps the only disease known to be fatal to aliens and it had been introduced into their world as an experiment.

Historian Pak watched carefully as the pieces of the puzzle clicked together in Mr. Ishioka's mind, prepared to helpfully clear up anything that might stand in the way of their eventual realization that Iwaski was single-handedly responsible for the presence of ADCs and Deathspeakers.

Historian Pak, an expression of abject apology plastered across his face, watched with the greatest satisfaction as the faces of the two men before him worked in rapid realization of the implications of what he had just told them. Historian Pak smiled. Eventually, they would, possibly together if their current reflections were any indication at all, come to the conclusion that Historian Pak wished to lead them to all along. That the deaths the aliens had been blamed for were in fact the result of another culture trying to save two warring Earth cultures who had between them inadvertently committed the genocide of another race.

Across the wide ballroom, used centuries before by a wrongheaded and stylized diplomatic corps for ritualized forms of dance and social congress, Historian Pak spotted the distinguished figure of Mr. Matsuda, reflected eternally—a small man punctuated by his full head of white hair—in the endless walls of mirrors. Historian Pak wished greatly that he could smile in happiness. He was a man absolutely at one with his world and with the pace of events unfolding before him.

He touched the shoulders of the two men whom he had drawn into his confidence. "So you see, I was hoping for some kind of confirmation. As I've said, the records are quite sketchy and incomplete. It is difficult to find anything specific." He drew out a glo-pen and wrote down several numbers on a piece of paper which he pressed into Mr. Ishioka's hand. "Please," he insisted, "if you could find anything out about this odd state of affairs, I would be most grateful. If you will excuse me, I would like very much to have a few words with Mr. Matsuda."

He left the two politely. Halfway across the ballroom, he turned and saw them still standing in nearly the same positions in which he left them, side by side, mute, still thinking. There had been enough eavesdroppers to ensure the spreading of the rumor, of that Historian Pak was certain. Even if Mr. Seiyoko chose to keep his mouth shut which, judging from his character, wasn't very likely.

Having moved among his guests earlier and exhaustively with the ease of the perfect host, Mr. Matsuda had earned a few moments to himself. He was using these moments, foolishly in Historian Pak's opinion, to smoke a Balkan Sobrani in relative calm.

Historian Pak approached him with great respect, as one should an enemy.

His enemy gave him an amused look. "And will you be reading, Historian Pak?"

"I am entirely at your disposal."

Mr. Matsuda's eyes crinkled with genuine pleasure. "You have already caused a great deal of trouble today."

"Sir?"

"Yes, I have gotten wind of the rumor."

"Your sources are most prompt."

"It's a Korean talent, the rumor. Used most effectively throughout history. Now I can see why. But, of course, it will be stopped before it can become too detrimental. And naturally, you have forgotten to attend to the fate of your remaining son."

"My remaining son has set his own course."

"But the gift of life?"

"It is also a gift of life to have an enemy you can respect. One who stretches and challenges you in every way. May I tell you a story?"

"My original intent was to host a party which was meant to be in your honor. But it seems many of the guests have left. Please, go on. An old story, is it? Old stories for old men?"

"It is an old story and a new story. Perhaps you remember it. Very likely, your nurse told you of the quarrel of the monkey and the crab?"

"Quarrel, is it?" Mr. Matsuda said. "Why I have always found quarrels most interesting, full of opportunities for increased self-awareness and challenge."

Neither Mr. Matsuda nor Historian Pak appeared to notice the crowd slowly gathering around them, though they stood in a shadowy corner of the ballroom which had been given a junglelike effect by several large hothouse trees with frondlike branches.

The great expanse of ballroom spread before the two of them, a beautiful blending of polished brass, oak, mahogany, and cut glass. Gazing at this monument to wealth and power made Historian Pak feel weary for the second time that evening. He stared into his glass for a moment and, from there to the nearest mirror, which reflected a three-dimensional world on a two-dimensional surface—so simple and yet holding intricacies of meaning he could not, with all his years and wisdom, begin to follow.

He smiled to himself. However his efforts on behalf of his son turned out, they were no more important than anything else. In fact, the futility of any action was most appalling.

He toasted Mr. Matsuda with the remains of his

mineral water, and his opponent saluted him in response. As Historian Pak began his story, Mr. Matsuda sipped from his glass.

"It is a tale of no deep significance. A fragment of the Monkey Tales, which have more variations than the switchbacks of a mountain trail. . . ."

Mr. Matsuda's glittering eyes regarded Historian Pak patiently. This was a Historian speaking, perhaps the most famous Historian of all time. If he chose to tell his little story in a roundabout way, still he deserved respect and, Mr. Matsuda reminded himself, it hardly meant his mind was any less sharp or direct. Unlike most audiences Historian Pak could have chosen, Mr. Matsuda turned his full attention to Historian Pak's face. The only thing we have in common, thought Mr. Matsuda, is a great tenacity.

Without benefit of computer enhancement, Historian Pak's voice, reedy with age, faltered slightly as he began to speak, and Mr. Matsuda found that he had to listen carefully to catch the story's hidden nuances.

"Many thousands of years ago," Historian Pak said, leaning conspiratorially toward Mr. Matsuda, "the monkey and his friend, the crab, were playing along the riverbank. The monkey found a persimmon seed, and, thinking himself extremely fortunate, was about to show off his good luck to the crab when he discovered that his friend had come across a far greater treasure, a large rice dumpling which the crab was tightly grasping in his claws. Immediately the monkey became hungry and he could think of nothing but how to wheedle the dumpling away from his friend.

"At first, he had trouble attracting the crab's attention because the little fellow's vision was greatly obscured by the dumpling he carried. But after a lot of scuffling, screeching, and jumping up and down, the monkey convinced the crab to set his dumpling down so he could listen to what the monkey had to say.

"The monkey waved the persimmon seed in front of the crab. 'Because I am your friend, I will trade you this persimmon seed, which has great value, for your dumpling, which offers only the prospect of momentary pleasure.'

"The crab looked at the monkey doubtfully. The monkey, being much quicker than the crab, immediately lost all patience with him. 'I can't believe you have so little regard for the future. If you plant this seed, in a few years it will become a great persimmon tree which will give you delicious fruit year after year. But your attitude makes me wonder if I should withdraw my generous offer of trading this fabulous seed for your pitiful rice dumpling. Perhaps I should sow it myself and forget about the joys of friendship and giving. After all, I am putting myself at a great disadvantage by offering you this seed. Just think of all the years of persimmon eating I am giving up out of concern for your future.'

"After several more monkey pyrotechnics, the crab agreed to trade his dumpling for the persimmon seed and the monkey grabbed the dumpling, gobbled it up, and stretched out on his back in the sand. The crab had to remind the monkey to give the persimmon seed to him, which the monkey, now that his hunger was sated, was hoping the crab would forget. But the crab got his seed and they both went home, the monkey jumping easily through the trees and the crab, now hungry and cranky, finding the trip a hard one with the persimmon seed dragging behind him."

Mr. Matsuda was beginning to see the direction of the story and his eyes, though hard as jet, had begun to haze over, as though the person hidden behind them had left. Historian Pak registered this information in a cursory glance, but he made no effort to speed up the story or make it more compelling by modulating his voice.

"Each spring, the crab was delighted to see the new growth on the persimmon tree until, finally, it blossomed. That autumn, the persimmon tree was covered with the ripest, juciest persimmons.

"It had become the favorite activity of the crab to sit in the sun in front of his persimmon tree and watch the fruit ripen before his eyes. Finally the day came when the crab knew the persimmons must be ripe. The crab tried to climb the tree several times, but he failed because his claws were made for scuttling across the sand rather than climbing tree trunks. At last he thought of trying to find his old friend the monkey, for he knew that monkeys could easily climb to the tops of trees and pick off persimmons with their paws.

"The crab set out to look for the monkey, running up the rocky bank of the river, dashing down several pathways into the forest until he finally found the right one which led straight to the monkey's tree. The crab saw the monkey sleeping in the tree, his tail curled around a branch to keep him from falling. In a faint voice, the now tired crab began calling and finally managed to wake the monkey up. As soon as the monkey heard about the persimmon tree, he could hardly contain himself for his quick mind had already worked out a plan to cheat the crab out of his persimmons.

"He followed the crab to the sandy riverbank, laughing and telling stories all the way until the crab was happy and content, for not only did he have his beautiful persimmon tree full of the choicest ripest persimmons, but he had his friend the monkey back after all this time, as well.

When they reached the tree, the monkey was astonished by the magnificent crop, but his astonishment didn't keep him from leaping up into the tree. The crab watched happily until, once in the tree, the monkey began to pick persimmons and eat them. Not one did he throw down to the unhappy crab whose tree it was. The monkey ate all the best and ripest fruit until he could eat no more and, by that time, there was nothing but hard, unripe fruit left for the crab below.

"Meanwhile, the crab's joy had turned to misery, for he had waited so long for the tree to grow and the fruit to ripen. Now his friend the monkey had eaten all the good persimmons and there were only the hard ones left. He was so sad, he ran around the tree begging the monkey to remember his promise.

"At first, the monkey ignored his squeaky, high-pitched voice but finally, irritated by the crab's persistence, he picked the biggest persimmon remaining and fired it down on the crab's defenseless back. One after another, the monkey threw persimmons at the crab until the crab was quite dead and lay crushed at the bottom of the tree he had worked so hard to grow.

"Once the monkey saw that he had killed the crab, he ran away like the coward he was."

Historian Pak nodded at a passing waiter who delivered a silver tray with a glass and a pitcher of mineral water. Historian Pak and Mr. Matsuda both knew who the figures in the story represented. They stood at the center of a crowd of distinguished people, all of whom had dropped their own conversations to openly admire the show. Fantasy animal stories, was it? The string quartet slipped from Bach to Vivaldi. Historian Pak paused to sip his mineral water, and Mr. Matsuda looked around the room, noting who was standing closest to them, and anticipating what purpose they might have in listening to the conversation.

"Now the crab had a son who had been playing with a friend near the spot where his father died. And when he came home that night, he found the body of his father lying under the persimmon tree he had cultivated and grown, his head smashed in, his shell broken and hard green persimmons scattered all around. At that, the son wept into the sand of the riverbank, but he gained no comfort from it. Only because his will was so strong did he refrain from throwing himself into the river. And then, in the midst of his suffering, the young crab remembered the story his father had told him about the dumpling and the persimmon tree. He remembered that monkeys liked persimmons more than any other fruit. And in that instant, he knew that the monkey was his father's murderer and he vowed to avenge the death of his father.

"At first, he wanted to attack the monkey himself but the monkey was very old and cunning and would surely get the better of him, and so the young crab decided to ask his father's friend the mortar for advice. The mortar sent to fetch the bee and the chestnut, who were also old friends of the crab, determined to enlist their aid in the matter. When they heard of the crab's death and of the monkey's greed and wickedness, they agreed immediately and wholeheartedly to help the young crab. They made several plans, settled on the most practical one, and the young crab went to bury his father. Meanwhile, as soon as the monkey saw that nothing would happen to him, he began to congratulate himself on his ability to cheat the crab every step of the way. He knew that if he were found out he would not escape punishment by members of the crab family, but he convinced himself that no one had seen him leave the persimmon tree and if he went home and kept to himself for several days, no one would be the wiser. This he proceeded to do, at least until he was completely bored to death at which time he told himself, 'Who can say I killed the crab? Dead crabs can't talk. Since no one could possibly know, what is the point of shutting myself up? Why should I spend my time brooding over any of this? It's all over and done with anyway.'

"So the monkey wandered out of the woods into the crab's village. He told himself all he wanted to do was to hear what the gossip was all about and to discover whether the crab family was still unsettled at the death of their leader and whether they had the least suspicion as to who the murderer was—for the idea of being pinched to death did not at all appeal to the monkey.

"His visit to the village was useless. He heard nothing at all and so he convinced himself that he need not worry and that his overactive imagination had upset him, nothing more. The monkey went home quite satisfied with himself and forgot the entire incident.

"Then one day, when the monkey was sitting at home, a messenger arrived in the service of the young crab. The monkey had no idea what this meant and he looked in surprise at the messenger, who was bowing before him.

"The messenger stared at the ground with the utmost respect and announced that he had been sent by his master to announce the death of his father, which had occurred as a result of his fall from the persimmon tree. In his fall, he had knocked down several unripe persimmons. 'As tomorrow is the seventh day since that sad event, it is the first anniversary of his death and my master invites you to attend the festival he has prepared in his father's honor. Please, as my master's father's best friend, honor the house with your kind visit.'

"The monkey began to fidget. He could barely contain his delight. Didn't this prove that all his fears of discovery were completely unfounded? He acted as though he were utterly surprised at the news of the crab's death, squeezed out some monkey tears, and informed the messenger of the long and devoted duration of the friendship between himself and the crab. In fact, he said, tilting back his head and closing his eyes as he reminisced, 'I remember how we once traded a persimmon seed and a lovely dumpling. It wounds me to think I was the cause of his death, trading him the persimmon seed for the dumpling as I did.' Squeezing out more tears from his eyes, the monkey accepted the invitation.

"But the monkey hadn't fooled the messenger, who was quite happy about the fact the monkey would soon be crying real tears, if the young crab had any say in things.

"On the feast day, the monkey put on his most solemn expression and set out to visit the young crab.

"Everyone was in the crab's home, waiting to welcome him. After the bows of greeting, they led the monkey to the great hall of the crab's house where he was met by the young chief mourner. The monkey was quick-witted enough to come up with some sincere-sounding condolences, whereupon they all sat down to the feast, at which the monkey found himself to be, to his surprise, the guest of honor.

"When the feast was over, he was led to the tea ceremony room where he was offered a cup of tea. The young crab himself took the monkey to the tea room, left him there, and did not return, even though a great deal of time passed. Finally, the monkey, impatient despite his great genius, became extremely restless. Unfortunately, he had drunk a great deal of sake at the ceremony and was very thirsty as well. He began to shuffle around the room in exasperation, because the tea ceremony took a great deal of time and the young crab hadn't even begun it yet. Finally, he could stand it no longer and went over to the fireplace. He took the boiling kettle and began to pour himself some hot water, when a hot chestnut burst from the ashes and hit the monkey directly on the neck. The chestnut, the crab's old friend, had hidden himself in the fire.

"Hiding in the screens, the bee, another friend of the crab, flew out and stung the monkey on the cheek. The monkey began to suffer. His neck was burned, his face was swelling up from the bee sting, and he didn't know what else to do but run off. The stone mortar, who had hidden himself on top of the crab's gate, fell on the monkey's head as he ran underneath. The monkey, now in great pain, was unable to get up when he was approached by the young crab, who now stood before him, holding his scissorlike claws over the monkey's head.

" 'You do remember that you murdered my father?' the young crab asked.

" 'You are my enemy?' the monkey moaned, astonished.

" 'Of course,' said the crab's son.

" 'The fault lay with your father, not with me,' howled the monkey.

"But the young crab had had enough. He cut off the monkey's head with his pincerlike claws.

There was a long silence when the story ended. The two old men stood side by side in the polished room, like two ancient friends buffed to their brightest essence by age. They looked like two finely crafted figurines, a pair made to complement each other, backed by the dark wainscoting and showered by crystalline light, caught in a momentary still life.

"You are saying, of course, that I had small expectations of your abilities for revenge when I allegedly had your son killed, am I correct?"

Historian Pak nodded graciously. It had been a most profitable evening. So profitable that perhaps he might have to revise his abhorrence for social gatherings.

Mr. Matsuda removed a finely hemmed linen handkerchief from the pocket of his evening clothes and carefully wiped his fingers. They were, Historian Pak decided, fingers which, were he to give them to a character in his Histories, would be described as belonging to a strong and predatory bird.

But he had no time to entertain himself with private musings. The French doors beside which he had been standing earlier in the evening suddenly blew into the room. Shattered glass lodged in the bodies of the nearest guests, the women in their gowns were the most affected: streaks of red broke out upon their arms, chests, and faces, and then they were streaming with blood like some kind of macabre blossoms.

The remaining guests rushed to the great doors, but not quickly enough. The doors burst open and a wave of black-suited Snakers rushed the fleeing guests, even as another group of Snakers streamed through the French doors, sandwiching the drugged and drunken crowd in a ring of terror. A slight, scarred man, who seemed to be the leader, with Snake Order tattoos burned into his cheekbones, began to circle the crowd while the terrorists held the guests at bay with an odd assortment of weapons and launchers that could easily have blown away half of Southern Japan.

Historian Pak turned to his host as Mr. Matsuda's bodyguards were led out in front of the crowd and executed. "A nice touch," Historian Pak said. He was not afraid of death, but the stench of human bodies acrid with fear and unable to flee made his stomach threaten to revolt. It would be most humiliating to lose control, he told himself sternly. Beside him, Mr. Matsuda's face was skeletal, the skin pulled tight and waxy over his skull, his eyes black holes burnt into his head. Since Historian Pak believed Mr. Matsuda's feelings on death mirrored his own—they were both old men, after all, and had to die sometime—he was shocked to see that Mr. Matsuda was shaking.

The leader of the Snakers continued to circle the room until he found the target he was looking for, Mr. Seto. Mr. Seto, Historian Pak was surprised to see, bore his capture with a certain defeated dignity. Most astonishing of all was the fact that Mr. Seto seemed to behave as though he had expected it.

The Snaker leader bound Mr. Seto's hands, although it seemed a completely unnecessary procedure, and marched him up the wide staircase to the half-landing that served as stage and platform.

He was met by five men, who stood behind the hostage.

"Our leader was recently assassinated," the little man began, pacing the length of the landing. "Our leader who did nothing more than to uphold Korea's demand for independence. We have waited too long for our freedom. Your very ruling family is descended from that of a Korean Prince. We, and the Ronin Historians, and the true musicians have banded together. There are more of us than you know, hidden among yourselves. I am sure that you are thinking this does not make a very great difference. But we will not rest until our goals are achieved. And we are not fearful of dying." He paused to stand directly behind Mr. Seto.

"This man was one of us, but he chose to parlay his knowledge and power into areas of self-interest. Despite his position, he is no longer useful. We have other means of obtaining the information he supplied us with for so long. The soyhan has demanded his public execution." And with that, he motioned one of the five men forward. The executioner withdrew an ancient ceremonial sword and, circling it above him, cut off Mr. Seto's head with one sweep. The man's body convulsed, sank to his knees, and the head rolled down the staircase, bounced across the floor, and, picking up speed through the splayed blood, careened across the ballroom till it came to rest at the feet of Mr. Matsuda. The rusty smell of blood filled Historian Pak's nostrils and he gazed for one moment directly into the eyes of the terrorist leader before the Snakers fled.

Everyone in the room stood in stunned silence. Outside, the sound of small firearms could be heard as Mr. Matsuda's men tried to chase down the invaders.

CHAPTER EIGHT

Dressed in a sterile scrub suit, Ewha bent over the cadaver. It had been three days since she'd first strapped the Korean engineer into her full-length dissecting tray and inoculated herself with germ shield, paltry protection against dissection of bodies that could carry diseases so ancient there were no longer antibodies to ward them off in the average human biological system.

The engineer had been ticketed with a strange flat tablet, which he wore around his neck like an amulet. It looked like a mah-jongg piece, greatly exaggerated, ruled once and dotted with black points arranged in a geometric configuration, three on top of the rule, four on the bottom. Ewha had removed it carefully and put it away in an airtight steropak for Dr. Bender's further study.

The Korean engineer had been a short, strong, compact man left behind in camp for a reason now completely unknown. Drukker and Bender found him in an excavated com station, bent over a vid screen which had long since ceased to work. Speculation had it that he'd been left behind to guard the camp, but it remained mere speculation. It seemed odd for him to have died. He'd obviously been sick, but there wasn't a great deal of deterioration in the body and Ewha doubted that he'd even known he'd had the disease at all. He had probably been under the impression that he was suffering from a lingering cold, or exhibiting allergic reactions to the environment. In fact, his body owed its perfect preservation to the mineral deposits that had almost completely covered him.

Ewha proceeded slowly. His body, though intact in every detail, was brittle and fragile. She worked carefully, keeping minute records and drawings as detailed as though she were documenting the discovery of a new species instead of the remains of just another poor Korean no one really cared about but her. Irrationally, Ewha felt a strange intimacy with her subject, as though he'd been driven to pass on information even at the sacrifice of his own body, having at the end no other means of communication left to him.

Ewha squinted as she aimed the laser beam into his small intestine. She told herself she was letting her imagination run away with her. She reminded herself to concentrate on the job at hand. There were enough real problems with the autopsy without reading into it the motivations of a man long dead, who came from an entirely different time. She honored his sacrifice by her attention to detail. Beyond that, she could do nothing, not even detect for certain the clues he'd left behind. All she could do was go through the motions of the search thoroughly and honestly. She cut away an intestinal sample adequate for the tests she needed to perform. She was, she decided, lucky that the body was dessicated. Although it made her work slower, it helped decrease the possibility of contagion.

If she were completely honest with herself, she had to admit she was grateful to have a straightforward task that demanded such concentration and could be performed alone, at her own pace, without interference.

She had isolated herself within her fiberlab, wanting desperately to distance herself from the rest of the crew and their increasingly erratic behavior. From experience, Ewha knew there was a time in each probe when things got a little crazy, a stretch that spawned chaos and confusion, when the stresses and pressures of being off-planet in a hostile environment and in the company of people one wouldn't necessarily choose as friends began to grate and the exaggerated and wholly unnatural exploration experience brought out the worst in everyone. This generally coincided with equipment and communications failures—something Ewha was thankful they had not begun to experience yet. And if the crew was coming unglued a little more quickly than she was used to, Ewha thanked the powers that be, and in her current mood didn't rule out the supernatural rulers of the planet, that there was nothing wrong with the generator or the water purification system, that the air was as sweet as the moment they had first set foot in the rusty bucket, which was to say stale compared to Earth's atmosphere, but mountain fresh compared to the air that surrounded them outside.

It was the "it could be a lot worse" syndrome, Ewha realized. Because from an objective point of view, things were certainly falling apart rapidly. Ewha sliced off another section of intestine 14 centimeters below the one she had just extracted and placed it in a cellular solution created to plump up cells and chemically restore tissue to its living composition.

Bender, as much as she appreciated his seemingly unerring reasoning faculties and his cold analytical logic, had been acting oddly. He had not been eating regularly if he ate at all. He had been spending the majority of his days poking around the Japanese mining camp and the one time Ewha had been dispatched to get him, she found him sitting on the floor of the Japanese mess hall, tears streaming down his face, dried salt pulling and scabbing his skin, rolling three human knucklebones around in his hands. She looked at him long and hard and, with that one look, managed to pull him out of it. She promised she would never tell anyone as long as he reciprocated by never letting it happen again. Although he agreed and had never broken down in that manner again, she wondered in the long dark nights whether even Bender knew he had been chanting Latin to himself. The sound of it terrified Ewha and, had she not already been thoroughly convinced she would never survive the probe to begin with, it would have made her fear for her own life. It was ridiculous, Ewha thought. At twenty, a probe crewmember went on his or her first probe completely entranced by the romance of dying heroically off-planet on some vital mission. By thirty, lifers began to worry over whether dying would take long and be painful.

Carefully, she cleaned out the abdominal cavity and began on the liver, sectioning it into fragments. Of these she sealed five sections for specialized viral tests. Two tests were routine, three were her own inspiration.

She was thankful to Kenjii—something she had never in her wildest dreams imagined would happen—for keeping Bender company during his days in the Japanese sector. As it turned out, Kenjii had a disciplined academic mind that was not easily distracted once it had something on which to focus. It was a mind that believed it could actually find the answers to the questions it sought, as though scientific method, if followed with enough dedication and unwavering attention to detail, must of necessity cause a conjuration of truth in all of its unrelieved horror. But, Ewha caught herself, it was quite unlike Kenjii to regard truth as any kind of horror. He believed in an ultimate truth that existed independently of daily exchanges and the fraying realities of life. He had been taking photographs of the mine structures, checking the use of equipment to verify that the Japanese had, in fact, been on the planet in a mining capacity and not for some hidden mission. Yeshe had been assigned to Kenjii's team but, in fact, Ewha knew that Yeshe had been keeping Bender in tow. And it wasn't an easy task. Ewha could forgive Bender's behavior, but she couldn't ignore the dark circles and hollow eyes that marred Yeshe's young face. She was no longer a beautiful woman, Ewha realized in surprise, as she put aside her laser and reached for an infinitesimally fine scalpel. She began shredding muscle tissue, placing it in small jars with mash of revitazine.

There was something odd going on there, and Ewha reminded herself to look into it as soon as possible, reluctantly admitting that her time in seclusion with the deep secrets of the mining engineer seemed to be coming to an end. With a start, she realized that she hadn't eaten with the crew for days. She'd been snacking on variations of dried tongue and mashed fish sandwiches. Ewha began to laugh to herself. She laughed even harder when she saw her deranged expression reflected in the dissecting pan. It was probably a record first that she'd managed, as ship's doctor of all things, to avoid the entire crew on a probe. She never would have thought it possible.

Then there was Drukker. Drukker was terminal and she worried Ewha the most. Two days ago, Savage had retrieved her from a landslide that caught her when she wandered off searching for Ahyrana, who, she claimed, was the soul voice of the mining camp who had first spoken to her through Bender. It was certainly possible—anything was possible once you got off-planet, Ewha reasoned, but probable? Not likely. Ewha resolved to give her more complete attention to the problem of Drukker.

She put the mash in a petri dish and stored it away for culture growth. If there were any dormant viruses, they would show themselves. She had come to feel companionable toward her engineer in what she concluded was a very sick way; he was her ally, they were the most ancient of friends and co-conspirators, and she was following his lead.

Ewha put down her scalpel, stripped off her surgical gear, and walked over to the stainless steel sink where she washed her hands and arms and, finally, her face. She threw back her head and let the precious water run down her face into her mouth and down her neck in an orgy of sensation before drying off her face and returning her attention to the cadaver. She replaced her steromask and gloves, braced her arms, and leaned over him, stopping herself before she actually started talking to him. He seemed to smile back at her and she picked up his dog tag, turning it over and over in her hands until it seemed like a small piece of paper fluttering to her feet in the chill of an autumn wind, a warning of the weather to come if only she had spent enough years in this atmosphere to read the weather.

Sighing, she touched the man's hand, gently running her fingers across his palm. What had he hidden away for her? His body was an intricate and beautifully complex labyrinth of secrets—for Ewha had convinced herself that the secret truth of the entire expedition lay within this one man, falling to pieces underneath her expert hands.

She peered at the man's face, wondering at the memories imprinted in the mummified tissue of his brain, at the last sights his dead eyes had witnessed.

Ewha covered the body and slid the body tray back into cold storage, wondering at the transient futility of knowledge sought after with single-minded purpose. What did it matter if he gave up his secrets to her? It was only a small bit of information retrieved and reconstructed. Information that could, at best, make a difference to the lives of only an isolated few. Yet were there any human secrets allowed to sleep safely for eternity?

She balled up the linens and heaved them into sterilization. Then she slipped her instruments into the burn bath. Carefully, she locked up the samples and cultures in the small, dark, temperature-controlled closet. It would do her good to pull herself away for awhile to clear her head and gain some perspective, never mind that she knew rationally all she needed was sleep. Not that she could manage it. It was probably important that she share her discoveries such as they were and find out how the digs were going. She needed a fresh point of view from which to consider her data. With all the best intentions in the world, Ewha combed her hair with her fingers, locked up sick bay, and set off for the mess. She'd get a cup of chia, watch the suns, and settle in for a good talk with whoever managed to show up.

As it happened, there was a spectacular sunset view from the mess hall and she felt herself relaxing as she gazed at the broad, open plain washed by the peach and green rays of light, the larger sun near and blazing, its sister distant, complementary in its watchfulness.

Chosyam and Savage looked up when she walked in. "Holy shit," Savage managed. "She lives. And here I was giving Chosyam a crash course in medicine, thinking we'd be needing a ship's doctor soon."

"Yeah, and we'd be in trouble if your medical lessons were on the level of your chess lessons."

A battered chessboard lay on the table between them. The board was an obvious veteran of many probes. It showed more wear and tear than Savage's face.

Ewha motioned to the board. "Heard they were rare," she said in appreciation.

Savage's hand curled protectively around the corner. "That they are. It's solid ivory from the time when elephants roamed the Earth."

"And they got their revenge, those elephants," Chosyam complained. "For generations they've foisted this bloody game on endless innocent individuals." He slammed down a rook.

Savage's clear eyes swept the board. "Are you sure you'd be wanting to put that rook over there in that space, then?"

Chosyam was annoyed. "What's wrong with it?"

"There's the castle blocking the way." Savage shook his head. "I thought you'd be able to be keeping track of the castles by now. Try it again," he offered generously.

Ewha could see Savage's magnanimity was torture to Chosyam, who only wanted the game to be over.

"Savage told you this was a war game," Ewha guessed.

"He did." Chosyam floundered with his move and decided to advance a pawn in an empty and remote corner of the board.

Savage watched sadly before tapping the rook that would take the pawn in Chosyam's foolhardy advance. Chosyam retrieved his pawn and stared blankly at the board again.

"You have a perfect opportunity right there," Savage offered helpfully.

Chosyam scowled.

"Just let your eyes get accustomed to the movement of the men for a moment and you'll find it. It's right here." Savage was trying very hard not to get excited at the move Chosyam seemed determined to throw away. Ewha, knowing Chosyam would never have an affinity for the game no matter how patient Savage proved to be, and she had to admit he was impressing the hell out of her. She hadn't thought he had it in him, and she tried hard not to smile at his predicament.

"No one else on board plays chess, then?" She drew off a cup of chia from the utility urn in the corner and sat at the table beside Savage, stretching out her legs.

"They do, they do. But only Chosyam has the time."

Chosyam looked wildly bored. He also looked like he had been up all night attending to important crises, all of which had been averted at the last moment due solely to his expertise and brilliance. His hair, standing up all over his head, was hardly blunted by a pillow. His utility flight suit hung on his body so perfectly molded to him that it was clear he hadn't taken it off in days. It was covered all over in multicolored glopen—drawings and slogans which seemed to have burst full-grown from Chosyam's brow to take up residence on his clothing. He looked, Ewha thought, quite rakish and cheerful, the epitome of a lifer; a colorful rebel surviving with flair, style, and daring in the outer reaches of an increasingly bureaucratic galaxy. It was odd how the myth of the personality had come about. After all, there was no more bureaucratic system on God's green earth than beginning space exploration.

Across the red chemwaste composition table, salvaged by Chosyam off some last-century tanker and probably from Galactic Archaeology or a similar warehouse in the Greater Newark Meadowlands, sat Savage in his faded blue navigation suit, his headphones and folded up cartographer's pieces shoved around his body in several pockets tailor-made for equipment originally shaped quite differently. Although Savage had probably worn his suit at least as long as Chosyam, his looked neat and freshly laundered. But his skin was pasty, his eyes were bloodshot, and his full round face was pinched around the cheekbones. His cuffs and collar were frayed. Electrical wiring and light pens dangled from his work belt. One of his huge, thick boots was propped up on the fibroblock chair beside him.

From the first, Ewha had liked the two of them, despite the violence they carried in their bodies like some tropical blood parasite. Violence had never frightened her. She understood it and even found herself curiously drawn to it. It had a cold, clear logic of its own and pure violence was as impersonal as an island storm. It was the undercurrents—deception, betrayal, and treason—that unsettled Ewha and made her skin crawl with fear. But she was better off not thinking about that and all the reasons she had ended up on the probe.

"Something wrong?"

She smiled at Savage and smoothed her forehead with the ball of her hand. "Just thinking."

"Too much thinking," he advised. "And you might do with a toss of the salt over your shoulder after being shut up with that dead body for days." He checked the board. "That's the final move?" he asked Chosyam, who nodded.

"You're quite sure?"

"Of course I'm sure, don't ask me that. You think I would have done it if I wasn't sure?" Chips of chemwaste fell to the floor in a shower from the table's edge.

"You think this table'll hold up until we get back to Earth?"

"Who says we'll get back?" Savage's bishop cut a wide swath through Chosyam's paltry defense.

"And this from the navigator? It's a sobering thought."

"You ever had a real thought that wasn't?"

Chosyam leaned back in his chair, crossing his arms over his chest.

"How are the others?"

"All fine." Chosyam blithely sacrificed his rook. "If Kenjii had his way, we'd be transporting the entire planet, both camps complete in every detail with every body of any poor sucker who happened to die in the wrong place back to home plate. Naturally, there's a reason for all this. I think he has it in mind to reconstruct the whole planet in some kind of air and space history site. He's been completely carried away by the possibilities. Every night he brings in bags of stuff to ship back and every day when he goes back to the dig, I take the bags out the back door and scatter them in back of the ship. Let's just say the sites have captured his imagination," Chosyam started to laugh, a deep belly laugh that filled the common room and made Ewha laugh as well.

Savage moved.

Chosyam picked up a bishop, looked at the board, and set the bishop down.

"For God's sake, look at what you're doing, man!" Savage hit the table with his fist and the chess pieces bounced across the board. Two knights and a queen fell over. "You have no respect for the game," he complained blackly. "Here I go out of my way to take the time to teach you this ancient game that's a symphony of thought and you jump all over the board like someone with no strategy in his bones."

"So that's the story on Kenjii," Chosyam summed up, letting Savage pick up the chess pieces.

"Bender, now I like Bender, don't get me wrong," Chosyam reached for Ewha's arm across the table, "but the man's been acting weird."

"That's a fact," Savage was suddenly agreeable. "Him and Drukker, the pair of them."

"Well, now come on. Drukker's been a little worse."

"Unqualifiedly weird."

"Well, that's it."

"Hold up a second."

Chosyam leaned toward her again, his face intent. "If I didn't know better, I'd say Bender was about to Deathspeak."

Ewha pulled at the neck of her T-shirt. "Don't go around joking about stuff like that. Deathspeaking isn't to be taken lightly."

"I'm saying what I see." Chosyam's eyes flashed and Ewha had a brief and intense moment of gratitude that she had never been on the receiving end of Chosyam's anger. With a little luck, God on her side, and a probe proceeding more or less on schedule, she would never have the opportunity. She held up her hands in what she hoped looked like a pacifying gesture.

"I was trying for specific concretes."

"What the hell is that, specific concretes?" Chosyam grumbled. "Anyway, who cares whether Bender starts Deathspeaking or not? I don't care. This probe's turned weird enough for it not to surprise anyone. At least he's quiet about it. The one drives me crazy is Drukker. Sheesh.'' He leaned so far back in his chair Ewha thought he was going to tip over and crack open his head on the red and black linotile. The mess hall ran deep, long, and straight as an arrow through the bowels of the ship, opening to a flared floor-to-ceiling viewing window that bayed out under the tail. Savage had set up the game about a hundred yards away from the window. The north wall held a long shelf and a storage unit with vats of brewed teas and minute food. There was no real luxury here, no formchairs, no drug or alcohol dispensers.

The light shifted, the suns' light poured through the view window and the living crystals growing in pots in front of the bay, threw rainbows around the room. Ewha blinked in the light and decided the world wasn't so bad after all. She told herself she'd just spent too much time in a sick bay which had been functioning as a morgue for almost two weeks now. It had given her a decidedly static outlook on life.

What she'd needed to do was just this, sit and look at the beauty of the planet before her in the easy company of Savage and Chosyam, watching them play a lame game of chess.

She took a sip of tea and realized her throat had been so clenched she couldn't have swallowed if she'd wanted to. She felt her entire body unknot.

Savage, still determined to pull out a game, locked his attention on the board. Chosyam got up, walked over to the window in one continuous catlike movement, and stood staring at the flat green and bronze landscape. Distant glassweave tents on the horizon, tinted peach, marked the location of the two excavation sites, but the ships were too far away for the three of them to see the tiny black dots that represented the figures of the rest of the crew. An ominous wind began to whine around the ship and the three of them listened, Savage bemused, Chosyam still searching for the words to describe Drukker's insanity, Ewha idly observing both Savage and Chosyam. Suddenly the door opened. All three turned to see the slight figure of Yeshe cross the room, her slippers kissing the floor. Savage put his chin in his hands, "Yeshe," he said.

"How are you?" Chosyam asked.

"Feeling any better?" Savage added.

"Yes, thanks."

"You've been ill?" Ewha asked out of professional concern, wondering why Yeshe's illness hadn't been reported to her.

"Well, yes." Yeshe drew herself a cup of quai dong and sipped it slowly. "As a matter of fact, it was Chosyam who brought me back to the ship. I was unconscious. Drukker had just laid me out with a piece of stainless steel pipe. Apparently she was trying to protect me."

Ewha tried to keep the alarm from her voice. "Has she threatened the well-being of anyone else in the crew? Why wasn't I notified?"

"She almost pushed Toshio off one of the ladders on the dig, claiming she was saving him from the marauding ghost of Denisovich, the poor sod," Savage said, taking his move. None of them answered Ewha's second question.

"Yes," Yeshe said softly. Gentle and distant, she struck Ewha suddenly as a woman who had her own obsessional reasons for being on this probe. Given that Ewha would probably never know just what those reasons were, she wished her well. But given the look in Yeshe's eyes, it seemed as though the knowledge was not something she wanted to have any longer and Ewha found herself wishing, not for the first time, that Yeshe were far more open and less cautious. She was like a flower blossoming in the night against a chainlink fence, its mesh imprinting the petals.

But Ewha was here to get some information. "Drukker," Ewha prompted Chosyam, thinking, how long has it been since I told her to report to sick bay? Two weeks, three? The Korean engineer had taken all her time.

"Yes." Chosyam turned around, walked back to the table, and sat down beside Yeshe. He put his arm around her, pulled her to him, kissed her on the side of her head, and let her go. Then, to humor Savage, he tried to concentrate on his next move. Yeshe rose and walked across the room to sit down beside Ewha.

"I suppose she thought the death of Denisovich wuld cause him to be a troublesome and unhappy ghost."

"They say an incident of great emotional intensity can affect a portion of the environment where the event took place," Ewha offered.

Yeshe looked at her hands. "I suppose it's possible. The Japanese believe unhappy ghosts become harmful gods. Perhaps they are right."

"But Drukker will go out into the middle of a sandstorm and sit there until she is encrusted with sand, swearing she must hear the cries of lost souls."

"Is she doing any work?"

"She thinks so. She thinks if she hears their story we won't have to do any more digging."

"Who's spoken to her about this?" Ewha asked, outraged.

Both Savage and Chosyam looked at her in surprise. "You've got to be serious."

"Someone should speak to her. She's not doing her

job. It should be So Pak. What is her area of research?''

''Sociology of late twentieth century mining camps.''

''You've got to be joking.''

''She's doing work for the European Archives. She is an Archivist. Supposedly, if we run into any trouble, she can catalog information for us.''

''There's really no reason for either her or me to be on the probe,'' Yeshe explained.

Ewha sympathized with Yeshe. It must be frustrating to be put on a probe to a planet with little to offer but geological specimens when your primary field of expertise was biology. It had been Yeshe who was responsible for the crystal arrangements in the windows. Sometime, she'd have to ask Chosyam just how they'd requisitioned the crew. In the meantime, Ewha decided to request Yeshe's assistance on the cadaver and medical experiments she had begun to conduct. ''Do you think Bender and Kenjii could manage without you?'' she asked the young woman.

Yeshe considered this idea. Ewha could almost see Yeshe weighing her own mysterious plans and desires against the goals of the mission. Though it was true that helping Ewha would let Yeshe make use of her own specialized knowledge, it would also curtail her freedom to explore the mining sites.

Finally, she said, ''I hate to abandon the others when I can't help but feel we're so close to finding some answers.''

Chosyam shrugged. ''How many probes have you gone on? Don't you know it's too soon for answers? Everyone's findings are still inconclusive. What can you expect? It can't be too surprising. We've only been at this a month.''

Yeshe drew a hesitant breath, "Actually, despite everything, we've found out quite a bit. I'm a little worried about So Pak though."

"Why?"

"He seems too personally involved. He wants to prove something."

"What?" Ewha asked.

"His theories."

"What theories?"

Chosyam made a move that had Savage reeling in appreciation and shock.

"So Pak is pushing, because he wants the probe results to undermine the power of the Historians by presenting purely scientific proof that the members of the two mining camps were merely tragic victims of an inhospitable environment," Chosyam said.

"Yes, he's right," Yeshe agreed. "But the more data we collect, the more seems to have been going on here underneath. Nothing makes sense. So Pak may have inadvertently stumbled onto something else."

Ewha was stunned. She tried to calm herself by immersing herself in the beauty of the planet, wondering how all this related to the body of the Korean engineer in sick bay. She had a wild and irrational urge to run back and protect him, but he had needed protection long before she'd been born and it would do him no good now. Now was not when he needed it.

"Drukker is merely responding to an imbalance," Yeshe said, returning to their earlier topic, squinting as sunlight struck her face. "Both excavation sites have lately become plagued by what can only be described as poltergeist phenomena.

"What do you mean?"

"Objects fly around, stones rain from the ceiling and are gone the next day. . . ."

"Might I point out that you are a community of scientists, not a bunch of parapsychologists?" Chosyam demanded.

Yeshe shook her head. "Toshio is determined to explore."

"Toshio?"

Yeshe turned to Ewha. "Apparently he has seen this sort of process at work in his ADC days. It's more to satisfy his own curiosity than anything else."

"I appreciate your reassurance, but . . ."

"What we do know is that the camps were placed far closer together than we would have had any reason to expect. Japanese and Korean feeling has never been that sympathetic, and strange surroundings don't seem enough to explain it."

"No, they don't."

"These miners were professionals, used to isolation and not particularly intimidated by inhospitable environments. They were career off-planet excavators, for God's sake."

Savage, delighted since Chosyam's last move to find that he had a game after all, looked closely at Yeshe. "You've really been thinking about all this, haven't you?"

"I've had a lot of time and not much to do but babysit Bender and Kenjii, listening to Bender's brilliant insights and wading through Kenjii's copious notes. You have to think about something. There are indications that it might have been a co-venture. We also know, at least according to Kenjii's notebooks, that the majority of deaths occurred much later than everyone originally imagined. Kenjii suggests this might be the case, or that the time of death might have been deliberately fudged. The Japanese died much later than the majority of the Koreans. Before the camp was completely deserted, the Japanese relayed the formula for ultrasound technology back to Tokyo."

"Right." The technical formula that was eventually responsible for putting the Japanese over the top economically," Chosyam added.

"We're not sure, but Bender and Kenjii seem to think the formula didn't originate with the Japanese. They seem to think it may have been stolen from the Korean mining camp. For one thing, the Koreans had manufactured technological equipment for ultrasound mining which they brought with them. They had a curiously low quota of miners for this sort of expedition. For another, it was clear the Japanese had set up a makeshift lab in an attempt to test the formula before the camp was completely abandoned. The lab seemed to have been constructed in an effort to prove the theory before they sent it on, but they didn't have enough time and ultimately had to send it along without finishing their tests."

"That's why Bender and Kenjii have been spending so much time at the Japanese camp," Chosyam said.

"Exactly."

"Does anyone else know about this?" Ewha asked.

"We haven't formally discussed our findings."

"And the formula?"

"The formula was apparently used as a way to mine from a distance by ultrasound without the need for human agents."

"And the Koreans had been using it here?"

"Apparently. The interesting thing is that we know the Koreans mined ore because we found their stock. But no one has yet found the mine. It must have been very far from the camp."

"It's just like the way the Iwaski government was mining in South Africa," Chosyam broke in excitedly.

"With the diamonds they mined and melted into film solely by ultrasound. What I heard was that approximately two years after the Japanese mining expedition on this site, they came up with a very complex ultrasound technology. It all makes sense. It was the same thing. They could never have researched and implemented the process if they hadn't had a formula. It would have taken too long."

They sat in silence, the implications of what they'd discovered weighing heavily.

"Shouldn't this be reported to the World Patent Commission as a patent violation?" Ewha looked at Chosyam.

"If it is a patent violation."

"Are we the ones to do it?"

"If we ascertain it is a patent violation, then we're the ones to do it. We have little choice."

"We could bury the information," Ewha said.

"We could."

"No one is really expecting any concrete information from this probe, after all."

"We don't know that," Yeshe responded.

"Oh?"

"Checkmate!" Savage gloated.

Chosyam looked at the two women, then at Savage. "Thank God that's one game over."

"Now, don't look at it that way, look how much you've improved."

"If you think that's going to convince me to play you again, you're very much mistaken."

"Well." Ewha sat for a moment digesting the results of their discussion. "We must have a meeting as soon as possible."

"Why?" Yeshe cautioned. "Wouldn't it be more

prudent to continue to pull in the information and put it together ourselves?''

''For one thing, something must be done about Bender and Drukker. We can't have Drukker running amok and putting the crew out of commission.''

''I suppose you're right.''

''But we could give it some time.'' And Ewha thought, Yes, indeed. Enough time for you and me to see if we can dig all the secrets out of the little Korean engineer I have locked up in the morgue compartment. Because there may very well be discoveries of equal importance yet to be made. Ewha found herself getting excited, so excited she wanted to get right back to work. But she had to slow down. First she had to rest a bit more. Then she had to arrange for So Pak to allow her to bring in Yeshe as her assistant. With the helpful addition of Yeshe's bright mind, and her much-needed new point of view, Ewha was convinced the work would go much more quickly.

Chosyam sat in the com room of *Arachne* and radioed *Bushido*. It was a full minute before Jaffe's face appeared on the vid screen. ''Yes, what is it now?''

''What's your problem? I'm late on the report.''

''I know you're late with the report. You're so late, I thought you'd give me a break and turn it in tomorrow. All right, what is it?''

''I have here,'' Chosyam shuffled through his screen, ''Bender's report on the Japanese site.''

Jaffee checked her screen, ''Got it. What're those little marks?''

''What marks?''

''In the corner. Your photo sender working?''

''It's working, it's working.''

''Doesn't look like it to me.''

"Look, Jaffe all you got to do is sit up there and take and receive. And we haven't exactly been jamming up the receptors, so you think you could be civil a minute? *If* you haven't anything better to do?"

"Whaddya mean? You think I'm up here picking belly button lint or something? The radio's jammed day and night with the infernal trackers."

"What're they doing back? The flight plan says they're not due for a couple more weeks."

"How'm I supposed to know? They're all jumping around up there like interstellar popcorn. Happened after you sent me those reports from So Pak."

"What reports?"

"The subliminals."

"What subliminals?"

"Well, isn't he down there decoding subliminals?"

Chosyam thought. He hadn't seen much of So Pak lately, but he hadn't seen much of anything except the landers' maintenance banks and Savage's chessboard. Nobody had seen much of each other; they'd split up to do research. It was an amazing event to wander into the mess and find anyone there.

"You there, cowboy?"

"Yeah, I'm here. I checked Bender's transmission. There's no operation error in transmission."

"Well, these guys are going to want to know what they mean."

"It's all just scientific data."

"Not what they seem to think. They've been accessing medical reports."

"Whaddya mean? They can't access medical reports. You've been transmitting them?"

"Excuse me, what else am I supposed to do?"

"Some kind of classified stuff got them going. That's why they're calling me every other waking moment.

It's got something to do with the subliminals, there's some kind of warning."

"What kind of warning?"

"Something to do with equipment technology. How the hell should I know? I'm not a subliminals expert. When are you running your next load of cargo?"

"At the end of the week."

"Can you be a little more specific? I got stuff to do up here, you know."

"Kenjii's tagged some stuff."

"Looks to me like he's doing his best to reconstruct the site in cargo bay. Let me know if I'm wrong here."

"The man's methodical. What can I say?" Chosyam wondered why he was defending him.

"Whatever. You want to finish transmitting?"

Chosyam loaded the photo sender. "Everything okay up there?"

"Quiet as a tomb. Ship's on automatic. Maintenance systems fine. By the way, Katz is quite impressed with your work. Thinks you're a genius. Okay, got it. Anything else you need from me?"

"One of those sweet-tempered good-byes would be nice."

"Get lost, buckaroo."

Chosyam's screen went blank. He shut down "transmit" and activated "receive," pushing himself away from the com console. All around him, the ship was still. He left the com room and wound his way through ship's quarters, his body tense, alert to the smallest sound. Oddly, there was nothing. Chopped light bars hung from the corridor ceiling, flickering in the gloom. Chosyam made a mental note to check the generators. Halfway down the corridor, he thought he heard footsteps behind him, but when he turned no one was there. He'd never been one to spook easily, but he found himself remembering Denisovich, throat slashed in his own quarters. He hurried to the mess. Maybe he'd have something to drink before he went back to *Lips III* for the night. Maybe he could ask So Pak about those subliminals, he told himself, trying to keep his mind on the matters at hand. Trying to keep his body from getting jumpy. Despite himself, Chosyam shivered.

CHAPTER NINE

Two weeks later, Bender sat in the makeshift location lab, the Plain of Holy Shadows stretching like a slow-breathing animal before him. He balanced on the edge of a duroplast camp stool, elbows resting on the cataloging table. It was his most prized possession, that table, it had been Bender's since he was eighteen, left to him by his father. The blue-green light characteristic of purite calmed him as it always had. Only the most elite craftmen used purite tables although a range of purite objects were utilized by aliens for scientific research. Purite, introduced on Earth around the turn of the century, was an alien mineral, rare in the extreme and the workmanship of Bender's table rendered it priceless. Meters and hectopoints were marked on the table's surface in horizontal and vertical alien markings, and a complicated border of planets and solar systems edged the surface.

Bender would sooner lose his arms than that table. It represented his father's confidence in him, and he had carried it with him all his life and that, though small comfort, had been all he was able to truly possess in his entire existence, his loneliness and fundamental separation from those around him broken only by the artifacts that crossed his path.

The reputation he had built and the knowledge he

had accumulated meant nothing to Bender. He lived his life to discover only one thing—what had killed his father. He had his suspicions. Then he learned that knowledge was an endless scouting trip into the unknown, reaching out and gathering pieces of data to oneself, each bit shifting and changing the overall pattern of information. And so, although he had his suspicions, the more he discovered, the more complicated the process became until it seemed that he was no closer now to understanding than he had been in his twenties.

Another fit of coughing shook his body, and Bender fought back the nausea and dizziness, managing to turn his head away in time to keep from disturbing the vials and medical equipment spread out before him in a fragile fan of glassware. He pulled his handkerchief away from his mouth. His handkerchief was as stained with blood as a Victorian consumptive's. Bender stuffed it in his pocket and returned to his research. He knew he didn't have much time, just as he knew the answer was before him somewhere in the midst of the chaos that threatened to choke him. It was through an effort of will that he had managed to keep himself in peak physical condition for this long in the face of the infantile disease that had destroyed 60% of his human antibodies and killed his mother in the bargain. His father had done his best to relate the Healing Teachings to him, but had himself been so ill toward the end that he had not finished the meditation instruction that would set the necessary transmutations to work. Bender was forced to put to good use the skills he'd learned imperfectly. From time to time during a particularly bad episode, the necessary entities crossed his path, but he had known before he applied for probe clearance that there would be no entity able to penetrate the Plain of Holy Shadows should exposure to the medical instruments result in activating the disease.

And yet, so far, he had managed to maintain his health since his first exposure to an environment as toxic to him as walking across an open nuclear wasteland was to anyone else on Earth. Still, he had to face the fact that he was no longer a young man and he had yet to prove his suspicions were correct. That alone was difficult enough to handle and now it was becoming more complicated because of the manifestations which had begun to occur. For one thing, he had been forced into too much familiarity with Drukker, whom he had not known was a sensitive and, in an effort to turn his energy from her, he suspected that he had upset something in the atmosphere of the Plain of Holy Shadows and caused it to boil up into dust devils, beginning as tiny tornados and picking up speed over time until they became howling dust storms.

The trick, Bender knew, was always in the focus. Throughout his life he had maintained focus. But between the Healing Teachings, his illness, and the novelty of the probe, he found he was having difficulty with his focus—something he had not had problems with for decades. Most especially, since he had last wandered too near an Alien Deathcamp.

Bender turned to his laptop, noting down the most recent findings and running though the prescribed cautionary instructions on handling Artifact Waste. The pink dome billowed around him in a gust of wind and he looked out of the observation window again to see another storm blowing up. Although the domes were as strong as spun steel, it was difficult to keep the specimens in exact order. He had secured as many as he could, but the fact was that no matter how he tagged and tied, they shifted out of their sections and he had to spend a good hour and a half rearranging them again every morning before he could begin to work. Several nights he had slept in the hut to save time in the morning, but he couldn't do it often because he had to appear as normal as possible in order to ensure his privacy. Already several of the crew members had asked after his health and it would only be a matter of time before Ewha began to suspect something. He had hoped to be further along, but Kenjii had taken up time cross-referencing with his reconstructions from the Korean site. Yeshe was the one to worry about. She was sharp-witted and little escaped her notice. Most of all, Bender knew that despite her assignment to the Korean site, she was bird-dogging Drukker for information and he blamed himself as much as Drukker for the injury sustained to Yeshe's head. The fact was that for almost half an hour before the occurrence, Bender had been thinking in his heart that more than anything else he wished Yeshe would let down her conscious observation for several moments. Drukker simply acted on the thought. He tried to slip her herbal drinks to break the bond Drukker seemed intent on forming with him, but it hadn't worked so far and the only hope he had was of getting better before his crisis of healing became too serious.

Bender was fairly sure at this point that the disease had been activated by the test tubes he'd been handling. The Japanese doctor had come equipped with some very serious test-tube matter that didn't seem to Bender to be routine equipment for a space probe. And these were artifacts that didn't fall into his field of expertise. There was a lot more going on here than a simple mining expedition.

He had just finished cataloging the contents of the locked medic drawer, a job he had been trying to complete on and off for almost a week now between other jobs so it wouldn't appear that his cataloging was slipping in any way, when Alice Drukker walked in the door.

He smiled. Despite her unpredictable episodes, she carried herself with grace and dignity. Had they known, the others would have been surprised at how well Bender and Drukker got on with each other, even though Drukker was, for all practical intents and purposes, rapidly becoming quite insane.

She sat down on the only other duroplast stool in the place, oblivious to the fact that it was covered with a week's worth of dirty lab coats. Bender looked into her cool gray eyes and waited.

"I believe there is a group soul at work here."

"This is not something to bring up at the general meeting," Bender suggested mildly.

"It's not as crazy as it seems," Drukker said, smoothing out her lab coat. "Phenomena have been known to occur on digs. Cosmic protestations occurring when well-meaning individuals hell-bent on discovery begin to poke around in places better left forgotten."

Bender looked at her in astonishment. "Better left forgotten? Surely, as a scholar you can't mean what you are saying."

But Drukker took scant notice of his protestations. "There were many documented instances at the pyramids. Accidents, manifestations, objects constantly misplaced. And the hauntings at the Babylonian excavations were apparently quite terrifying."

Bender, once again bent over his work, said nothing.

"They all died here," Drukker said. "Every single one of them. It's a mass grave of secrets."

The Plain of Holy Shadows, Bender thought. The woman wasn't all wrong, but there was no hope in encouraging her. It would do no good and it wouldn't contribute to the well-being of the group at large. Still, to completely deny her observation would give it greater importance in her mind than it deserved because she would concentrate on justifying her position. That factor, combined with her already considerable intellectual powers, made him feel it was better to head her off.

"Be that as it may, that is only one very small part of the data we need to consider here. You know as well as I that we need to take each piece of information and give it equal importance until we get a structure going."

"I am not talking about our research," Drukker said desperately. "I am talking about all of us here. I am talking about whether we're going to make it out of here alive."

"That is not something that need concern you overly," Bender said as soothingly as he could. "Your job is to do the work."

"My job . . ."

"As a responsible Archivist."

"But we need to alert . . ."

Bender sighed wearily, sliding his glasses down his nose so he could look at her straight on. Her face was pink. She was indignant. She knew something was not right, she was embarrassed enough as a scholar to have to be talking about forces neither of them understood. "You have your responsibility to your profession. It is our job to make the necessary entries and to document everything so thoroughly that, if something happens, others will be able to pick up the trail and use our objective information to understand what we have seen here as clearly as if they had been here themselves. So, God forbid, if our conclusions are altogether wrong, others after us can reconstruct."

He waited a moment before continuing.

"We must make objective observations." Even as he said it, he felt he was lying. What was so objective about what he was doing?

"Of course, you're right," Drukker said, looking at her hands.

"Pet or personal theories have no place in our research. Our job is just to state the facts." Bender cursed himself for his hypocrisy. He wasn't exactly approaching his own work without personal motivation or bias and he never had, were he being honest with himself. Perhaps it was this flaw in himself that explained his empathy and tolerance of what others might term Drukker's ongoing insanity.

Still, Drukker was stubbornly insistent. "There is something here, I feel it."

"Feel what you must, but I remind you feelings have no place in objective research. Where is Toshio?"

"Working with Kenjii. I believe it is Toshio's opinion that . . ."

"Toshio's field of expertise is alien studies."

"Exactly my point, if you will let me finish." Drukker tapped her wrist against Bender's worktable. "Toshio has made an interesting discovery."

"Yes," Bender said wearily.

"Kenjii let slip that Toshio believes there are pieces of purite scattered among the ruins of the Korean camp. Not just scraps, but fashioned purite made into objects, tools, the very kind of thing a race would leave behind, supposing it had to leave quickly after a prolonged visit." Drukker stood up and began knocking around the cramped tent, crowded with objects yet to be classified, with an intellectual's physical clumsiness. "Tea?" she asked.

Bender made a noncommittal sound. No matter what his wishes, he knew he would be getting tea anyway. He might be able to manage a few swallows.

Drukker knocked over a catalog of glassware dating and notes and papers hidden in the papers scattered across the floor. "Not necessarily one of those to whom neatness is a calling, are you?" she asked. "You know, it's odd. When the probe began, I could have sworn you were one of those obsessive types. Just goes to show how wrong you can be about people. I always distrust people who say they can tell about people right away."

Bender's hands began to shake. Imagine her noticing the progression of the sickness. He'd counted on her being so involved with her own processes that she didn't have time for anything other than monitoring her own feelings and observations and doing her work. However, if he was deteriorating fast, she was deteriorating equally quickly.

He wanted to bury his head in his hands and weep. Lately, he'd come to find himself overcome by emotion over the smallest things. He knew he was not himself, but he had no idea of what he was becoming. When he woke up mornings, a taste of spent blood, like copper pennies, lingered in his mouth. If none of the other symptoms alerted him, that one certainly did. He was nearing the end much more quickly than he'd thought possible. Despite the fact that studying the disease had been one of his lifelong hobbies, he understood that soon it would kill him and he didn't know nearly enough about this thing that was a mortal enemy to his body.

It was a strange thing, knowledge, Bender thought

as Drukker thudded around the room making tea on an old bunsen burner. It could give one such great daily joy and pleasure. Exercising it tuned one so thoroughly to the world that the planet itself was experienced in sharper detail, in perfect moments of discovery and understanding strung together like beads on a brave thread of courage. It could get a person through life. But once the courage was gone, all that knowledge was inanimate and brittle, little comfort in the end.

"Entertaining morbid thoughts again?" Drukker asked as she came up behind him and attacked him with a hot mug of tea. Obediently, Bender sipped and winced. Another of Drukker's questionable fortifying blends. She pulled up her camp stool next to his and drank her tea hot, straight down. Bender wondered that she didn't scald her entire digestive tract . . . he had never seen any living organism possess the powers of digestion of this woman. His body sagged in the chair. He felt weak and shivery inside and the air pierced his lungs so uncomfortably that it was a constant reminder this was not his home planet. But, Bender reminded himself, when had it ever been different? Sitting in the fiberglass dome, pink and orange, packed with objects that held within themselves more knowledge than he could unearth, the dome so full there was only a tiny trail through the wreckage to the worktable, storage shelves and compufile, he felt at once overcome and satiated—as though he need go no further, ferret out no other mysteries than those contained in this room, to know everything. He was absurdly grateful for Drukker's irritating company at his side, but that wasn't really the point. The fact that he had someone else to help. . . .

Through an effort of will, he stopped himself. He

had to sever the link, not make it stronger. Already, it seemed too far gone. He looked at Drukker's profile as she sat watching the setting suns of Zeta Reticuli, her face raised to the light and her eyes closed against it. Her hair was polished bronze and her skin luminous but why should that surprise him? Did he really expect to see her marked by his suffering? People hoped for that, Bender knew. They hoped to bear the marks of pain, thinking it might save time in the explaining.

But what did all this thinking and speculation matter? No matter how linked he became with Drukker, she was dangerous as long as her psychotic episodes continued. There wasn't a great deal anyone could do about foreseeing continuance, frequency, or intensity of the episodes. For his part, he must accept the fact he was terminally ill. He had to accept that it would get worse no matter how hard he tried to hoard his energy. He had to keep all this a secret from the rest of the crew, particularly from Ewha, for as long as he could, and not count on the fact that she would not have the expertise to diagnose him correctly. At the same time, he had to focus concentration on unraveling the clues before him. He knew that he had at last arrived at the place to which he had been journeying all his life. All of his considerable experience had been a dry run for this final test of time and place.

Bender and Drukker sat before the small window of the flexdome watching the suns set and the moons rise on the horizon. Layers of dust and sand filtered the light and broke the harshness of the day into soft bands of color against the smoky sky. The sand shimmered before them in ribbons of light so delicate and insubstantial that not even Bender's eyes could pick up all of the nuances of the changes of shifting sand, the blur of vegetation, and the smear of the sky. All things,

Bender was reminded once again, had their beauty, even the Plain of Holy Shadows. When they set up the flexdomes, Bender positioned his to look out across the ancient plain about which so many stories had been told him as a child. It was the place where his people had been massacred, strangely, of their own volition, and with their own consent. Bender remembered the story well. It had been his father's favorite bedtime story. His father, in particular, loved to act out the death, so enthusiastically he'd jump off the bed on which he'd been sitting and reel around the room in the half-darkness, his hands scrabbling at his throat, a dim shadow shape wrestling with true shadows for his son's edification. As it happened, it had been a horrible enactment of his own death. All Bender's childhood nightmares about the place were uncannily accurate. Now, sitting in front of the serviceable window, he watched the Plain of Holy Shadows and was comforted by Drukker's awkward, precognitive company.

She lurched toward him, almost spilling her tea across his uncataloged medical vials. "What's that?"

The suns bathed the sky in lemon yellow; bottomless inky night sky bled into the horizon. The sand-washed valley was tinted gray and streaked in black and silver. A stain of beige swept the foreground and cross this leaking color, a figure tottered toward the flexdome.

Drukker leaned further forward at great peril to the samples, peering out into the landscape. "Who is it?" she asked. Bender, unlike Drukker, wasn't particularly curious. Drukker poked him. "Toshio?"

"Sorry?"

"Toshio?"

"Isn't Toshio back at the lander?"

Drukker slammed her tea down on the table. Bender watched as she methodically pulled on her atmosphere suit, jammed on her helmet, took an automatic reading and set the controls. She stepped into the air lock and headed toward the lone figure on the horizon.

Much as Bender usually enjoyed her company, he was relieved he no longer had to pretend. Sickness swept over him in waves as he eased himself up from the camp stool. The degenerative disease was settling into his joints, his pelvis, and shoulders, and it had been weeks since he'd lost the 180 degree rotation in his left shoulder joint. No matter what he did, he could not regain it. On a good day, he was lucky to manage one third of the movement. He rotated his head and his neck snapped like a string of firecrackers going off at New Year's. Worst of all were the afternoons when he was so exhausted he dropped off to sleep. When he woke up, he had to work at his joints for several hours until he could get back the most limited range of movement.

The close stillness of the air was broken by the sound of Drukker's shoes scuffling across the sand. Bender straightened, fighting off the dizziness that grabbed at his forehead and blurred his vision. Flaming red balls seemed trapped inside his eyes and wherever he turned his head, he saw them. He took several deep breaths and began agonizingly pulling on his own atmosphere suit so he could follow Drukker out.

He tried to push worry about the fate of the crew from his mind, the worry that dogged him every time he had a full-blown episode. What chance did the crew have of surviving when at least two of them were burdens of time and technology on the already threatened probe? He was losing vitality so quickly, he doubted his ability to make it off-planet. And if he didn't make the break soon, Drukker would undoubtedly go completely mad. They would have to either kill her, imprison her, or turn their backs and let her wander off as she would demand. None of them could afford the time to supervise her and, if they tried to lock her up under electronic surveillance, her superhuman strength would be difficult to contain. Bender forced himself to stop. It was an integral part of the disease that an individual characterized by extreme rationality in personality should suddenly become clairvoyant and Bender had been fighting it for some time. He couldn't decide whether or not it was the intention of the Japanese to booby trap the probe with the likes of Drukker and himself. He would probably never know the truth of it, as if the knowing mattered anyway. It was not often that one was allowed the luxury of knowing the whole story in this life. Speculation brought on by sentiment only led to erroneous conclusions.

On the positive side, his own findings were now fairly well cataloged, and, from what Toshio and Kenjii said, they were making real progress also. So Pak had been shut up in his quarters for weeks, working on classified material, but once he emerged and gave his approval to their preliminary reports, the mission could be classified as at least a partial success. After all, even though they hadn't yet studied the sites as thoroughly as they would like to—time, supplies, and planetary conditions permitting—they had gotten some concrete information.

Shivering with fever, Bender turned and went out the dome's air lock, thinking, as he did so, about the story Toshio had told two nights ago at dinner after observing Bender's shaking hands. Only Yeshe, So Pak, Ewha, Drukker, Toshio, and Bender himself were still sitting around the table. It had been half an hour after dinner and the rest had already gone off about their own business. It was Ewha who had gotten Toshio to tell the old tales, the more sardonic, the better, and, after a couple of obvious Korean stories, Toshio settled into what he termed a Japanese medical tale.

At first, Bender had laughed with the others. His fever had been bad that night and he was pleased with anything that created a distraction. Yeshe and Ewha were halfheartedly warming cordials and listening to Toshio's stories. For the moment, Drukker seemed relatively docile; food appeared to make her feel better. But Ewha was keeping a wary eye on her activities. Toshio, seated to the left of So Pak, shoved his chair away from the table to stretch his legs, and began to relate the story of the tapeworm.

"This is a Japanese medical tale," Toshio said, "that begins with a beautiful woman who had a tapeworm. Invisible it was, living inside her. One spring, a courtier saw her walking under a canopy of apple blossoms, married her, and gave her a son. The son grew up and became a government official and, naturally, the family prospered.

"His first assignment was to a post in Sinano Province. He was met at the border by an entourage sent to greet him. At first, the new governor was flattered and he enjoyed the prestige the huge banquet afforded him but, as he was ushered to his table, he happened to notice that it was laden with walnuts. Not only did the walnuts cover the table, but when he knelt before it they dropped into his lap. All the other tables were also covered with walnuts and there was not a place where he could avoid them, although he was feeling a strong need to escape from the nut meats. He felt extremely uncomfortable as though he were being strangled. Finally, he managed to ask why the tables were groaning with walnuts and was told that walnuts were a major export of the province. He felt worse than ever yet could not explain why even to himself."

At this point in the story, Bender noticed Toshio looking pointedly at him so he smiled good-naturedly and leaned forward, encouraging Toshio to continue.

"The new governor was becoming so nervous that the deputy governor noticed it and, driven by curiosity, decided to try an experiment of his own. He mixed some ground walnuts, aged wine, and water and heated it until it resembled a kind of cloudy mash, which he poured into a cup, placed on a tray, and carried with the greatest respect to the governor's table. He placed the cup in front of the new governor, who looked even more uneasy than before.

" 'Why does this wine look so strange and cloudy?' the governor asked, thinking he might vomit any minute.

" 'It is our custom to offer each new governor a ceremonial drink made of three-year-old wine and ground walnuts,' explained the deputy.

"For several minutes he waited, watching the governor shake uncontrollably. 'You must drink it, sir.' he coaxed.

"The governor swallowed hard and raised the cup to his lips dashing it to the floor and confessing, 'I'm really a tapeworm. I can't drink this.' A minute later, he turned to water, slumped to the floor, and trickled away. Confused and dismayed, the guests packed up and went home with the words of the deputy ringing in their ears, 'All this time and you didn't suspect,' he told them all. Naturally, the governor's wife and children were very surprised, but everyone who heard the story got a good laugh out of it."

Everyone at the table had a good laugh as well, but Bender's had been a little less hearty than the others.

Now, as he rushed toward Drukker and the other figure on the horizon, he wondered again about the fate of the mission. What he got in response to this thought was a sudden flash, a picture of So Pak's brother, Kim, a very unhappy ghost, tracking So Pak down across the galaxy. Then Kim's wife's round face drifted before his vision like a gardenia flowering unseen in the night. He saw a European official signing papers. When he closed his eyes against the vision, it burst in his brain like a great blood-ripened fruit.

Drukker reached the intruder and recognized Yeshe's face behind the helmet. But Yeshe, frightened by Drukker, backed away, tearing herself from Drukker's grip. She tried to run back into the desert with great lurching steps, but, as Drukker grabbed for her, a holo dropped from Yeshe's hand. She dove for it on her hands and knees, raising a cloud of sand that threatened to choke her, scrabbling for the holo before it disappeared forever beneath the shifting granules. Despite all of Drukker's efforts, Yeshe found the holo, stuffed it down the front of her atmosphere suit, and only then did she allow herself to be led toward the flexdome.

Bender gripped his hands tightly behind his back for balance and composure as he waited for the other two to reach him, determined not to have so much as a flicker of a vision until this episode was cleared up.

Yeshe came to a stop ramrod straight in front of Bender, eyes lowered, body tense.

"Aren't you assigned to the infirmary today?" Bender asked gently, hoping it were true and grabbing at any hope of keeping Drukker in check. It was because of him and his lingering self-pity that the bonds hadn't been adequately severed, and there was no telling how Drukker would act in the face of spirit association which, if Bender was correct, was exactly how Yeshe had planned on spending her day. In fact, he would be surprised if spirit trails didn't hang from her fingers and stream from her hair—but before he himself fell prey to this image, Bender quickly brought himself back to the reality he could see directly before him. It was more than enough. No use clouding the waters.

Yeshe wasn't about to answer him. She stared at her feet, her eyes suitably downcast in humility and subservience. Bender realized that, now that the holo was in her possession, she didn't care what happened.

Bender was beginning to find himself at a loss. "Isn't she?" he asked Drukker.

"Chosyam sent me to get something." Yeshe held out a wire splicer, vintage from the last probe. "He said he was sure I'd find one of these on the Korean side and to just haul it in because he needed it to repair the generator."

Bender blinked in the sun and his arms began to twitch. He gripped his hands to still them, his fingers wanting to tendril in the chaos around him, sensing, probing. He thought of his dreams, great horizons dissolving into fire and smoke, and looked at Yeshe, who seemed puzzled; and Drukker, whose eyes had taken on a glittering unholy righteousness.

"Let her go," he ordered Drukker, but softly. He didn't want to startle Drukker. He had to get her back to the *Arachne* and settle her in before she started. That was more important than anything else at this point. He had no desire to know what Yeshe had been doing at the Korean mining camp. Weren't her ancestors Korean miners on off-world sites? As far as he was concerned, that was reason enough in a world swiftly going mad.

His father could never have envisioned this, that was the worst of it, his father who had always tried to protect and provide for him. Yet here he was, truth-bonded, on Zeta Reticuli with no help at hand. He had been holy all his life, what justice was there in this?

Yeshe was much stronger than he. She was behaving as the veritable bamboo, bending but not breaking before the wind.

CHAPTER TEN

"Chosyam?" So Pak sat on the flight deck at a drive console, which had temporarily been converted to an administration desk for their ground stay. Supply lists, requisition papers, ship's log, schedules, and progress reports filled the desk. The vid screen flickered with static every time Choysam jiggled the wires on the communications station. "Where's Yeshe?"

"I sent her to the Korean camp to get some equipment."

"You did what?"

"Equipment. I figured the Korean camp was as good a place as any. She's assigned to the Korean camp."

"She's been reassigned to Ewha. Ewha needed her today. Chosyam, the Korean camp is a historical site. It is not a motor pool and supply junkyard for your various projects here," So Pak waved his hand around vaguely, indicating the ship itself. He tried to forget all the nights when he'd tossed restlessly in his bunk, staring at the ceiling and sweating over the possibility of something happening to Chosyam, whose insane creations the ship and landers were. It was transportation that looked official enough on the surface, but wrench away a panel or two and So Pak suspected the guts of the ship would come oozing out like so much shaving foam, and no one would be able to do anything about it because only Chosyam knew where everything fit and why. Biweekly, So Pak requested that Chosyam update the ship's plans which had once been sketchy. Now they were so convoluted it was difficult to tell a pod from a set of oxygen packs. And he also knew that, if he gave Chosyam his head and a couple of weeks, the entire campful of Korean relics would be incorporated into the workings of both landers as new and improved ship parts. Keeping Chosyam completely away from it all was impossible. "Look, you have to give the teams a crack at undisturbed finds before you go in there and start scrapping those ships. Even then, it might be a good idea for you to ask their permission to enter certain restricted areas."

Chosyam shrugged. So Pak didn't know why he was bothering, Chosyam would do what he wanted anyway.

"Does anyone have a current status report on how the studies are proceeding?"

Chosyam didn't turn around. "The copies are circulated every week. I photosensor them back to the *Bushido* every night. I can't read them for people."

"What about having someone write up a little summary of the reports every week?"

"Are you kidding me? A summary? Someone is supposed to read all that drivel and write a summary on top of that? Call a meeting."

"Meetings take up a great deal of unnecessary time."

Chosyam grimaced at So Pak.

"I suppose you want to know why my time is so valuable."

"You got that right." Chosyam muttered to himself. There was a long silence before Chosyam turned around and began to wave his wrench. "Could solve all this just by having people stop by every week and tell you what happened.''

So Pak considered this. It wasn't a bad idea. Everyone was far enough along in their work that there should be some real substance to their reports. Tentative conclusions could surely be drawn. He watched Chosyam ratchet off a piece of pipe, slam the panel back in place, and count to ten slowly before pounding open the adjoining panel and wriggling a sound pipe.

''How are you handling the tracker ships?'' Chosyam asked.

''Jaffe's been doing a good job. She files complete and very chatty status reports and her tone is impeccable. One thing's for sure, they're bird-dogging us more closely than I thought they would. It's puzzling. The news of Denisovich's death didn't seem to surprise them.''

''Yes. All very strange.''

''Strange is the order of the day with probes. You never know what's going to go on.''

''Excuse me, sir,'' Chosyam advised, ''but if I were you, I wouldn't let the crew hear me say things like that.''

So Pak threw down the faulty glo-pen that was dribbling ink down the sides of the paper. ''Most of them are lifers. They know it. You think this is some secret?''

''Knowing it and hearing the captain say it are two different things, sir. Totally different things.''

So Pak stared at Chosyam. ''So who do you think did it?''

''Did what, sir?'' Chosyam thought So Pak was really jumping around today. His brain was popping quicker than a pan of hot beans. For weeks he'd been locked up in his quarters, coming out only to check on ship and crew, and disappearing again, squirreled away with original documents supplied him by Toshio and Bender from the site records.

''Do we have anyone on board with Snaker connections?''

Chosyam almost dropped his wrench. This time, he turned around and looked the captain dead in the eyes. ''You saw the reports, sir. You know them all as well as I do. Why would Terror Two send a Snaker on an ill-omened probe like this one?'' Chosyam scratched the corner of his eye with the tip of the wrench. ''Terror Two is a tiny organization. . . .''

So Pak looked sharply at Chosyam and Chosyam stopped. Something was going on here. He didn't know what it was, but he damned well better find out.

''It seems odd about the trackers.''

Chosyam sighed. This was just his day to have So Pak take it into his head to start interrogating him. ''What about the trackers, sir? You just told me that Jaffe was looking after business perfectly well.''

''As far as she can. But last week the tracker ships started to access the crew's reports. Two or three times a day, they come up on the screen. They're accessing the crew's medical records.''

If that was all, Choysam decided, turning back to his work, there was no problem. ''No one can access records. I constructed a perfectly safe system before we left.''

''Yes, I know. The problem seems to be that it's safer than the trackers had been led to expect. Do you know of any reason why that should upset them?''

Chosyam could think of quite a few, but most had something to do with the fact that operations managers on probe ships were not particularly well-endowed with brains. Or beauty, either, for that matter.

For half an hour the two men worked side by side, Chosyam's butt on the level of So Pak's elbow as Chosyam patched the wall back together and So Pak sorted through paperwork.

"Do we have any idea of what the tracker ships are actually tracking?" So Pak asked, picking up the conversation again.

"Pardon, sir?"

"What are the trackers actually looking for?"

"Well, the one thing you can be sure of is that you will never know exactly. Unless, of course, you are unlucky."

So Pak flicked one of the wretched glo-pens against his temple. It left a streak of ink over his left eye. Chosyam thought about telling him, actually telling him the truth, and then decided that eventually So Pak had to come to it himself. "Is it just the medical records they are going through, sir?"

"Yes. I have no idea why. They must have duplicate records in some other computer, not to mention the fact that there's nothing surprising about them. If there is anyone on this ship with a degenerative illness that could affect the probe's chances of survival, the Japanese conglomerate would have been efficient enough to have planted them for a specific reason."

"Paranoid as hell, but most likely true, sir." Chosyam agreed.

"One more question."

Chosyam seriously doubted that, considering the frame of mind So Pak was in. Chosyam wished the captain would just go back to his quarters and leave them all to the vagaries of fate.

"Chosyam, if we had to get out of here on a dime, would we be able to do it?"

Was So Pak joking? They hadn't been able to get

out of Newark on a dime, much less off-planet. "Of course, Captain. No problem."

"You're quite sure?"

"Yeah, sure." He would most certainly kill himself if they actually had to because if he didn't manage to kill himself cleanly, he'd certainly live to regret it.

"You know something, Chosyam?"

"Sir?"

"I have dreams of the face of a woman I saw once for only a few moments before we left Earth. She is as familiar to me as my own hands. It's almost as though I have known her for years, have lived with her as part of my own household. . . ."

"It is in the nature of women to seem to be familiar," Chosyam said. Somehow he had to steer the captain around to the business of the morning. Better yet, he had to get off this beater ship and get away somewhere so he could have a little time alone. The place was getting too crazy even for him, and his insanity threshold was exceedingly high. He was saved from saying anything more by an annoyingly loud buzz. "Incoming vid, sir. Do you want to take it in your quarters?"

"Identified?"

"Historian Pak, sir."

"In my quarters."

Chosyam looked at the man's face, frozen on the vid screen until So Pak picked up. How much did the man know? He bent over the screen and peered into the man's eyes, seeing only a canny old man. When So Pak picked up, Chosyam switched Historian Pak off and went back to fixing the pipes. Maybe later, he'd let Savage talk him into playing and losing at chess again.

At about the time that Bender was trying to think of

how to disengage Drukker from his own symptoms, So Pak was propping himself up in the corner of his quarters and listening to the sadness in his father's voice. So Pak looked at the man's face and felt a rush of tenderness for the blurred, wavering outlines. So Pak swallowed. He wanted to ask his father to forgive him for adding to the sadness.

So Pak straightened. "You do not expect me home, Father."

"No," his father said wearily. "Son, I believe your probe is . . ."

So Pak read his father's face and actions carefully. He was being warned. Desperate as he was for the information, he couldn't let his father continue. The line was undoubtedly tapped. "We are having great success. We've discovered that the members of the two mining camps are merely the tragic victims of an inhospitable environment."

"Your goal was to undermine the Historians, then?"

"Yes. Nothing happened here."

Historian Pak knew better, was not about to be thrown off. "I have recently returned from a small party given on the estate of Mr. Matsuda." He began to tell his son all that had happened. Anyone listening would know anyway, he had waited several days for gossip to make the rounds. It would have been considered rather odd, in fact, had he not told his son anything of the party and the news he received at it. By the time he finished, although he did not say it in so many words, So Pak knew he should be looking for some kind of advanced technology in one of the two camps.

"Apparently, it seems some sort of serendipitous discovery was made through use of a musical instrument. Or perhaps that is merely a romantic notion."

"We have found nothing to indicate this, Father."

His father opened his mouth to speak, but his face suddenly split into eight sections and then the screen went dead. So Pak was thankful that the transmission signal had lasted as long as it had, but he was sorry he hadn't had a chance to say good-bye.

So Pak swung around in his chair and accessed his notes on the records taken from the Korean and Japanese camps. He displayed them side by side. He was staring at them when he heard a knock on the door.

"Come in."

"Captain?"

He was surprised at how delighted he was to see Ewha. "How're things in sick bay?"

"Between storing viral strains and the autopsies, let's hope there is adequate contamination protection."

"You want any of that transferred to cargo bay?"

"Let me freeze-dry samples and get them ready for storage. How are you?"

"Everything is fine. Interesting findings from the camp records. There are subliminal messages from both, one to do with a seeded disease and one with a technology for mining having to do with sound."

"I brought you some somapowder and you look like you can use it."

"There isn't time."

"Captain, you can't get sick."

"And the crew?"

"I'm worried about Bender. And there is something wrong with Drukker. She hasn't been in for her checkup." Ewha looked as if she was about to say more but instead she reached for the door.

"You are doing a grand job of keeping us all healthy."

"I don't know about that," she said, and hurried out.

So Pak went back to the subliminals on his screen. They were so layered with censorship flags and codes that it was difficult to get to the bottom of them but, from what he could see, it looked like what he'd guessed was right on the money.

CHAPTER ELEVEN

At the same time the subliminals were boiling up on So Pak's compuscreen, a small figure dressed in flat black scurried through the Kleinhaupt Terminal in Newark. The figure was slight, resembling nothing more than a backlit wedge of shadow as it moved quickly through the hangars and across landing strips. It was dressed in black footless tights, a tight, seamless blendex weatheroff jacket, high-top black climbing boots, the tiny razor-sharp blades embedded in the soles suitable for climbing and quick grip traction on any surface and particularly effective on the wet, oily surfaces that infested the terminal, black fingerless gloves with the same tiny razor blade implants in the palms, a black kid leather face mask and the thinnest fiberglaze helmet made to withstand the same impact and pressure as the old riding helmets of the last century.

She held a belt full of laser explosives which she had unstrapped from her waist, and a bracelet of guide-path paraphernalia, meant to guide the explosives with pinpoint accuracy, flickered on her wrist. At the Iwaski Terminal, she began working carefully and quickly, rappeling herself onto the nearest carrier, poised like an aerial stingray against the red sky of the Newark night, and wiring explosives through the passenger section and along the tail and wing sections. Once the activator was triggered, the passengers would be exterminated and the wings and tail would appear to drop off the body of the plane after the brief appearance of a surgical red line of fire.

The woman worked quickly and silently and the first plane was finished in under twenty minutes. There were six ships in all. Twenty minutes was too long. The next ship was set in fifteen minutes and, in another hour, the shadow slipped unseen past the security guards into the waiting room of the terminal itself, having set six ships to explode.

It was more difficult to pass unnoticed inside the terminal. The halo lights pierced every corner of the long walkways and everywhere there were robos, security personnel, and wary passengers, all on the lookout for suspicious behavior. Security was tight now that three kelp bars had been blown up and fifteen holocard waiting rooms pulverized, all by people claiming responsibility as members of Terror Two. Airport officials hired security associations to infiltrate the organization, hoping Terror Two was more easily penetrable than the Snakers, which didn't seem to have any permanent location from which to operate in any kind of stable fashion. "In fact," the chief of security was heard to say on Activid News, "it was a wonder the organization had managed to operate for as long as it had, given their lack of centralized location and leadership."

As soon as Reoke hit the light bathing the outskirts of the terminal, she pulled off her helmet, flattened it, and shoved it and the face mask into the waist of her tights. She pulled back her hair with a five-inch band and straightened, yanking a piece of inflatable luggage from her sleeve. Hoping it looked considerably more substantial than it was, she struggled through the front entrance.

If anything, she acted too well. Three spacecaps came running toward her and she waved them away, frowning. They didn't stick around too long insisting on helping her, and she quickly adapted her walk so as to be not quite as noticeable. The idea, she had been taught, was to be just noticeable enough that people avoided and forgot you. The best disguise was one that put you right in front of people's faces and gave them the option of paying little or no attention to you. Usually, they didn't. Particularly in Newark. Just last week two women had been simultaneously raped in a terminal walkway as 150,000 people passed by. When interviewed later, some of the passersby admitted to hearing screams, but from such an "undesignated area they couldn't actually pinpoint the site of the trouble even had they wanted to help." Newark papers had the story plastered all over the front pages but, as Reoke knew, the same sort of thing had been happening for the past three or four years to poorer women all over Newark. That, and a marked rise in the murders of musicians in the district, in plain sight of tourists and residents alike, none of whom even stopped to watch. Reoke assumed someone of prominence had been the victim this time, although, as usual, victims remained unidentified to protect their private lives. At least if the rape victim was the wife or daughter of someone prominent.

She walked through the lobby and headed toward the Interzone flight pods, dragging her suitcase behind her, but when she heard the first shots, she flung the suitcase aside and took off down the hall. It served her right. Her concentration was slipping, and she was behind schedule. Reoke ran, the only person upright and moving in a corridor crammed with people flattened to the floor, their faces ground into transit dirt. Arms pumping, thighs pounding her feet into the ground, Reoke raced along feeling as though her lungs would tear for want of air. She hurled herself through a door marked "KEEP OUT, POWER STATION" minutes after her four comrades left it behind and glimpsed their backs as they headed toward the loading platform, spraying anything that moved with high-impact bullets. The walls were mottled with blood, like the finger painting of a demon child. As Reoke slipped through the door and slammed it behind her, the sudden image of a placid lake full of white water lilies, limpid under a summer rain slammed into her brain. Two blue herons, grayed and graceful, caught in flight between water and sky burned her memory and a physical pain caught at her heart for the husband she had loved. Though it couldn't be said she was doing this completely for him, she was certainly doing it for more than herself. She narrowed in on the pain and pulled the energy into her body where she needed it the most. Minutes later, she found herself on a gray plexi platform, which turned to the left and right beyond the door, catwalking fifteen feet above the room beneath her. Five people were seated in front of their vid screens below her. Not one of them was alive. There was a sweet smell of blood, the ripe odor of human bodies cut open. Reoke threw the rope over the railing of the catwalk and let herself down to the ground level of the power center for the entire terminal. It had taken her weeks to memorize the grids and switches.

With barely a glance at the dead control workers, Reoke flipped switches, rewired circuits, and crossed terminals until three-quarters of Kleinhaupt and all of Iwaski were shut down. And, she thought grimly, it will take at least several days to get everything back in working order.

She lit a phosphate torch and made her way back to the fiberglass rope that hung from the railing. She had only minutes to activate the explosives. If they didn't go off, two of the planes would make it to safe zone distances. Grabbing the rope in her hand, she was beginning to wrap it around her leg when she heard a scuffling from the darkness in the corner, obstructed from view by a tangle of pipes. Reoke killed the phosphate torch and was peering into the corner when she felt a glimmer of movement behind her and spun around, managing to untangle her leg from the rope just in time to avert being knocked to the floor by a flashing knife. She grabbed the man's chest in a bear hug and felt the sickening crack of his ribs. He was smaller than she was, but not by much. On the strength of her legs alone she managed to flip him over and she managed to kick the knife out of his hand, but not before he slashed at her ankle, partially severing her Achilles tendon. She raised her hands, clasped them together over her head, and brought them down behind his ear, or at least where she judged his ear to be, given the darkness of the room. She was rewarded with a grunt as he dropped to the ground and, in one swift movement, she grabbed the pencil from her wrist pouch, reached for his open mouth, and rammed the pencil through the roof of his mouth and up into his brain. She felt for a pulse, making sure he was dead in order to eliminate any surprises. But she had no time to frisk the body. She had to get back to the runway and she was crippled now. She limped back to the rope and managed to shinny the length of it using mostly calf and thigh muscles. She imagined her Achilles tendon surrounded by clear white light and when she collected enough of the light in her mind, she imagined a laserlike knife blade penetrating the frayed ends of the tendon, then shrinking to needle size and sewing them all together in a hypnotic back and forth motion with a thread of light into which she tried to rest and relax. She had only an instant to repair the tendon before she got to the catwalk.

Minutes later, she was up and over and limping. She cut the band from her hair, wrapped it around the ankle, and tied it together. The thing to worry about was the rest of the tendon ripping. If she lost the tendon, she wouldn't be able to walk. But what choice did she have? If she did not fulfill this mission it hardly mattered whether she lived or died. She clamped her lips tightly together and headed over to the terminal pod.

Fifteen minutes later, she was hiding herself away in the drain duct, staring through the grating, chemical waste slopping around her ankles as she hunkered down, her arms wrapped around her knees. She couldn't stand up straight. The best she could hope for was a kind of deep knee bent shuffle. At first she tried to avoid the slime-covered ceilings and the garbage-slicked sides of the waste tubes but, soon realizing that was impossible, she tried only to keep everything but her feet out of the chemical waste pooled at the base of the conduit. It seemed as though she waited several people's lifetimes. She couldn't lose her concentration or let her muscles cool down, so she sat systematically clenching and unclenching them, muscle group by muscle group, stilling her mind as best as she could. There was nothing left to do, there was no stopping the outcome of action, right or wrong, and she watched the people before her, all of them completely unaware of their impending deaths, living as though they were immortal. It wasn't the first time Reoke found herself marveling at the world of ordinary people who lived as though death would never catch up with them.

A distinguished businessman in his sixties, looking to be at the peak of his career, pulled down a VIP lever seat. Moments later, after seating himself carefully and rearranging his briefdesk, he was yelling something that sounded vaguely like "Aikeewa. . . ."

The caretaker of the VIP seat, mildly annoyed, paused to look at him. "It collapse on you?"

The businessman said nothing, merely brushing off his raincoat and abandoning the pullchair.

Near the grating, Reoke could see their torn-up can-mold shoes as two dealers stood talking.

"Well, I'll give you two of them, but don't take them both at the same time."

A rank bosky odor penetrated even the fumes of the chemical waste river in which she crouched.

"I don't want you ODing on this shit."

"You mean this is actually shit you're giving me?"

"Of course it is. You think there's anything good on the street these days? Like, actually good?"

"Yeah, but shit?"

"By the time it gets at you, there'll be a 'Man Dies, ODs on Shit' column in the Newark paper, featuring a new dynamic death every week."

"Lost on me, man. Lost on me."

Reoke crouch-walked down the drainage tube and came up at the next grating about a hundred yards away, where she looked out at the same scene of people hurrying by, unmindful. She watched the homeless using words to cover the humiliation of their begging. It was a horror in desperate need of changing, which is how it all began, Reoke remembered. She, like her husband, would never be around to see it all when it became different, if it ever did. It didn't matter. Nor did it matter if their legacy was left the world at all. If they passed through, childless and faceless. Long ago, Reoke had decided to make invisibility her strength. She would move through it all like the wind and no one would be able to see her or see where she was going, although everyone could see the trees bending to the wind's will, the wheat fields swept with the force of it and occasionally, like tonight, the wild force let loose without restraint. Terrorists must be nameless, faceless, placeless. They must be the most common looking people in a crowd, so that no one could pick them out. They must never be beautiful, nor slovenly, nor extreme looking in any way at all. And Reoke had the good luck to be born that way, plain, nondescript, with an obedient nature but a compulsion for the unexpected.

She flexed her ankle and rubbed at her tendon, hoping against hope that it would not burst. She checked the watch embedded into her skin. She hadn't more than a couple of more minutes of waiting in the Kleinhaupt Terminal cesspool. She'd wired the Japanese and German embassy stations in the terminal, Iwaski corporate headquarters, the ticket gate and runway, six ships, and part of the control center. Who they thought was responsible was their problem. She wasn't about to vidphone anything into them. She had two more checkpoints left to go, the cache was positioned and all she had to do was check and activate the wiring. Two hundred yards to pass there and back unseen with her Achilles tendon extremely questionable.

And then it was time to move. Reoke pulled her arms tightly to her body and ran, crouching, her back muscles swelling against the pipes strapped to her body, double-belted and wrapped again in plastifoam, which peeled away when she pulled at the plastic velcro ties.

She emerged from a discharge duct near the floatcar entrance. There was enough entryway activity that she was reasonably certain she was safe and unnoticed. She hugged the wall and made her way to the shadowed corner where the cache was buried, a small ball of explosives wrapped in a waterproof cloth. She removed several pipes from the strap against her back and stuffed them with explosives, buried a wick halfway down to the plastene, wired the pipes together, and leaned the whole thing against the wall, covering it over with loose brush and scraps of airport debris. Then she set the timer and moved several yards away to see if she could discern any change or oddity in the corner where the explosives were placed. There was nothing. She moved to a supply depot. It was hardly ten minutes before she was running again, slipping between shadows, the detonator in her hand. She ran behind a quonset hut and pushed the detonator. An answering pain shot up her leg as six planes, one wall, one supply depot, the Iwaski office, the Japanese and German embassy suites and four runways exploded into the air.

Reoke turned and slipped away across a Swiss corporate runway, diagonally dodging planes whose passengers were being let off despite the chaos in the terminal. She mixed with the passengers and, as soon as she was able, slipped onto the Kleinhaupt walkway, mixing with the foot traffic of Newark until she meandered off to the southeast to a row of torn up tenements, where men and women sat on their stoops and spit onto the sidewalk, their gazes distant.

At number 64, Reoke pulled out a key and let herself in the door. She stumbled past a wicker chair by the steps in the entryway that stank of age and cat and decay, and walked slowly up to the fourth floor, using the railing to haul herself up limped down the hall to 4F, where she unlocked a double lock and let herself in. The room was spare, bare, and painted dirty cream. Fiber agate curtains diffused the glare of light in the main room. To the left was a cramped sleeping room and a kitchen, bathroom, and tiny study in which a terminal, vidphone, and comlink were hidden in built-ins in the wall.

Reoke went to the study, pressed the lever to disclose the comlink, and typed in a private access code. Carefully and thoroughly, she reported on the effects of the mission, to be confirmed once she could catch the media reports later. She stressed that she had acted independently and that the standard communications codes were not to be trusted. Using language code, she tipped off her contact that, although the Japanese had attempted to throw the group into chaos by assassinating its leader, this morning's actions would have proven them misguided in thinking they could do any such thing.

The message then suggested as little communication as possible, referring to the tracker transmissions. Reoke asked verification of the message and left the comlink on as she went into the bathroom to run a bath for herself. She stripped and she was sinking into the scented bathwater in the sunken tub, the apartment's only luxury item, regarding the spray of cream-colored orchids growing in the window of the bathroom, through the steam, when the comlink began to click on in response.

It suggested a series of alternate contacts and support people and left a track of addresses and com numbers. It inquired politely after her health and, in the event she had suffered discomfort during the strike, recommended a homeopath, herbalist, and chakra alignment specialist. It respectfully suggested that she lay low but bowed to her greater wisdom of right action, giving the impression that the writer knew his advice was falling upon deaf ears. Finally, it informed Reoke of Denisovich's demise. Denisovich, the comlink informed her, had to be exterminated because it was clear his loyalties were no longer uncolored by other alliances. Such sacrifices, the comlink concluded, were necessary in a society not yet stabilized.

By the time Reoke had turned on the vidcaster above the bathtub, the message, from thousand of light-years away, had clattered to a stop. As she inspected the partially slashed tendon in her ankle, she tried to cope with the knowledge of Denisovich's extermination. She had never felt more alone in her life and she hated herself for the self-pity that brought tears to her eyes. It was surprising that she wasn't beyond all this. She read the papers and hit the comlink.

On the empty flight deck, a lone figure picked up the receiver of the comlink and slipped into shadow. "Angelis."

"Retro 1," Reoke code spoke. "A success. And you?"

"One Deathspeaker, one death."

"Yes, Denisovich."

"A back-trapper?"

"Confirmed?"

"Interestingly so."

"Good work." Reoke tried to hide her sorrow and exhaustion. "Anything else?"

"Not yet."

Reoke flushed with anger. What the hell were they doing up there anyway? "There isn't much time."

"Yes."

"There are more strikes to come. I can't be certain I will survive them. You must find it. It will bring down Iwaski once and for all."

There was a crackling on the line and Chosyam quickly pocketed the small transmitter that sent com signals through another frequency than that used by ship's communications. Unfortunately, it was a frequency that wouldn't stay open indefinitely.

The line went dead. Reoke switched off the comlink and went downstairs to get a floatcar to take her to the garage, where a doctor with Snaker sympathies agreed to use laser surgery to clean up and mend what was left of her Achilles tendon, providing the chemicals hadn't eaten it away.

All in a day's work, she reminded herself, but a very good day as long as one managed to keep in mind the fact that success was its own mine field.

CHAPTER TWELVE

Yeshe looked over her shoulder to make sure she wasn't being followed and gunned the sea-land vehicle toward a specific hill of sand. She brought nothing with her but a small pack and whatever she could fit into the pockets of the flak vest that she'd managed to fit over her atmosphere suit. She wouldn't need much, she wouldn't be staying long. In two and a half hours she would have to show herself at sick bay sterilized and ready to do what Ewha told her.

With the rising suns over her left shoulder, the world around her fresh and new, even the sand seemed comforting in the morning light. She didn't have far to go. She had found a quick route to the Korean mining camp since the day Toshio first recruited her, and she used it all the time now. She jockeyed the vehicle through a pass cut between two sand-hardened cliffs and gunned it as the sand dragged at the wheels. It wasn't long before she saw the hunkering camp on the horizon.

Other than being partially dug out, it had hardly been disturbed, despite Chosyam's forays into it for ship parts, Toshio's document lab, and Kenjii's systematic removal of necessary bits and pieces to be used in his dioramas. There was a comfortable familiarity about the camp that struck Yeshe the very first time she chanced upon it. It was quiet, quaint in its simplicity and lack of technology. The members of the crew had brought along enough personal items to individualize them from one another and there were pictures, books, toys, pocket knives, pieces of earth, rocks, and coral, and here and there a child's toy or shoe. There were one or two musical instruments and several varieties of small finger games. Perhaps, Yeshe thought, the camp seemed comfortable to her because it was like rummaging through the attic of her family home, the huge old attic full of generations of her family's things.

It hadn't taken Yeshe much rummaging to find her great-uncle, Oly, almost perfectly mummified and lying on his back on a cot with a thin cotton sheet drawn up around his neck. He had apparently been left alone to die, for the sheet hadn't been pulled over his face. His name was taped to the blanket and he wore a tablet around his neck with his name repeated, like the one Ewha found attached to the Korean engineer. His hands had been folded across his stomach, his legs crossed at the ankles and there was a small arrangement of beaded flowers before him along with the key to his steamer chest. Yeshe, used the key and opened the chest to find an extra pair of socks, pictures of his family taken at a ceremonial event at her father's ancestral home, a small packet of firecrackers, Buddhist burial cards, and red banners in case of death. The one real oddity was the pitch pipe clutched tightly in his hands.

Yeshe took out the banners and the ribbons and arranged them around the body according to Buddhist ceremony. She couldn't bury him officially until So Pak gave her permission, and she couldn't get permission because, even though everyone on board knew of her excursions to the Korean camp, she wasn't officially visiting it. So she used the banners and ribbons and set up an ancestral shrine around the body and, every day, or whenever she could, she came to pray and light candles and bring offerings of rice, noodles, and tea. There were no real vegetables or fruit to be had, let alone flowers, or she would have brought them as well. What she did bring were small palm-sized cards on which she drew pictures of persimmons, bananas, orchids, and chrysanthemums. These she arranged around the body until such time as she could bury it.

Yeshe was not naive enough to suppose her ancestral great-uncle spoke to her or offered any guidance whatsoever, but she felt a great peace and a sense of overriding calm in his presence, such as one gets when alone for several days in a forest. Perhaps this was due to the unnatural stillness of the abandoned mining camp. Or perhaps it was simply the result of being away from the rest of the crew. But even had she gotten nothing out of her visits, Yeshe would have stubbornly continued to come out of respect for tradition.

She parked the sea-lander near the communications shed and made her way along paths in the sand as yet unmarked by human footprints. She walked easily, pack thrown over her shoulder, her feet pointing directly before her and not toeing either out or in. She would have said, if asked, that she liked to disturb the world at her feet as little as possible.

Once she reached her great-uncle's resting place, she began to move around quietly, changing the offerings and lighting candles. Finally, she removed her shoes and knelt down in front of him to pray. Fleeting images passed by her as she looked at the man's strange, dried face, the skin like the petals of dried paper narcissus, pulled tightly around the skull, papering the neck, peeling from the hands.

He had been twenty-four when he died. He had not, except perhaps in the time just before his death, had a life of sorrow or difficulty. He had known little enough in his lifetime, yet the fact of his death made him ancient, wise in his dead distance, unburied, his spirit all-knowing and wandering.

Yeshe sighed at the weight of the burden placed upon her. Now that she had found him, she must somehow bring him back to Earth so his spirit could rest peacefully. She thought of the others who must remain here in unconsecrated ground with no one to bring them the pledges and offerings due ancestors, and she sighed again, this time for the pity that touched her heart. Then she regarded her ancestor coldly, appraising the difficulty of convincing So Pak of the need to bring him home.

She kneaded her hands as she set out to make a plan. Chosyam would never allow it. He was a man lacking in sentiment and all ties to tradition. Ewha would insist the body be cut up, its parts preserved and labeled. Toshio would be fundamentally against bringing diseased bodies back to Earth. Savage wouldn't care, nor would Bender. And she could expect no help from any of the others.

Yeshe had arranged the shrine at the north end of what had once been the camp's sleeping quarters. Forty-five bunks were lined up in two rows. Now collapsed, some covered by the sand that seeped through the duroplast windows, which had been blasted out at the corners in some ancient explosion, the hall was a strange combination of preserved neatness and the chaos of natural reclamation. Bodies once carefully laid out on the bed were scattered about, capsized in the drifting sand.

Torn between rearranging them and leaving the site intact for the others to find, Yeshe had forced herself to touch her Great-uncle Oly, the navigator.

Yeshe had reinforced the northern wall, pulled the weatherproofing sheets as tight as she could, and lashed them shut against the sand. She'd moved the navigator's body against the wall and laid him out on a pallet, which she brushed free of sand whenever she came to visit. Lately, she came more to calm her mind than to attend to the body and, most recently, it occurred to her to wonder what forces had brought her here and what it was they wanted her to do. For all of it was no good unless she cleared her mind with obedience. Sometimes, she found herself wishing that her great-uncle would turn his head and tell her. She imagined he would open his dried eyes and after a moment of recognition, begin to speak. But, as she ran her fingers across the objects she had placed on the altar before the body, she realized she had learned little from him other than the fact that he valued the pitch pipe. Yeshe reached across to the small table and pulled the pitch pipe toward her. It was much too large for a standardized pitch pipe and had irregular notes hidden away inside the disc, called up by half mouthpieces, which were placed around the perimeter at quarter centimeter intervals.

Idly, Yeshe turned the large, flat disc in her hand, palming it from one hand to the other as she looked at the body of her great-uncle. Had she been another kind of person she would have set herself to daydreaming, but she sat with fixed attention, her senses sharpened, fingering the pipe until she suddenly became aware of the tiny irregularities on the disc in her hands.

She looked down, watching the disc move through her fingers like the large flat body of a fish, silvery and strong, fleeting as magic. Mesmerized by the slipping disc, the light feeling of it in her hands, as clean and efficient as a weapon, she began to read the markings on the surface.

Sliding over the floor, she held the object up to the candlelight. In the weak flame, a flickering of light against the gloom, she peered closely at the minute Korean characters. The entire pipe was covered with markings, instructions which, if performed, would bring about some result. As she read, Yeshe saw the instructions had little to do with the actual playing of the pipe. They had, rather, some kind of meaning beyond that. The playing of the pipe had been put to some purpose.

Curiosity overcoming the rules of worship and burial, Yeshe backed out of the makeshift ancestral shrine, pipe in her hand. In the waxing morning as the suns spread their heat across the surface of the planet, Yeshe stood in the middle of the compound and began to read the pipe.

There was a clear series of steps, which if followed would bring about the desired result. Squinting against the harsh sunlight glittering off the surface of the pipe and dancing in the discs of reflected light at her feet, Yeshe pressed the pipe to the flexible mouthpiece of her helmet. She stood at the edge of the camp, a small figure hunched against the great expanse of horizon, and blew. The first note was tenuous. She blew harder and a high, nearly inaudible note pierced the air. Seconds later, a two-foot canyon appeared at her feet. Yeshe jumped back, alarmed.

Her hands began to sweat. What was she to do now? Was she in danger? Perhaps the area was subject to fault lines. But there had been no tremor and, if the area was unsafe, wouldn't the camp have disappeared years ago? It was still standing. The ground must be safe. She would worry about reporting this and her presence in the camp later. The important thing was that she had begun a course of action. It would be the most extreme ill-luck to stop in the middle, particularly when the action had been put in motion by her ancestor.

Feeling less confident, Yeshe read off the second command and obeyed it. This time, she heard nothing. The sand at the bottom of the fissure parted, exposing two smoky crystals, cubes of some unknown material. Yeshe sounded the third note, after rotating the pipe a quarter turn as instructed.

Open-mouthed, she watched the two exposed crystals spin upward in the air, revolve, and turn away from the fissure before floating through the air and landing in the sand at her feet.

The crystals were long, bulky, and flecked with an incandescent blue-white light toward their tips. They lay nestled in the sand as though it were the most natural thing in the world for her to have stumbled across them.

Gingerly, Yeshe pulled off her backpack and put the crystals in the inside pocket, holding the pipe between her gloved fingers. For a moment only she stood in the hot sun, clutching the bundle. Finally, she walked a good quarter mile away from the fissure to a smooth stretch of sand.

Trembling, she pressed the pipe to her helmet mouthpiece, and managed the first note. Again a fissure opened at her feet. At the second note, two more crystals appeared, rocking a little as the sand swept away from them. At the third, they levitated through the air, lifting themselves from the fissure and landing, like the previous pair, at her feet. Yeshe stared at the pipe.

When she glanced down at the sand beneath her, she noticed that the crystals were half-buried again, sunk back into the sandy skin of the planet. The fissure, however, showed no sign of closing up.

Yeshe headed toward the barracks. She went inside and looked at her great-uncle, knelt down before him, and stretched out her hand to the slivers of cloth across his chest.

"Thank you," she whispered, "for this gift you have bestowed on me. And guide me as you were guided in its use."

Then she stood up, inspected the shrine to make sure everything was in place, and went to what passed for home on this godforsaken planet.

Yeshe reported to the captain as soon as she returned to the *Arachne.* As he looked at Yeshe standing before him, eyes downcast, much as she had looked in her initial interview, So Pak saw that she had changed. She had found what she was looking for, and something else. As far as she was concerned, the mission was over.

"Yeshe, the Korean camp cannot be visited alone. Too many things could happen to you and, if you got hurt, there would be no one to help you." This was getting him nowhere, he was not sounding like a probe captain. And Yeshe only stood before him rigid and unmoving. She would do what she wanted to do whether he approved of it or not.

"I know your great-uncle is in that camp. We will get him out. I'll apply for clearance to get him back to Earth. Beyond that, I can do nothing. And you must comply with probe rules. That's what they're there for.

Next time you're found there, I'll be forced to put you in the brig. And if you keep it up you'll sweat it out in there until we land.''

Yeshe, without lifting her eyes to his, nodded, her back and shoulders rigid and unyielding. Slowly, obeying duty, she reached into her canvas sack and brought out the pipe, which she offered him. ''This is what I found. A relic of my great-uncle.''

So Pak quickly found the inscription and lifted the pipe to his mouth.

''Don't,'' Yeshe stopped him. She reached into her bag again. So Pak couldn't stop watching the brush of the sun on her face as she walked to the flight console. There she spread out the crystals, her hands strong and worshipful, reverent as those of a priestess. Against the prefab flight deck, the two crystals glimmered like dark eyes, too deep to understand.

''Purite,'' muttered So Pak. ''Raw, uncut purite.''

''The pipe brought it to me from the earth. The land fell away and the crystals came to me.''

''A primitive ultrasound mining process. Which explains why the Japanese mining ship came equipped with standard equipment and the Korean ship had none. But we haven't found the actual Korean mining pits yet, so we don't know what they were using. This corroborates the plans we found in the Japanese engineer's cabinet, Pages and pages of notes which we couldn't understand.'' So Pak handed the pipe back to her. ''Make a copy of the characters and give it to Chosyam. If what I think is true, it's good evidence that the Koreans had ultrasound techniques before the Japanese.''

Yeshe bowed formally and turned to go. ''And report to Ewha in sick bay.''

Once Yeshe handed them the inscription and someone on board compared it to the Japanese engineer's notes, the proper authorities would have to be notified of patent infringement and reparations would have to be paid. And it might put Iwaski out of operation. It had been decades since they'd begun illegally operating without a proper patent and the implications of this discovery were unimaginable. There was a nagging fear in So Pak's mind that his goal was about to be thwarted. Even if the members of the two mining camps were victims of an inhospitable environment, he had stumbled across information which ensured that the ghosts of the probe wouldn't rest any time soon. And the information had been stored and handed over by a dead man's hand. It was almost a certainty, So Pak now knew, that someone had facilitated the probe, someone other than Iwaski and Mr. Matsuda. They had not necessarily been sent off to die. The silken ghosts of the miners, and of Kim and Denisovich seemed to crowd the flight deck, pressing closer to him, obscuring the view of the planet, the sounds of the afternoon detail returning, of Bender's steady, insistent coughing, and the keening wail of Drukker's voice.

CHAPTER THIRTEEN

Toshio and Kenjii were eating noodle soup in the *Arachne* mess when Bender and Drukker arrived. The last person in the world Bender wanted to see at the moment was Toshio, but when Toshio looked up from his crabbed writing in the notebook propped against his tea bowl to look at the two of them, it wasn't Bender he began to study.

He stared calmly, his therapist's training slipping into place from Death Camp days. "Good evening, Ms. Drukker." He took in Drukker's blotched face and watery eyes, her nervous agitation and wild appearance. She looked like some kind of self-styled romantic heroine home from a day of storming the moors rather than an academic working on a strenuous probe site. Bender sat as far away from them all as possible and took out his pipe. Kenjii brought him a cup of hot tea. "Chosyam made the tea."

Chosyam's tea was generally undrinkable; they all had to drink it.

"Ms. Drukker, perhaps I might have a word with you." Toshio half-rose from his seat at the table, his noodles forgotten.

"Certainly."

"Perhaps you would like to have a seat?" He pulled

out the chair beside him and Drukker settled herself on it.

Toshio put a calming hand on her arm. "How are you feeling?"

"She looks like the last person in the world able to answer that," Kenjii muttered under his breath.

Drukker turned toward Toshio gratefully. "I have been feeling somewhat at a loss."

"Have you been experiencing periods when you black out?"

She looked at him blankly. "Perhaps that would explain it."

"Times when you haven't been able to remember what happened? When maybe you could have done something, something violent you might be feeling guilty about."

Shakily, Bender got up to leave. He couldn't sit here and watch this any longer.

"In my long experience in the Camps, I don't recall anyone who killed out of pain and desperation, but I suppose it could happen. It's the sickness, it foams up under the skin. I understand," Toshio said. "It will help if you can talk about it."

"You going, Bender?" Kenjii asked mildly.

"I suppose so." Bender felt sweat beading up on his body.

"Going to get some rest?" Kenjii's face swam before him.

"Yes. Yes, that is exactly what I intend to do."

Kenjii nodded sympathetically. "I haven't been sleeping well lately, either. It may be something in the life-support system. This recirculated air doesn't help one to work at maximum efficiency."

"The air's fine. There's nothing wrong with the air." As Bender swayed unsteadily on his feet, Chosyam walked in and flung himself down in the nearest chair where he propped his booted ankle on his left knee and began picking at his hair. "What would you know about it? Always complaining, the lot of you. You'd think you'd never been on a probe before."

Bender was beginning to feel quite ill and Kenjii's eyes were flashing, which was not a good sign.

"What's he doing?" Chosyam jabbed the air in the direction of Toshio and Drukker.

"He's worried about her health."

"So send her to sick bay. What's wrong with her anyway?"

"I'm sure I don't know."

Kenjii folded his hands in front of him. "If you will excuse me for saying so, you are a gigantic pain in the butt."

"Oh? And what would you know about it? What exactly is your job on this probe anyway? Maybe population control?"

Drukker and Toshio looked at Kenjii.

Bender tried very hard to distance himself and fight it off. Denisovich's death swam before him. He saw a hunched person bending over the man, heard a gurgling rattle, and smelled death. He dove straight into a sensate flood and saw a young woman sitting in a peach bathroom. Scars tracked her arms, her foot was badly injured, and she would never walk again. A comlink was listing herbalists and chakra alignment specialists, and nonsensically informing her of Denisovich's death.

Bender began to sweat more profusely. He tried to hold back the words but they rose to his teeth like vomit. "Who is Reoke?"

Chosyam spun like a yo-yo on a string. "Who?"

Bender stuck his pipe in his mouth and coughed.

"I believe he said Reoke," Kenjii said.

Chosyam leaned over Bender, who had begun to twitch. Chosyam pressed his lips to Bender's ear. "Not here, Deathspeaker," he hissed. He slid his arms under Bender's and pulled him up. "Let's take this up at sick bay."

Calmed by the touch of Toshio's fingers on her arm, Drukker only watched. Toshio looked at Kenjii with a guarded expression. Kenjii sat, arms apart, fists clenched on the table.

Savage, walking in with a transmitter in his fist, looked at Chosyam and nodded at Kenjii, "What's with the Whiz Kid?"

Chosyam didn't answer.

"As a matter of fact," Savage said, "what's with you?"

"The man's a menace," Kenjii said. "He's going to kill us all."

"Oh?" Savage asked. "What would you know about it?"

Toshio continued to stare at Kenjii. "What would you know about Denisovich's murder?"

"Oh, Jesus, Mary, Joseph, do we have to go through all this again?" Savage demanded, beginning to clean the transmitter with a pocket knife.

"Kenjii, where were you when Denisovich was murdered?"

Yeshe looked startled when Chosyam clattered into sick bay with Bender draped across his shoulders. "Here." Chosyam dumped Bender into the chair in front of Yeshe's desk. "Where's Ewha?"

"So Pak called her to the bridge."

"She needs to look at Bender."

"What's wrong?"

"He's Deathspeaking."

"What?" Yeshe stood up, shocked. "Well, don't put him there." Weaving her way gracefully through the confined space, she motioned toward a tiny cubicle. "Put him in here. He'll be in isolation."

"He won't stay," Chosyam warned. A look of deep sadness crossed his face. "Anyway, it hardly matters. We don't have much time anyway."

Bender began to thrash around.

Yeshe smiled up at Chosyam. "Thank you."

"I don't deserve your thanks."

"What did you do?"

"You don't understand."

She pushed him out the door. "How long have you know? Have you known for the entire flight?"

"It's not true."

"And did you kill Denisovich?"

"No."

"Your murders are cleaner? Endangering an entire crew by burdening them with a Deathspeaker."

"I didn't. . . ."

"How could you not have known?"

"I didn't choose the crew."

Yeshe turned her back on him. There was nothing more to do here. Tonight, when she finished her shift, she must go to her quarters and put things to rights. Unless she was very much mistaken, none of them had long to live.

Ewha was preoccupied with the electroscope when Yeshe got to sick bay the next morning. She looked worried and busy, as though she were trying to distract herself with work.

"Bender have a bad night?" Yeshe guessed as she pulled on the sterogown.

"It wasn't easy for anyone. Drukker had an episode." Ewha stared shrewdly at Yeshe. "I'm glad you're here. I need your help. Put on the gloves over there on the chair. Check the gloves to make sure there are no holes. I'm beginning to suspect that no matter how dried out these samples are, they may still hold contagion and it's always better to be on the safe side. There's no blood to take, but I've scrapings under the electroscope. Take a look and tell me what you think. I'm especially interested in viral strains. You'll find notes over there on the lab table that'll help you know what to look for. If you get to a good stopping place, bring those records over. I've a few things to add. And Yeshe?"

"Yes."

"Please get here on time tomorrow. I need you desperately. This may be the key to it all right here."

Yeshe nodded. "I'm very sorry, Ewha. I had planned to be back."

Yeshe washed and sterilized her hands and walked over to the lab table. Following Ewha's cool directions, she sliced fragments of bone and dried flesh, storing them away in tiny bottles, some filled with a liquid solution which would expand the tissues. As she worked, Yeshe began to notice that Ewha had collected an extensive series of sample bottles from the Japanese ship's sick bay. Several of them were scabby looking, but two or three looked carefully preserved. Japanese characters on the labels identified the contents as viral baths, housing experimental strains.

"Although," Ewha commented in exasperation, "I don't know what they could have been thinking of, importing experimental viral strains to a new planet. It's entirely beyond me, that kind of irresponsibility. I could have sworn that the injunctions were in force even then.''

Yeshe admired the efficiency with which Ewha worked in the tiny two-room area, separated only by a fiberweave curtain. The section in which they worked was a small quarantined operating area, surrounded by mirrors to facilitate the access of light and make the room look larger. Freezers built into the wall lined the south side of the room, along with centrifugal force microprobes, dryer stretchers, and controlled atmospheres for herb storage and culture experimentation. The adjoining room was set up for crew members who were sick or incapacitated. It was now occupied by Bender, who was shouting and muttering.

''Let me take a couple more samples. I'm almost through here,'' Ewha said, maneuvering around the operating table. Maybe you can clean up here when I'm finished. There are some interesting things to follow up here. Some kind of implanted inorganic virus seems to have killed most of those in the Korean camp. It was undoubtedly introduced by the Japanese and is related to the samples in the tubes over there,'' she said, motioning to the ancient vials. ''I don't know to what end, but I can guess. The Japanese seem to have arrived very well equipped, shall we say?'' Her cool eyes flickered over the vials and there was compassion in her glance, as well as, deep curiosity. Ewha, Yeshe suddenly realized, was a person driven by a need to know, as well as a person who had long ago come to terms with the fact that this could very well be the last probe for all of them. Yeshe felt a sense of freedom in this room after spending so much time with the secrets of her great-uncle and his crew.

''My analysis of tissue samples and results of enzyme revitalization are not quite completed, but what

I am certain of is the existence of a mutated strain of virus which is responsible for almost all of the deaths. Or, at least the deaths I've studied. There's a rictus and a paralysis, a strangeness about the position of the hands. . . ." Unable to be more specific, Ewha shook her head. "What is interesting about all of this is the fact that the virus mutated on this planet and its greatest extent of mutation occurred in a host body that had no humanoid characteristics. And, oddly, it's almost as though something had consciously willed the strain to change in a certain direction."

Yeshe wiped her hands on a surgical towelette. "What do you mean?" She began to set up the electron centrifuge in the lab area, working carefully and as quickly as Ewha, the equipment dancing into place in her hands.

"It looks almost as though the structure of the virus was altered by a conscious mind. There's a logical progression of alteration, almost as though someone were running through a chemical formula. And there's another thing. The virus seems to have been artificially created, as I mentioned before." Ewha paused. Her gaze locked with Yeshe's in the mirror. Yeshe felt surrounded by death, outraged by a kind of perfect preservation. Her heart lurched in longing for life though she knew it was not to be hers. She found a kind of comfort in Ewha's clear vision.

Thankful she'd been assigned this work detail, she entertained a high, wild, momentary hope that Ewha's clarity as well as the nature of the job would offset the dark, hidden secrets of her ancestor's makeshift shrine, which she was already beginning to feel tighten its grasp upon her and drag her down into a vortex of unconsciousness.

A shrill scream, answered by Bender's guttural muttering, rose in volume and swept through the lab. Frantic footsteps careened past the door and Ewha wiped her hands and threw open the door in time to see Drukker disappear around the corner. Mumbling, "That woman," under her breath, Ewha grabbed her bag and ran after her with long, loping strides. In her absence, Yeshe finished setting up and packing away the body of the cadaver. It was a full ten minutes before Ewha returned, her arm around Drukker, who was now heavily sedated. Ewha guided Drukker gently into the patient area. "Lie down here a moment and relax. You'll just have to sleep it off, I'm afraid," Ewha informed Drukker, who put her hand on Ewha's arm.

"It's Bender," Drukker was muttering. "Very ill."

"Symptoms," Ewha asked mechanically, although she doubted she'd learn anything particularly useful from Drukker in the state she was in.

Drukker closed her eyes, succumbing to the effects of the 10ccs of sedative Ewha had used to quiet her. "Arthritis, upper respiratory congestion, spasmodic muscle weakness, fever. The man is very ill." Ewha made sure she was sleeping and then she pulled the curtain and returned to the lab. "Drukker is going to be a problem," she said.

Yeshe, watching Ewha, saw fear darken the doctor's eyes.

"She can make him worse."

"She said he was glowing. Yeshe, it is not outside the realm of possibility for Bender to be an alien."

Yeshe considered this a moment. "Not very probable."

"My dear, always believe the improbable," Ewha replied. "It is very often the only thing of any truth." She got ready to leave. "Watch Drukker. She should rest fine. I pumped quite a bit of X-T-Doze into her. While I'm gone, compare those tissue samples and make up some preliminary reports for me. If I'm right, this is exactly where he should be, perhaps even in complete isolation."

"Yes, all right," Yeshe agreed. She stared through the neutron microscope at the virus slides and wrote down her findings. At first she worked mechanically, her mind on any number of other things. But her attention snapped back to her findings as she noticed the progression of the mutation of the virus. Ewha was right. All samples had been taken from the bodies of various hosts. It was the later deaths that contained the mutated cells. And they mutated in such orderly progression as to be almost a perfectly logical lesson in theoretical progression. And, Yeshe realized, her fingers trembling with discovery, there was one step missing, as though one host had been completely eliminated from the chain. She scrawled down her findings and checked the samples. Ewha had run tests ranging from the bacterial bath stored in the Japanese ship's sick bay to the members of the Korean crew, to the more recently deceased members of the Japanese crew. It was enough to trace the development of . . . the discovery stopped Yeshe cold. It seemed as though what they had run across was a designer virus created solely for the purpose of viral warfare. Somewhere along the line, the virus met a host which was in the process of rendering the virus harmless to human beings. They had stumbled onto a medical laboratory for successful viral experiment. That's all the mining community was set up to be. That a few irregularities showed up, contributed by people taking it all on faith, had only been an aside to the focus of the probe. Yeshe shivered. But what happened to turn it around? Even though there had been no survivors, ultimately the virus had mutated through various hosts to the extent that it was no longer fatal to human beings. But what had been the crucial bridge?

Yeshe shivered as, next door, Drukker wrapped in a cocoon of sleep thick with portent, stirred up dust devils outside the ship and in the desert beyond, giant whirling columns of heated sand and dust that floated across the desert as though called to destruction. And gathering more particles of sand and goofer dust to them as they progressed in obedience to Drukker's dreaming.

That's when Yeshe heard Bender speak from the other room.

"It's a disease with simple parameters," he was saying. "Rare enough, but it runs in the family and we know what to do for it."

"Only one will make it off the ship holding the knowledge discovered in a driven journey."

Yeshe's blood ran cold. She flung open the door and stared at Bender. His face was glowing with knowledge. He had begun to Deathspeak. He must be isolated. Then she caught herself short. Why? They were not on Earth and did not have to obey the rules of quarantine unless Ewha invoked them.

"Bender, listen to me. . . ."

Bender tried to explain to her that he must not be kept too close to Drukker, but Yeshe could make nothing of it. He began to babble about some bedtime story his father had taught him, that during the time of the mining expedition, when the crews were struck with disease, aliens coming down for purite had run into the virus, internalized it to neutralize it as they had been taught by their medical people, and failed.

unfortunately, because the virus was a designer virus, they couldn't neutralize it organically. Something was out of sync, the virus turned fatal. Neutral to humans, it was the deathblow to the aliens.

That was all Yeshe managed to get out of Bender before he began Deathspeaking in earnest and Ewha returned in a rush.

"Drukker's doing it." Ewha was frantic.

"What?"

"Do you hear it?"

Yeshe listened. Then she heard it, a violent duststorm had begun to batter the ship.

"We have to get her calmed down. If we don't, she can tear the ship apart." Ewha was wrestling Drukker into sick bay and forcing an injection into her, but it wasn't enough. They tried all night to calm her down.

The storm raged throughout the night, the *Arachne* rocking in its relentless clutches so that most of the crew had little or no sleep. By 10:00 the next day the sky was as dark as the night before. There was nothing to see but swirling sand and wind funnels dancing across the plains. The wind pummeled the ship until it seemed as though it would pick it up like a child's toy and cruelly hurl it across the desert.

It took both Yeshe and Ewha to control Drukker, whose strength, echoing that of the winds outside, seemed superhuman. By the time Toshio and Kenjii showed up at sick bay to relieve them, Bender was staring glassy-eyed at the ceiling and Drukker was calling down destruction upon the crew, the Snakers, the Iwaski government, Ronin Historians, and cursing out the tracker ships which, she kept insisting, she could hear circling above them like vultures over a kill.

Despite the storm, Toshio and Kenjii attempted to leave for *Lips III* to scavage what they could, but they were forced to turn back to the *Arachne*, reporting sand and goofer dust twisters over one hundred stories high. The storm raged apace with Drukker's ravings until Savage accused her of causing it and shouted her down. Oddly enough, as Drukker lay sobbing, the storm seemed to let up a little. Bender, silent, thrashed mutely with the pain twisting his joints. In desperation, they all filed reports. Jaffe, watching the storm from orbit, threatened to come in and get them. Later, So Pak thought he should have let her try.

Two days later, there was nothing left of the research site at the Japanese camp. It seemed the storm had veered around the Korean camp, but for how long was anyone's guess. Katz tried valiantly to take weather readings from the *Bushido* but all the ground sensor equipment had been put out of commission by the sand. They huddled in the *Arachne*, tempers frayed, to wait out the storm, using the time to catch up on their reports and to inventory their findings.

So Pak, Drukker's prophecies ringing in his ears, called the World Patent Office through a relay on the *Bushido* to report his findings.

Over the static on the line he heard a low-level clerk, "World Patent Office."

So Pak cursed his luck. "I'm calling from Probe 789 on Zeta Reticuli."

The clerk seemed to brighten somewhat at that, interplanetary calls were still unusual enough to be interesting.

"I need to speak with someone in authority. It's urgent." So Pak paced the bridge, comlink in his hand.

"Department?" the clerk queried.

"Incorrect filing?" So Pak guessed.

"One moment please."

It was, indeed, only one moment. A cool feminine

voice answered, "You want to report an invalid patent?"

"Yes." So Pak reached for the Japanese file and extracted an ancient patent request. He read off the numbers. Then he waited, listening to the clicking of keys as the official took her time hunting up the information on the compuprompter. There was another moment while she registered controlled surprise. "The Iwaski ultrasound mining technology process?"

"Correct."

"And what have you found, sir?"

"I am reporting from an investigative probe on Zeta Reticuli. There are two mining camps here: one Korean, one Japanese. We have found a relic, a small set of pipes with inscribed directions and a filing number."

"The number please."

"X568-6430-800."

He waited as the clerk called up the file number.

"A very old mining patent filed by the Korean government before the World Patent Office came into existence."

"I would like to register a formal complaint. I believe the patent corporately stolen and request an investigation," So Pak began. "It's my belief that the matter must be reported to the World Bank and reparations paid to the Korean government."

The voice on the other end of the phone became impatient. "We will investigate the patent infringement and take the necessary steps, sir."

"Thank you."

"Is there some place where I can reach you with this information?"

So Pak evaluated the danger involved and looked at the twisters tearing up the surface of the planet in front of his window before, unhesitatingly, he gave the woman his father's vid number.

Yeshe and Ewha, meanwhile, spent the time doing Bender's bloodwork while Drukker and Bender both slept uneasily, screaming down destruction and loss on all of their heads until Ewha threatened to gag them with surgical tape. At first it was easy to ignore, but after a time it began to wear on the nerves of both women. Still, they worked until they were done.

Ewha jammed her fists into her pockets and began to pace the length of the small operating area as Yeshe cleaned and cleared away equipment. For a few moments, Ewha said nothing. Bender's blood structure was identical to that of the samples taken from aliens in Deathcamps. And traces of the virus, altered so as to be nonfatal to humans, were present. The missing link in the bloodwork she had pieced together as best she could from the two autopsies and the bottled cultures.

"I don't understand this."

"We don't have to understand anything." Yeshe meant it to be soothing, but it came out brittle and hard.

"It explains one thing that always puzzled me."

"Oh?"

"Why aliens were given clearance to die on Earth."

Yeshe shrugged. "A cover-up. Maybe the Japanese were trying to silence the aliens. Maybe they worked out a deal."

"But wasn't it the German Alien Aid Society that finally worked out the deal?"

"We don't know what kind of involvement anyone really had."

"Maybe none."

"Maybe."

"But how could Bender have lived all these years holding the disease inside him like that?"

"You heard what he said. He said he'd been given techniques for regulation."

"Why didn't they implement those techniques in the Deathcamps then?"

"Maybe the information was exclusive. Maybe it was suppressed. Maybe the aliens who arrived were too far gone and could no longer put any of it into practice."

Yeshe regarded Ewha carefully. Her eyes were clouded with anger. "What are you going to do?"

"There's nothing I can do now. But if I get a chance, what I am going to do is make sure I live long enough to get the story to the proper authorities."

Drukker screamed. She sat up in the sick bay bed, hair streaming out around her, face chalk white, the skin pulled back from her mouth in rictus, snarling imprecations. The warning bell couldn't have rung more than two and a half seconds before the sound of a great rushing wind filled their ears.

"The door!" Ewha was already dragging a storage chest across the floor, shoving it against the metal door. "I wish they'd thought to vacuum lock the damn area," Ewha muttered, slamming a table against the chest. "At least there aren't any windows in here." As the door began to buckle, she threw her shoulder against it in desperation.

"Help me," she ordered Yeshe.

They stood, shoulder to shoulder, palms pressed against the door as Drukker howled behind them and the door convulsed beneath their hands. It seemed an eternity of pounding wind and beating hail. Once, Yeshe turned around to see Drukker, hair streaming in the electric storm field, calling down Earth gods, demons, and vengeance until finally, her English gone, she began muttering in alien. "A telepath. She bonded with Bender," Ewha explained.

Tears streamed down Yeshe's cheeks. She didn't think she could hold back the door much longer, her arms were trembling with exhaustion. It seemed as though she had arrived, fully conscious at the gates of hell.

Behind them, Drukker gathered strength and, as Bender looked on in utter horror, she threw herself out of bed and jumped for Ewha's shoulders, tearing her backward, away from the door. Outside, the storm redoubled its fury and Bender, with the last of his wheezing breath, lunged for Drukker. She whirled upon him as Ewha, released, raced back to the door. Drukker turned on Bender and seized him by the neck, throwing him against the wall as easily as a child hurling a cookie. She broke his back.

He stared at them all, and Drukker, refusing to break the bond, flung herself against him.

Almost instantly, the doors stopped buckling and there was a tremendous quiet but for Yeshe's sobbing as she dragged her arms away from the door. "It's no use, Ewha." she shoved the cupboard and table away.

"We have to find what's left."

Yeshe, with no desire to find what was left, patted Ewha on the arm, then pulled her away. It was odd, Yeshe thought, that she couldn't bring herself to look at Ewha's face.

Distantly, the two of them could hear street jazz playing from the direction of Chosyam's work area and, determined to take inventory of the choices left them, Ewha began to make her way toward the sound.

Even as the music drew the two women on the ship toward Chosyam, Reoke, transmit-hooked from Earth, softly hung up. He'd called as she had expected, his voice surprisingly calm.

"Retro 1?"

"Answered."

"Object found. Am relaying data. Apparently it is a small pitch pipe. Already reported to the World Patent Office, my dear. And, Retro 1. Denisovich was killed in error. Kenjii killed him; Kenjii was an industrial plant. So Pak never did want him. Man has good instincts.

"Denisovich wasn't the leak. He was only a misdirected subversive. It's better he's dead. He was a threat to the organization and would have brought it down eventually. Funny ideas, he had."

"The leak?"

"Jaffe. Com officer. They paid her, it was simple. Some interference and static about the alien virus originating here on the same expedition, would you believe, but it's all background noise to the main issue. I believe we are finished. I also believe the ship will be destroyed in the storm that has begun on planet. Stress points can't hold out. it's a beater ship, after all. Saves me the trouble of blowing it up and killing myself anyway. The ship wasn't designed to get any of us back. I just built it to get us here."

"Angelis, you all right?"

"As a matter of fact, the storm's really torn us. If there's another side, Denisovich will be waiting although I'm sure he must have forgiven us all by now."

After that, the line faded to unintelligible mumbling in the background, jazz the only thing coming over the line clear and clean and finally, although she would rather have held onto the receiver all night, cradling it against her chest, because she knew once she hung it up she was forever severing all connections with Chosyam, Reoke softly placed the receiver on the hook.

It was only a setback, Mr. Matsuda told himself. He called for the Office Girl, who looked particularly pleasing today. Her skin was glowing like it had been underlit with soft peach light.

He played back the conversation between Reoke and Chosyam. If only there were a way to find out who the woman was. As for Jaffe, the best thing to do would be to completely disengage. He smiled at the Office Girl. He tried to find solace in the sight of her body, her hair, her skin, and her smell. His eyes wandered over her, but there was no true appreciation. Her wrists were too large. Her eyes were dull and stupid and she moved so delicately he wanted to smash her. He would have to get a new Office Girl, someone who would excite his senses.

"Please pull all files on Jaffe Potter and have them destroyed. Contact the information and marketing bureau and have them come up with some other explanation for her activity. If they ask, we did not promise protection. The girl was too idiotic to demand it from us. And tell them to reconstruct events to prove that she was working for herself, or better yet, for some terrorist group. Perhaps a terrorist group involved with the Snakers."

The Office Girl bowed her head. "Yes, Mr. Matsuda."

"This must be done very quickly." He watched as the Office Girl turned to leave the room. "Suki."

"Yes, sir."

"You are awkward and impossible. Please do something about it."

Mr. Matsuda stood up and walked to his window.

There was nothing he could do about Kenjii. Kenjii had acted in an extremely unfortunate manner. There was no way to cover the fact that he had been a plant. Mr. Matsuda had had to tell the German and European Federation as much in order to get on the probe against So Pak's wishes. The murder of Denisovich would be investigated and wouldn't become a blot on So Pak's record.

Mr. Matsuda reviewed his options. Iwaski, not So Pak, would be blamed for the murder on board ship. The German European Federation must have known that Iwaski had built its power on a stolen, unreported Korean patent, while employing germ warfare under the guise of chemical testing. That was why they had signed ship's clearance. He had been smoothly set up. He would have to endure an Atrocity Investigation and, most likely, a World Patent Office suit. If he was lucky, he would have to pay reparations that would bankrupt Iwaski and the government, as well as him personally.

Had Mr. Matsuda had any trustworthy and honest advisers, they would have told him he couldn't survive. But he had done away with them all. And he had become so accustomed to power, he believed himself invincible.

He picked up the vidphone and dialed Historian Pak. Historian Pak's line was answered promptly. "I would like you to know that your son is coming home," Mr. Matsuda said. It sounded like a threat.

"Heaven be praised," Historian Pak watched his enemy warily.

"He is coming home in defeat."

"But he is coming home," Historian Pak repeated.

"He has found out lies that cannot hurt me. Only four of his crew are left."

"I appreciate your sharing this information with me," Historian Pak said. "Although I doubt very much whether what you are saying is true." Historian Pak leaned into the vidphone. He looked like some shaggy, aged creature who had learned wisdom through survival. "I would take care to preserve my winnings, sir."

And with that, Historian Pak shut Mr. Matsuda off. He was no longer a worthy enemy, an opponent against whom to pit one's intellect. He had lost. Worst of all, he had played the game so badly, he no longer knew his true position. For the first time in their long association, Historian Pak termed Mr. Matsuda a man to be disregarded. Historian Pak was shocked at his own lack of judgment.

For the next several weeks, he heard rumors of internal unrest at Iwaski. The company was in turmoil. Stock slid on the market and shareholders began to hold investigations.

Then, on a particularly cool winter evening, Historian Pak received a call from Mr. Matsuda.

He refused to answer with respect, but he did answer politely.

Mr. Matsuda's face was drained of blood. He tried to speak, moving his mouth around words which did not form. His gaze, dark and distant, reached through the vid screen before he dropped the scanner.

Historian Pak watched in horror as Mr. Matsuda lifted the ceremonial sword and slashed his own throat. Pinkish, watery blood spilled over his chest and down his samurai robe, across the horizontal gash through which his entrails slid.

Beside him, a dead woman lay, the brilliance of her young face blurred by death.

CHAPTER FOURTEEN

"Where's the light coming from?" Yeshe glanced at Ewha, as they turned toward Section 8 of the ship, where Chosyam's work area was located.

"Must be here." They stepped through a twisted mass of metal into a well-lit room that looked as though it had been caught and crushed in an angry fist.

Ewha looked sharply at Yeshe's face. "We don't have much time. The *Bushido* will come for us before we know it."

"If we live that long."

"Of course, we'll live that long." Ewha's voice was irritable.

"All of them gone," Yeshe said, under her breath.

"We don't know that!"

Yeshe looked at Ewha in surprise. Who did she expect to be left?"

"Come on, then," Ewha squared her shoulders and made her way across pieces of the sharded ship toward the sound of music. Yeshe looked around her and at the comprehensive destruction of a natural disaster that, subsiding, left complete tranquillity in its wake. It was as though all that was required for survival was an ability to somehow make it through the disaster itself until all could be righted again, ultimately knowing, in the face of all mortality, that there would be one time and one time only when a person would not be able to survive. That one's life would be claimed and the world would go on as it always had.

They picked their way through the debris, carefully avoiding the ragged edges of the ship, careful of their footing, until they found an entrance to what seemed to be the remains of Section 8. By bending and squatting, they were able to walk through the four-foot gash in the outer wall into Chosyam's workroom. It was strewn with ship parts, diagrams, and bits of shredded technotoys. The vid screen flickered with blue-white light until Ewha turned it off to save whatever power was left. The compuprompter was running. Ewha turned that off, too, before silencing a drill bit that was snaking its way across the floor.

Chosyam lay in a corner, thrown there like a free-form chair, a metal beam through his chest and his body twisted around it as though his last moments had been spent trying to writhe out of its grasp. It seemed he had succeeded in detaching himself partway, but there was still a hand's length pinning him to the floor. The vid com receiver was in his hand and, on closer inspection, the still running com tape was operational. Ewha slid it out of the cartridge and put it in her pocket, the case no bigger than two fingers laid side by side. She pulled her keys out of her pocket and threw them into the room. It wasn't likely she would be needing them anymore. The locks had sprung open or twisted shut beyond the use of keys. When she switched off the tape, a silence greater and more dense than anything Yeshe had ever experienced, descended on them.

Yeshe bent over Chosyam's body and tried to pull it straight, the sound of the body scraping across the floor like the drag of wet leaves across a dry riverbed. But they were too late and the body had already stiffened. Death-cramped, it refused to realign. It seemed the most important thing in the world to give Chosyam a position of rest, even if she had to break his bones to do it, but Ewha put her hand firmly on Yeshe's shoulder. "Leave him," she ordered.

Yeshe followed her blindly, crawling out of the hole in the room and was grateful to follow Ewha's purposeful striding toward what she guessed to be the flight deck. She saw So Pak, standing on the bridge, staring at them wordlessly, looking up from the pages of an instruction manual as though he expected his crew to come and find him and help him piece the ship back together. There was no one else on the flight deck.

In his hand was a remote he was using to operate the cameras which relayed the extent of the damage on the viewer before him.

"It's always good to have a ship's doctor," So Pak said, the greeting the only evident softening in his bearing.

"We knew the risks, Captain," Ewha said calmly.

Yeshe watched them in horror, their behavior incomprehensible to her. They were acting as though this were all just another problem to be solved, as though it hadn't crossed their minds to mourn for the rest of the crew, who undoubtedly lay dead around them. When she could stand it no longer, and when it was quite evident that they did not plan to move from the bridge, she asked pleadingly, "Can't we look for the others? They may need help?"

In answer, So Pak pressed the remote and the cameras passed through frames of death, one after another. Toshio and Kenjii crumpled against the air lock,

Kenjii clutching samples against his chest as though through them he could keep his life as well. Savage was jack-knifed over his console, Drukker and Bender were dead in sick bay. Yeshe took it all in, dying a little herself with each new image. Another ship haunted by ghosts.

"Do you know what caused the storm?"

So Pak turned to Ewha. "My only thoughts on the matter are so outrageous they would be unacceptable in a report. You saw Drukker. She was mind-linked to Bender. Both were in great psychic pain. And the atmosphere of Zeta Reticuli is known to be unstable, any disturbance enough to set off raging destructive storms in the environment.

He no longer cared who thought him mad, Yeshe suddenly realized.

"The *Bushido* will be here for us tonight. We can't stay here. Fortunately, everything has been prestored in cargo bay. Chosyam made early storage runs."

Ewha flung herself into a flight chair. "I do not look forward to the flight home."

So Pak looked at her bemusedly, "You prefer death?"

"It hardly matters anymore."

So Pak shrugged. "An irrelevancy."

"Clearly," Ewha agreed. "So we simply wait?"

"Yes, and piece together as much as we can before we leave while we still have the evidence around us."

"It seems you have already done that."

"Yes, quite a bit of it. And sent through the reports."

"So we wait, then."

"Find what you can and I'll set the emergency flares around the area. Then if we still have time, we can gather the records that are left for the final flight report."

"All right."

So Pak's face softened. "Yeshe, we won't be able to bring back the body of your great-uncle."

Yeshe nodded.

That night, after they had done a full day's work, Yeshe slipped silently out of the ship and stood for a moment, looking at the wreckage as night surrounded her as sweetly as a lover. She shouldered her quilt and water bottle and began to walk across the sand. It seemed to take her hours, her footsteps dragging through the mineral-rich crystals that grabbed at her ankles and stretched before her like some highway so broad it had no boundaries. It was a bright night and she had no trouble finding her way to the Korean camp. By the time she arrived, she was exhausted, grateful that the camp was untouched despite the carnage of the probe site she had left. For one last time, she glanced around her, then walked into the barracks. She felt her way to the back, to the shrine of her great-uncle, lit a candle, and said a brief prayer asking forgiveness for not being able to bring any offerings. She spread out the quilt at her great-uncle's feet and, taking a sip from her water bottle, lay down to die before the burial shrine she had so carefully made for them both, wondering how long it would take and if it would be painful in the end. However long it took, she knew that neither So Pak nor Ewha would interfere.

CHAPTER FIFTEEN

Two and a half months later, Jaffe, Katz, So Pak, and Ewha landed in Newark. They were held and interrogated in the Newark Judiciary District, a place of blasted-out cement and busted water mains. The news holos were shocking. Two weeks later, when they were allowed to go home, not one of them could pass a public transmitter without seeing themselves staring, wasted and hollow-eyed, into the holocam. They looked like political hostages. After a three-week leave, Katz and Jaffe were immediately reassigned to five-year tracker duty under tight supervision. The *Bushido* was confiscated along with the comtapes and all records, findings, and reports. The ship was taken apart bit by bit and destroyed. Findings were passed through endless comlinks and analyzed by specialists. The probe survivors were told nothing.

Historian Pak contemplated the ornamental garden outside the window of his study. The garden was deep in the first flush of spring. The ginko trees were backlit by natural light, the sun trapped in their translucent lemon green leaves, as delicate and still as tiny upside-down fans poised against a windless sky. The fresh-raked sand moved in ripples around the sentinel stone to the west, and a tiny bed of wildflowers danced in profusion against the black bark of a fully blooming ornamental cherry tree.

It was for moments like these that one lived, Historian Pak reminded himself. Moments of serenity and completion that held the promise of rebirth. All the rest was nothing more than chasing after the wind.

He pressed his gnarled hands against the desk and regarded with satisfaction his eldest son, who stood by the window that overlooked the garden. He had done well, his son. So Pak returned home with wonder, the odd birthright of the prodigal. And with a woman who, although she hadn't stayed, was possessed of the talents of the Historian: a quick, intense mind, an eye for detail, and a flexibility of vision born of familiarity with human nature. If he taught her slowly, if he stopped her from rushing ahead, inflamed by an idea; if he taught her that all things came in fulfillment and dignity so long as one did not pull the plant up by the root, she might make a fine History some day.

It was a difficult test, holding on to passion while waiting for the good, but it was the only way to live life without regret. There was an infinity of wisdom at work in the Universe that went about its business acknowledged or not, and Historian Pak's greatest happiness lay in observing it at work. No one could have brought him a more worthy successor and she had come to him after following a long and bitter path. Why shouldn't he be happy?

"I was notified of the World Bank's decision on the evidence presented by the World Patent Office" Historian Pak began. He had the immediate attention of his son.

"Due to the evidence presented through the findings of your probe, they have determined Iwaski was at fault. Iwaski has been found guilty of corporate and international patent theft in stealing the ultrasound mining patent from a preexisting Korean patent. Several other countries have also been named in the suit. The World Patent Office has demanded reparations be paid."

So Pak grinned.

"Reparations will be quite substantial. To be paid directly to the Korean government. It will bankrupt the Japanese corporate structure and make way for the enviro-experimental companies. Korea will be on a new economic footing on a par with Germany. It seems Korea has won more than independence. We must take care not to sink into power the way the Japanese Conglomerates did. One can only hope we learned a lesson from Japan."

"Hope?" So Pak demanded.

"It was an understandable human error on the part of the Iwaski group," Historian Pak said calmly, thinking regretfully of his old foe, Mr. Matsuda who, despite himself, he sometimes missed. In the same way that great athletic rivalries formed and developed an athlete's performance, personalities were often formed by their rivals or enemies who pushed them to perform beyond themselves. "It goes back centuries."

"Of course."

"You think this is my bias."

"Isn't it?"

"Listen to me."

"I am listening."

"In order to survive being battered by the Western nations, the Japanese worked magic. They learned well from their conquerors and took it to be a lesson in power. They reinterpreted the industrial power of the Western nations, developed it fully, and used it to essentially Kung Fu their conquerors. Power is gained and lost and traded in the great dance.''

''This is, of course, only your opinion.''

''Well, let's just hope that the endless tears of Korean history have taught us not to incorporate the ways of our conquerors.'' Historian Pak chuckled. He thought of his daughter-in-law. ''Now Reoke will have to teach her fingers to do other things than terrorize corporations. It seems the role of the Snakers, let alone that unfortunate offshoot, Terror Two, who killed Reoke's second-in-command that day in Newark, has been eliminated. In my discussions with Reoke, however, I do not remember very many alternative plans.''

''Discussions?''

''Oh, yes. We had a great many talks, Reoke and I. I can't say we were close, but I gave her options. Her mind, needless to say, was already firmly directed in its course. Not unlike yours, as I recall.'' he finished.

''And Kim?''

''Oh, yes.''

''You knew of his involvement with the Snakers? Living a lie in your own house, using you as his cover?''

Despite So Pak's evident indignation, his father continued to regard him blandly.

''Who are you to judge your brother?''

''He showed you disrespect.''

''I forgave you. Can you not forgive the dead?'' Historian Pak's eyes twinkled.

''He and Reoke were nothing but butchers.''

''And you? Could it not be said you led your crew to their deaths? As I recall from the tape you smuggled back, Chosyam was planning to sacrifice himself and the ship, no matter what happened.''

"I didn't know that, did I?"

"Then you were an ignorant leader, despite the ruling of the Negligence Trial." Historian Pak's face softened. "Do not be too hard on your brother."

"And the aliens?"

"I was slipped the analysis of your reports. An interesting problem: After great deliberation, it has been decided the Japanese exported a virus to be tested on their own men. Both mining probes encountered another mining community on Zeta Reticuli. It was a community of aliens who had trained themselves to chemically alter disease until it was no longer fatal to their systems. They did this internally. Apparently, they had been doing it for decades, traveling from planet to planet. But the virus they happened upon on Zeta Reticuli wasn't organic, it was chemical. And they couldn't alter it completely outside a laboratory. It became an epidemic. Interestingly enough, it was humans who developed the immunity.

"I've had access to the Atrocity Report. It has been decided the aliens will be allowed sanctuary on somewhat more humane terms. After all, there are many living among us already. Perhaps some of us will listen to what they have to say now that Deathspeaking is no longer outlawed. I don't know if entities close to death have more to say than the living about truth, but Deathspeaking seems to be something from which we can all learn." Historian Pak looked at his son carefully. Then he turned his full attention back to the garden. It was a pleasant day. There was much to learn and more to do. Historian Pak determined to let nothing disturb his appreciation of life. People would do what they did. He was responsible for his own peace, despite the events that raged around him.

As if in answer, a faint breeze stirred the ginko trees and the distant sound of wind chimes chasing the demons from the compound came to him from the very back of the garden.